Winston & Baum
and
The Secret of the Stone Circle
by Seth Tucker

To Cyndi,
Beware the goblins,
they'll steal your
socks!

-Seth Tucker

To Caralyn, who takes my madness in stride and loves me anyway.

Intro   Dan Winston stepped carefully through the doors inside of the old farmhouse into what had been a bedroom. There was a moldering scrap of cloth that at one time had been a mattress. The room was barren other than that. Other than the lantern he had fastened onto his belt there was no light from outside. A small noise came from somewhere in the house. Crossing the empty room, he opened the door to what had been a closet. A portion of the back wall had been ripped away leading into another room of the house. There was a cackle from inside the house. It was loud and gruesome, like nails on chalkboard. "Goblins," Dan said. "I hate goblins."

Crouching down he looked into the other room. It was empty just like the room he stood in now. He knew better than to crawl through the space, but the goblins knew he was there now. "Why have you come?" A voice called.

Dan looked about the room; he was unable to tell which direction the voice had come from.

"Brought us nice shiny toys," a different voice answered.

"Like hell," Dan said under his breath as he knelt down and crawled into the other room.

The large brass pneumatic pack on his back caught for a second and then tore a piece of the wall off and allowed him to pass. Standing once more, he adjusted the straps of the pack. He also shifted the gun belt with the twin revolvers hanging on it. "What do you want here?" Said another of the otherworldly voices, they all sounded mischievous and malicious but this one had a certain venom to it.

Holding his hands up, Dan turned to the darkened corner. He saw the goblin. It was only as tall as a small child with sharp teeth lining its mouth, a short flat snout sat on its head. It dressed in rags made to resemble human clothes. What caught the attention of Dan was the single shot black powder pistol that the diminutive figure held. The pistol was old and worn, the brass had turned green and Dan estimated that the last time it had seen action was in the previous century, most likely in a duel. The goblin aimed the gun directly at Dan. "I ask again, why you come here?"

"Let me speak to the leader," Dan said. He knew goblin hierarchy, only the leader of this group could decide if Dan should be killed. Unless the goblin was able to persuade Dan to parlay with him, but Dan was not that stupid.

"Tell me what you have to say and I pass it along," the goblin said smiling, revealing more of the razor like teeth.

"No chance," Dan said smiling. "I know the rules. Now take me to the big chief."

The goblin pulled back the hammer on the pistol. "I don't like you," the goblin said.

"I have that effect. But I'm about done talking." Dan threatened.

"Really why? You about to start screaming," the goblin said laughing.

Dan gritted his teeth at the unholy sound. "No," Dan said. "You need a percussion cap to shoot that piece."

The goblin's eyes darted back to the pistol. Dan took the opportunity and lashed out with his boot. The hard sole of his boot made contact with the goblin and lifted it off the ground. Bouncing off the wall, the goblin came to rest on the floor. It tried to raise itself up. It was pushed halfway up on its arm and then collapsed back to the floor.

Behind Dan came the sounds of pistols being prepared to fire. "I want to see the chief," Dan proclaimed.

"Well then I guess you in luck." A voice said, this one was deeper than the other goblins.

Dan turned. There were now five goblins in the room, four smaller ones like the one he had kicked. These four stood two on each side of one that was just as tall as the others but had a large potbelly protruding forth; here was the leader of this clan. "Hello clan leader. I apologize for your clansman," Dan said motioning toward the unconscious goblin on the floor behind him. "I've come to speak to you of matters that will affect your clan."

"Sit we will speak," the leader said.

Dan sat cross legged across from the goblin. His four guards did not lower their pistols, all of which were newer and in better repair than the one belonging to the first goblin. "I have come to ask you to leave this place," Dan said.

"Why should we leave?" The clan leader said. "We have been here many seasons no humans stay here that long."

"About that," Dan said choosing his words carefully. "You wouldn't know anything about what drove out the last few people who wanted to live here, would you?"

The goblin leader bared his teeth. "You accuse us?" He screamed.

The goblins surrounding him began to growl. "I would never accuse the clan leader of such," Dan said keeping an eye on the armed goblins around him. The one truth to all goblins were that they loved being flattered, Dan decided to exploit this. "I merely asked knowing that goblins are wise in such things."

9

The growling slowly subsided as the clan leader sat back down. "We are wise, but we do no know what would cause people to leave palace."

"People want to live here again and they would like you to vacate the premises." Dan said resting his hands on the floor.

"Too bad, we no go." The goblin leader said, crossing his arms.

"If you don't they'll send one of the humans that hunt your kind," Dan said. "I felt it my duty to warn you."

"What human fool challenge us?" The clan leader asked laughing, drawing laughter from his minions.

Dan cringed. He didn't think that there was a worse noise in the entire realms of this world or the next. The goblin leader stood and stepped closer to Dan. "I ask, who challenge us?"

Dan smiled. "Me," he said drawing his revolvers and firing into the nearest two goblins.

Their small bodies crumpled as the lead struck them. The two remaining guards fired but with Dan jumping up into a standing position, they were not able to aim and control the kick of the pistols. One bullet whizzed high and struck his bowler from his head. The other missed entirely. Two more shots from Dan felled the remaining two guards. The clan leader was reaching into the belt that hung around his waist, trying to retrieve a weapon. Dan holstered his pistols and hoisted the small figure into the air by his throat. "Heavier than you look," Dan said. "So I'll ask you again are you going to move or do I need to end this quickly and violently?" Dan squeezed to emphasize his point.

Something clubbed him in the back of the knee and Dan dropped the chief and fell to his knees on the hard wood floor. He turned in time to see the first goblin run through the missing portion of wall into the other bedroom. A quick cackle sounding as the goblin retreated. He heard a match struck and then a loud hiss. He turned and saw the small spiked orb with a fuse on top. There wasn't time for him to get out following the goblin. The chief had already made his own escape after dropping the bomb. Running Dan leaped through the nearby window. He fell from the second story as the small room exploded. The brackish water of the nearby pond surrounded him as he fell and then the silt at the bottom cushioned his fall. He stood up dripping wet and covered in mud as one of the new steam powered velociters slowed in front of the house.

He walked toward the velociter, headed in the direction where he had parked his own velociter. Instead of the metal and glass cabin with the large steam engine on the rear and the gears that controlled the three wheels he found only fragments of the vehicle. The approaching velociter stopped beside him. "Problems?" Asked Lee Baum, Dan's partner.

"Goblins," Dan said.

"I see they dismantled your vehicle." Lee stated.

"Apparently so," Dan said.

"So I don't really need to ask, but what kind are they?" Lee inquired.

Dan picked up a small fragment of the bomb that had destroyed the second story room from the ground. He handed it to Lee. "Black powder, what else."

"Yes judging by the condition of the velociter, I assumed as such." Lee said tossing the bomb fragment over his shoulder.

"They're armed with pistols as well. Old dueling ones it looks like." Dan stretched as he removed the pneumatic pack from his back. "Will you take a look and make sure it's still in working condition."

Lee knelt beside the harness and inspected the gears and copper piping on the pack. He took the greatest care in looking at the rubber hose that ran from the pack to the attached shotgun. "It appears that everything remains sealed off and I don't detect any type of leaks. Still let me replace the hose, just to be safe."

No one knew the pneumatic pack and shotgun better than Lee; he had designed and built both of them. Lee retrieved a replacement hose from the cargo compartment under the operator's seat of the velociter. Removing the old hose, he connected the new hose to the pack and then the stock of the shotgun. "All ready," Lee said hoisting the pack up.

"Let's wait a second. We don't know how many are in there, or why they won't leave. Also I'm soaking wet and it's chilly out here."

Lee motioned Dan over to the velociter. Climbing into the passenger seat, Dan felt the warmth envelope him as he sat in the compartment. With an adjustment to one of the gears that cluttered the control box, Lee increased the flow of heat from the engine into the compartment. "Thanks." Dan said as he felt the moisture in his clothes start to dry. With his clothes drying, Dan could feel the silt from the lake creating a layer of grime over his body. It reminded him of working the fields back home.

"So what is our next step?" Lee asked.

"We can't leave them for too long. Lord only knows what kind of trouble they'll make with the velociter parts. You didn't bring the Tin

Man did you?" Dan asked looking out the rear of the velociter. "Never mind, I see his trailer his missing."

"He's too heavy would have fallen directly through the floor and then he's no good to us." Lee explained.

"Right, well I guess what we'll need to do," Dan thought for a moment. "I guess I'll get to go room by room and clear it out. You have the Winchester, right?" Dan asked.

"I always do," Lee said sounding annoyed by the question.

"Good post up out here and don't let them take the velociter. It's a long walk back to town." Dan opened the door and started towards the farmhouse.

He emptied his revolvers of their shells and tossed them into the high grass covering the front of the house. His hand stopped just above the bullets lining his belt, the realization that they had also gotten wet had eluded him until this moment. "Here," Lee called from behind him.

Lee tossed him a box of shells for the revolvers, and another box of shells for the shotgun. Withdrawing a large metal breastplate, Lee made his way over to Dan. "Don't forget this." Lee said.

"It's too heavy," Dan said taking the breastplate.

"It also stops bullets," Lee retorted.

Grumbling under his breath Dan slid his arms into the loops on the shoulder of the breastplate. It was iron and heavy, but it would stop most knives and bullets. At least the kinds these goblins used. Lee tightened the straps on the back of the breastplate and then helped Dan shoulder the pneumatic pack once more.

"Might want to move that contraption over by those trees," Dan said referring to the velociter.

"I will, now be careful and try not to make too much of a mess," Lee chided.

"You ain't my mother," Dan shot back.

"No, I would have taught you better manners." Lee responded.

Lee went back to move the velociter. Dan once again stood outside the farm house, this time a little dirtier but knowing what he faced. He wasted no time in surveying the outside this time, with a swift kick he knocked the door from its hinges and stepped in.

His lantern had extinguished when he landed in the pond. With the lights from the velociter on, he had not noticed the lack of light. Now however, the dark was too great to see through. Stepping back out and standing beside the door frame, he lit one of the magnesium flares he carried, wet or dry they sparked and fired just fine. The magnesium ignited and Dan tossed it into the darkened house. This time he knew there would be no warnings or seeking to speak to the chief, his intentions had been made clear. Reaching over his shoulder, he detached the shotgun from its harness attached to the geared pack and stepped once more into the farmhouse. The rooms were illuminated by the flare but cast shadows into all of the far corners. Dan trusted that the goblins would follow the traits of their race and betray their position as their kind normally did.

Lee watched from the far side of the velociter, the Winchester rifle lay across the seat, his finger on the trigger. Lee could easily fire on any enemy coming from the house this way without having to hold the rifle at the ready the entire time. His arms had once been accustomed to holding weapons at the ready for long periods of time, but after the war in India he had left the world of the professional soldier and taken back up designing and inventing. With the business he and Dan had, his training with firearms had proven quite beneficial.

Dan stepped cautiously nearer to the flare, waiting as the dark corners held their secret. "How is a goblin like a mule?" He asked, even though he saw none to hear the question.

Whispered voices came from the rooms near the rear of the house. "I'll tell you. They're always too stupid to keep quiet." Dan said closing on his prey.

This brought a cluster of outraged shrieks from the small group of goblins. Stepping into the hallway that led to the back of the farmhouse, he pushed open every door with the barrel of the shogun and shoved the flare in front of him to insure that none of the goblins could sneak up on him. Finally, he came to the door at the end of the hallway. He could hear the scurrying sound that the goblins made as they moved about the room. They were also snickering. Swiftly he pushed the door open and tossed the flare into the room. He saw the boiler from the velociter and several of its copper pipes rearranged and soldered into a larger pipe from some other source that had been laid down in front of the boiler. Inside the pipe, Dan saw glittering metal. "Now!" One of the goblins shouted.

One goblin wearing goggles and sitting atop the boiler turned a small valve on the side of it. The dials on the boiler raced into the red. Dan turned and dove onto the floor as the goblins laughed and their new device blasted bits of nail, glass and metal shards into the hall sailing over Dan's lowered head. Looking around he saw the walls torn to shreds by the shrapnel. "That's it." He said gritting his teeth and lunging into the nearest open door.

The goblins were cocking back their old fashioned black powder pistols and drawing their small but sharp knives. Reaching behind him, he felt the small wooden handle. It was attached to a string. Holding onto the shotgun, he pulled the handle around in front of him and heard the gears start to turn. The piston on the side began to churn and the sound of industry was clearly heard. Stepping out into the hall once again, he squeezed the trigger of the shotgun and with the additional power of the pneumatic pack on his back it was fully automatic. Buckshot flew out in a constant stream. The shotgun had been modified to increase its rate of fire and additionally both sides of the chamber had ejection ports that alternated with each shell to prevent jamming and overheating. The fifteen round magazine that Lee had designed cycled through the shells quickly.

As the last spent casing ejected, Dan saw the goblins running past him in the hall. He watched them run past screaming and looked up. Several broken goblin bodies lay on the floor, but the boiler taken from the velociter was shaking and its dial was breaking past the red point. The valve that was used to turn it down was bent and broken, by the blasts from the shotgun. Dan also turned and ran for the exit of the house. As he exited the hall and made his way toward the door, the boiler detonated, the concussive wave carried him out the door and dumped him onto the hard packed dirt of the walkway to the house. He felt his breath leave his body. Several of the goblins were running frantically through the tall grass and into the nearby woods. Several more lay dead on the lawn. Lee held the smoking Winchester looking down the barrel at the devastated state the house was in.

Walking around the velociter, his mouth gaping Lee exclaimed. "What did you do?"

"Nothing, they built a blasted blunderbuss out of the boiler and well it may have gotten damaged." Dan explained pushing himself up off the ground and taking a few deep breaths.

"You blew up the boiler," Lee said.

"It blew up. I may or may not have helped it." Dan turned to face the farmhouse.

The entire back half of the house was missing. The field behind it was littered with the flaming wreckage from the farmhouse, as the remaining standing portion of the farmhouse began to tilt toward the missing rear half. Lee watched in shocked amazement as the house tilted. Dan just closed his eyes and waited for the expectant sound of it collapsing to the ground. After several seconds, he opened his eyes. The house was tilted back but the portion that had not been destroyed in the blast was still standing. "See it wasn't a total loss," Dan said slapping Lee on the shoulder.

"They paid us to get rid of the goblins not to destroy the house." Lee said turning to face Dan.

"Which we did, the goblins just took more of the house with them than expected." Dan said. "Did you bring some bags?"

Making a frustrated noise, Lee stalked back to the velociter and came back carrying three empty burlap sacks and a fresh lantern for Dan. He tossed one of the sacks and the lantern to Dan. With a big smile, Dan fastened the lantern to his belt and looked about at the dead goblins. "I'll see how many I can dig out of the house," Dan said. "I don't know why they even have those guns none of them even shot."

Lee cleared his throat and pointed at the breastplate. "Look again," he said.

Dan looked down and saw the small dents that the balls from the goblins' pistols caused as they had hit the iron and fell off. "Maybe I was mistaken." Dan said.

"There's also a knife in the stock of the shotgun," Lee said.

Dan looked at the weapon and saw that Lee was right. One of the goblins had thrown it at him as they had made their way out and instead of hitting Dan had landed it firmly into the oak stock of the shotgun. Pulling it free, Dan threw it into the tall grass and secured the shotgun in its harness beside the pack. "Take the pistols, just to prevent anyone from coming back and getting them," Dan said as he walked around the destroyed remains of the farmhouse.

"Not my first time doing this," Lee called after him.

Lifting the first of the crumpled small bodies, Lee dropped it into the bag tossing in the small antique pistol nearby. As the wind changed direction, he caught the first whiff of the dead goblins. He recoiled in disgust. "Nasty blighters always need a bath," he said to himself in revulsion.

Scouring around the destroyed portion of the house, Dan found more pieces than entire bodies. Still, if he had enough parts he'd get a bounty for the full body. He found a lot of limbs and a few torsos, most without the heads still attached. Investigating in the direct ruins of the farmhouse, Dan found the leader of the clan. The body was still intact a large shard of wood had impaled him. Most of the bones had been broken and from all appearances, it had fallen a good distance onto its head. Looking about Dan took note of the destruction to the upper level of the farmhouse. He concluded that the chief had remained upstairs expecting his clan to finish off Dan. The plan had not apparently counted on their new weapon exploding. The chief had taken a shard of shrapnel to the chest and been dead almost instantly, his body had fallen from the upstairs when the house shifted back. "Told you to leave peacefully," Dan said to the small lifeless body.

Three more of the small bombs fell from the pouches hanging on the side of the clan leader's belt. Dan stuffed them into storage pouches of his own, and then stuffed the body on top of the mass pile of parts that were filling his sack. After a half hour of searching he could find no further substantial goblin parts. Tying a rope around the top of his sack, he went back around the front of the house. Lee was waiting for him leaning up against the velociter, the Winchester resting in his arms. Tied beside the boiler at the rear of the vehicle were the two burlap sacks Lee had kept. Dan stowed his with the others and placed the pack into the cargo cabinet underneath the passenger seat. Climbing into the seat, Dan looked at the controls for the velociter. There were gears to be turned on the control panel that adjusted speed, a stick coming up from the floor between the driver's legs to control the front wheel and in return control direction, the two pedals on the floor controlled the forward and backwards motion of the vehicle. Lee had insisted that they purchase the velociters and Dan had to admit it had been easier than maintaining horses, given that most of the things they hunted would eat horses if given the chance. Most things did not try to disassemble the newer technologies, except black powder goblins.

Lee sped the velociter on its way back into London, and as the velociter kicked up dust and spread the dying leaves from the trees, a small lone figure emerged from the farmhouse. It was the first goblin that Dan had encountered. In its hand it held a business card, one that had fallen from Dan's pocket while he had been collecting the goblin dead. The goblin had been watching waiting until the man had left; one of his eyes had swollen shut. After the boiler exploded, he'd been knocked unconscious but safely hidden in the upstairs, near the clan leader. He looked at the small piece of paper in his hand and tried his best to read the business card. In a clear legible font was printed:

Dan Winston & Lee Baum
Exterminators of the Strange & Weird

1   The velociter sped through the cobblestone streets of London, lit by the orange glow of the street lights. Lee and Dan rode through the streets in silence while the city bustled about full of life even at this late hour. Children were going about to the factories to work on the late shift while women of ill repute were displaying large portions of flesh to tempt the men coming from the factories, their faces covered in dirt and grime. "Deplorable," Lee said.

"What is?" Dan asked looking at some of the women they passed.

"The women you seem so interested in," Lee said.

"I'm looking not buying," Dan said.

"See to it that you don't," Lee scolded him.

"I've never paid for the company of a woman yet, and I don't intend to start," Dan said turning from the side window and looking directly ahead of them.

Lee nodded as he slowed the velociter. They were entering into the more crowded section of town. The throngs of people leaving the pubs that were clustered near the factories were overwhelming. The velociter had to slow to a crawl as the people milled about in the streets going from one pub to another or stumbling off into the darkness to their homes. Finally, they made their way through the people and were able to once again pick up speed. They were headed not to Scotland Yard but the short squat building beside it. Known locally as "Glorianna's dungeon," the Office of Abnormal Affairs was a small branch of the government that paid bounty hunters to deal with any threat outside the normal realms of police work. They would also recommend bounty hunters to private citizens wishing to deal with any abnormal threats.

Dan and Lee were one of the more successful bounty hunter teams out there.

Lee and Dan locked the velociter and retrieved their burlap sacks of goblin carcasses from the rear of the vehicle. The large wood door strained as Dan pushed it open, the hinges needing oil. Inside, the building was lit by the much brighter turbine driven lighting system that most government buildings had been retrofitted with. Long tubes of filament were attached to the ceiling where they were charged by the constant turning of the massive turbines located in the basement of the building. Upon entering the building, there was a wooden partition with doors on both sides, in between the doors sat a pudgy little man. Tiny spectacles adorned the bridge of his nose, resting just above the busted capillaries that indicated his love of a good stiff drink. He looked at the two men with the burlap sacks over their shoulders.

"Roger?" He asked.

"Of course sir," Lee said smiling.

Pulling a wooden shutter down over the opening, the man left Lee and Dan to wait in the foyer of the building. They looked around at the different photographs on the wall. Each displayed different interactions with humans and the different fey and abnormal beings. The later pictures depicted Royal Marines standing with captured dark fey or around their trophy kills. The most sickening one contained the depiction of thirteen Royal Marines standing on top of a mass grave of dwarves and goblins. "Indiscriminate massacre," Lee said shaking his head.

"You'd think somebody would have asked what started the whole mess, but they didn't did they?" Dan said.

The Limestone massacre, as it had been dubbed at the time, was the first revelation as the reality of supernatural beings. Both sides of the fey had been upset at it. Queen Victoria had worked long and hard to apologize and see to it that precautions were taken to prevent it from happening again. Of course, that was not good enough for the dark forces of the fey. They had tried to assassinate the Queen. It had failed but not before the Queen had been savaged. Fortunately, new technology had given doctors the ability to save her life.

"To what do I owe the pleasure?" Roger asked opening the door on the right of the partition and looking at the two men.

"A good night of hunting that's what," Dan said stepping up to the man.

Roger's thick bushy mustache was well trimmed and fitting with his black suit. His posture and speech were impeccable portraying the true English gentleman, he was their dealer. His actual title was regent warden; there were several of them in the office. Each bounty hunter was assigned to a regent warden, Roger had been lucky enough to be assigned Dan and Lee.

Turning away from the men, Roger led the way through the small desks and offices that comprised the building and finally settled in at a small wooden desk. Lee and Dan sat across from him dropping their sacks onto the floor with a muffled thud. "So what's in the sack?" Roger asked.

Lifting one of the sacks onto his desk, Lee removed the rope from the top of the sack and held it open. Roger drew back after the smell reached his nostrils. Retrieving a handkerchief from a pocket inside his coat, he moved closer to the bag, using the handkerchief to cover his nose and mouth. "Goblins?" He asked.

"Yes," Lee said, his smile never faltering. "Black Powder."

Roger looked up from the bag to the man holding it and the other man seated beside him.

"Are you sure?" Roger asked.

"Positive," Dan said. "They tried to shoot me, stole a velociter and built a blunderbuss out of it. Oh yeah also left a nasty little present on the floor for me, black powder bomb."

The sound of Dan's colonial accent always made Roger cringe. "Indeed," he said sourly. "How many?"

"I have at least fifteen in the two sacks here, Dan?" Lee asked looking at the bag with goblin blood seeping through it.

"You've got to assemble the pieces but I'd say at least another seven or eight of them, including the clan leader." Dan tossed his sack on Roger's desk where the goblin blood leaked out onto the oak surface.

"We'll have to confirm that of course, weapons?" Roger said.

"As many as we could find," Dan said. "Go on and confirm it, we ain't got all night."

Lee closed his eyes embarrassed at the manner in which Dan addressed their regent warden.

"Certainly," Roger said, placing the three sacks onto a small wooden rolling cart and pushing it toward a locked door at the back of the room.

"I wish you wouldn't speak to him like that." Lee said sitting back down.

"I wish he didn't take so long, why ask us how many if you're gonna count them anyhow? Just doesn't make sense, unless they're trying to cheat you." Dan said.

"They are not trying to cheat us," Lee said. "Besides it would make it so much easier if you would be more polite to him. He does impact our eligibility to renew our bounty license."

"Bah!" Dan said. "After what we did for queen and country you think they'll take our license?"

"Perhaps not, but still I would rather not tempt fate," Lee chided his partner.

"I lost my hat," Dan said changing the subject.

"It's just as well. It was a poor excuse for a hat." Lee said.

Dan looked over at Lee an unfriendly expression on his face. Opening his mouth to reply, Dan was cut off by Roger's return.

"Twenty-four confirmed goblin kills gentlemen." Roger said returning.

Sitting behind his desk he sat down and retrieved a book of payment slips from his top desk drawer. He filled out the form and asked Dan and Lee to both sign off on it. Tearing the slip from the booklet, he handed them their copy of the form. "Good evening gentlemen. I am sure you will be back soon." Roger said as the two men left the desk and headed towards the cashier's office.

"That is a lot of money." Dan said as the cashier continued placing bills on top of one another.

His smile grew wider with each bill placed on the stack. Finally, after the appropriate fee had been counted out the cashier slid the money through a small slot in the iron bars that guarded his desk. "Sign here?" He asked handing a small clipboard through as well.

Lee and Dan both signed that they had received the money. Placing the money in a silver money clip, Lee placed the large wad of bills in the front pocket of his pants. "Wait a minute!" Dan protested following Lee outside.

Approaching their parked velociter, Dan stepped up in front of Lee. "Hold on, where's my cut?" Dan asked. "I got an awful big thirst." He explained.

"Then I suggest you drink some of the tea we have." Lee said. "I fear that your portion of our profits will have to pay for damages."

"What damages?" Dan demanded. "The goblins blew up the back of that house, not me."

"True, but unfortunately, that is not going to bring back the velociter we will need to replace." Lee said getting in the driver's seat of the vehicle. "Now are you riding home or would you prefer to walk?"

Dan mumbled under his breath as he climbed into the passenger seat.

"Would you quit mumbling?" Lee said exasperated.

"If I don't mumble, you ain't going to want me riding with you." Dan said crossing his arms and skulking as he looked out the window.

A bolt of lightning shot across the sky, followed by the familiar boom of thunder. It always reminded Dan of cannon fire. It always made him uncomfortable. Then the skies let loose a torrential downpour. "See even the weather thinks you shouldn't be withholding my money." Dan said.

"If that were true it would have started raining before we made it into the velociter." Lee said pulling away from the small squat building located next to the illustrious Scotland Yard.

"No, because I shouldn't be punished anymore than I already am." Dan said.

"You'll be all right without taking rounds at the pub. We have several bottles of beer still in the new cooling receptacle at the flat." Lee said.

"We don't have dancing girls and it's called an ice box." Dan said.

"There is not any ice in it and I refuse to call it by such a ridiculous name."

They rode the remainder of the way in silence. While Lee navigated the now empty streets, the rain poured keeping the people in the pubs or homes where they were. It was London and since the advent of the steam and coal driven engines, the rain was welcomed as it washed the ash and smoke from the air and off of the buildings. The air was clear when they returned to the second floor flat they rented from the widower, Ms. Edwards. Pulling the velociter into the small overhang that they had built for both of the devices when they purchased them, Dan and Lee exited the vehicle. Dan taking his weapons with him, while Lee carried the Winchester and a large canvas bag on his shoulder; they made their way inside and started up the stairs.

Ms. Edwards opened the door and looked out at the men. She had her dressing gown drawn close around her and a stern look upon her face. Her features softened as she saw the men. "Good evening lads," she said to them.

"Good evening," Lee responded.

"Ma'am," Dan said with a nod of his head.

"I trust everything went well, you both appear unharmed." She said.

"Yes, it was a very good evening." Lee said.

"Good night then." She said pushing the door closed.

The men continued up the stairs. Unlocking the door at the top of the staircase, they entered the main living room of their flat. It was full of books on engineering and folklore. Dan's desk was converted into an ammunition center with the black powder press used to make bullets. Lee's section of the room was filled with engineering books and schematics of the devices he had designed or planned on designing. Removing their coats, Lee hung his on the rack by the door, while Dan tossed his over the nearest chair. Frowning, Lee retrieved Dan's coat and placed it on the rack beside his. Dan went into the small area that was a kitchen complete with a small stove, oven and the latest a rather large chest that produced a chilled air to keep food from spoiling, known as the cool box or ice box as Dan preferred. Opening the door to the cool box, Dan retrieved a large brown bottle and pulled the top from it.

He smiled as it popped from its place and he took a giant drink from the bottle. "I'll say this you boys can make a good beer." Dan said.

"We do more than that." Lee said.

"Some of you do, but on the whole most of you boys ain't worth spit." Dan said. "I still say you've got more American in you than Brit."

"I've already told you the only time I've ever been to our former colonies was for a two week trip, in which you met me when I was returning via steamship." Lee explained.

"Well, we must've rubbed off on you." Dan said. "Take your love of that rifle."

"It is a very dependable accurate weapon that is all." Lee explained growing more frustrated.

"All right didn't mean to touch a nerve." Dan said taking another long pull from the bottle, finishing it. "I'm getting a shower."

Dan walked into the small room that comprised the bathroom. There was a large tiled area that was lower than the rest of the floor a large grate sat in the center of the tiled area. Stripping out of his soiled clothes, Dan turned the handle that started the gas boiler above them warming the pipes the water was about to pass through. Turning the other handle, the water began to flow.

Standing under the flowing warm water, Dan felt the grit and grime from the farmhouse wash off of him. Fatigue set in as he shut off the water and wrapped himself in a large plush cloth robe. Droplets of water still hung in his unruly moustache and his thick dark hair. He settled down in a chair in the living area where Lee was busy working on a new design. Turning to speak to Dan, Lee stopped noticing his friend's head leaning down onto his chest and the slight sound of snoring that he made.

Taking a quilted blanket from the large pile near the sofas, Lee covered his friend and turned out the lamps in the room. Lee went to his own room, where he continued working on the schematics for several hours before climbing under the covers and falling soundly to sleep.

Dan knew he was asleep in the great chair in the living room of the flat, but despite this knowledge, he found himself on an open plain. The first tentative drops of rain were falling from the sky, stinging his skin. A strong wind was blowing in bringing the storm with it. The tall blades of wheat and barley danced in the wind. "Why can't it be the dream where I'm on that island?" Dan asked no one in particular. "Wake up." He commanded himself.

"Help!" Cried a small voice from the other side of the field.

Scanning the flailing wheat, Dan saw a small red headed figure running through the tall plants. Dan started off at a walk toward the few strands of red hair that he could see above the wheat. "Help!" The diminutive figure called again more urgently than before.

Dan quickened his pace. He was not sure why he felt this urgency to reach the figure his own mind assumed it was so the dream could end sooner. As far as dreams went he was finding this one disappointing. Normally, he dreamed of dancing hall girls from back home or Lee and him stumbling onto an old dragon's horde of gold. This was mundane by comparison. Picking up speed, until he was at a full on run Dan tried to reach the small person in the field. His foot hit something and he went sprawling into the dirt hard. It took a minute for his eyes to focus on the objects littering the ground. They were dwarves, elves, fairies, brownies, sprites and some of the small satyrs that haunted England's woodlands causing young love, all of them dead. The dead eyes stared at Dan as he tried to stand.

"Please help me," cried the now familiar voice.

Dan started to stand when something latched onto his ankle. He turned and saw the hand of one of the dead dwarves clamped onto him. "Protect the girl," the dead body said moaning.

The other dead fey moved, coming near him. "Protect the girl!" They echoed.

"Let go and I will!" Dan said kicking at the dwarf holding his ankle.

"Dan, what's going on?" One of the dead asked, only the voice that came from the dead body was Lee's.

"Lee?" Dan said surprised. "What are you doing here?"

"I live here, what are you doing to the ottoman?" The dead body with Lee's voice demanded.

Dan opened his eyes and looked around; he was back in the flat. Lee was standing by the kitchen stove staring at Dan. Looking down, Dan saw the ottoman stool. He had been kicking it and splintered the wooden frame supporting the lush cushion. "Sorry," Dan said looking around the room.

Sun light was peeking in through the haze in the sky and barely pushing into the windows of the flat. "Where you sleep walking or kicking as it were?" Lee asked.

"I suppose so," Dan said still unsure of his surroundings.

They could both hear the knocking on the front door of the building. Ms. Edwards would answer it. Within the next few knocks they could hear Ms. Edwards addressing someone at the door. Then the familiar sound of feet heading down the hall and up onto the steps. "Company," Lee said.

Lee was dressed in a smoking jacket with a pair of slacks. "You should put on some trousers," Lee said looking at Dan, who was still wearing the bathrobe.

Dan hurried off to his room to clothe himself. There was a strong knock on the door, as he escaped into his bedroom closing his door behind him. Lee hurried to the entrance of their flat. Opening the door, he saw two burly men in overcoats, hats in their hands. In front of the men was Ms. Edwards, wearing a high collared dress. "Good morning," Lee said smiling.

"Good morning sir." Ms. Edwards replied. "These gentlemen asked to speak with you and Mr. Winston. They claim it is urgent. I trust you don't mind."

"Not at all." Lee confirmed opening the door wider and stepping aside. "Do come in. Thank you Ms Edwards."

The older landlady turned and made her way back down the stairs. Lee watched her go and closed the door once she had reached the foot of the stairs. Turning to his new guests, Lee was surprised to see that they stood side by side not far behind him. "You Baum?" The larger of the two said. He had a scar running down the side of his left cheek.

"Well?" The other one chimed, whose head seemed too small for his body.

"I am Lee Baum," Lee confirmed. "And how can I help you?"

"You're in an interesting line of work, aren't you?" Scarface said.

"One might say that." Lee responded.

The two men were blocking his way around them to any defensive articles he might be able to procure. Such as the pistol in the top of his desk drawer or the dagger located under the sofa cushions. Lee tried to sidestep around the men, but they moved in unison to block his path. "Gentlemen, I really must insist that you let me to my desk. If I don't take the appropriate notes, we cannot assist you properly."

Little Head put a hand out onto Lee's chest. "You're going to need assistance," he said and shoved.

Lee hit the wall hard.

Dan watched from his bedroom as the two men entered. As soon as they shoved Lee, Dan retrieved the pistol he kept by his bed and also a small iron rod. Throwing open the door, he let loose a loud: "Yee-haw!"

Bounding over the couch, he struck Scarface squarely in the cheek with the iron rod. Little Head turning at the new combatant was not prepared when Lee pushed off the wall and tackled him. Scarface sat up, his face bleeding from his freshly opened cheek. Spitting blood and teeth onto the floor, and with hate in his eyes he began to speak. "Loit loit loib elbbub," Scarface began his voice no longer masculine but the voice of an old woman.

Dan saw the shoes on Scarface and Little Head's feet, the toes were squared off. "Shoes," Dan called.

Lee saw the shoes on Little Head and let go. Smiling at him, Little Head started to raise up. With a strong kick to the head, Lee sent the man back to the floor rattling the windows with his impact. He lay where he was, unconscious. "Nordluac nrub, nordluac elbbub," Scarface continued.

"Here!" Lee called tossing Dan a small tin.

Catching it Dan began sprinkling a red and white mixture around the chanting figure. Finally completing a circle, Dan gave the tin to Lee who formed a circle around the unconscious figure on the floor. "Now that you've been bound by the circle, what've you got to say for yourself Meg?"

"Meg?" Lee said surprised.

"Remember I gave her that scar on the other side. Congratulations, now it's a matching pair." Dan said laughing.

Meg lunged at him and stopped as she bounced off of an invisible barrier. She looked down at the glowing circle around here.

"You know why we have come and what we seek?" The haggard voice said from the man's body.

"So you and Peg came seeking revenge?" Dan said.

"Our sister's body was broken, destroyed by you mortals." Meg said spitting at him.

Her spit bounced back toward her, held in place by the circle around her. "We gave you a chance." Dan said. "You were just playing tricks until you took the children."

"They were succulent, what right did you have to stop our meal." Meg screamed.

"Last I checked; Keg wanted to ignore us." Dan smiled. "Needless to say we don't like to be ignored. Speaking of which, we still have some of the hawthorn branches. Want to see them?"

"No," shrieked Meg and Peg, who had regained consciousness and found herself also contained with a circle.

"Make your oath," Dan said. "Make it to where we believe it and you won't be roasting alive."

"Sister, we must." Meg said to Peg.

"Before any oaths are made please drop the disguise." Lee requested.

"Mrofeurt," both of the witches said.

The male facades vanished leaving two old shriveled hags in their place. Faces withered and wrinkled by decades and rotting teeth filled their mouths. Lee could hardly stand to look at them. Dan shared the sentiment but refused to turn away. "Now make your oaths," Dan said.

"Fine," Meg and Peg said in unison.

Each raised a hand before them and with the long nails from the opposite hand's thumb cut their palm open. "By the black blood within my veins, no harm shall we cause. No mischief we make. These walls are a sanctuary against us. We denounce our powers within these walls." The old hags had made the oath in unison. "Now will you free us?" Meg asked by herself.

"If ever you try anything like this again." Dan threatened. "Or if we have to come out after you. We will see to it that you are proclaimed a witch before the court and burned to a crisp."

Meg and Peg shrunk away from the anger in Dan's voice. "Lee," he said as he removed a portion of the circle.

Lee did the same. Peg and Meg rose together and took hands. They tried to use their powers to leave the flat. "You renounced your powers here, remember?" Lee said smiling.

The two witches gave him an expression full of malice, yet peacefully made their way to the door. They opened it and ran down the stairs, out the door, slamming it behind them. Dan knelt by the door after he was sure the witches were gone. Lifting up a loose board that ran the length of the door, he looked in the groove left there. "No wonder," Dan said taking the tin and refilling the groove with salt and brick dust. "That'll stop that."

"Good thing you came in when you did." Lee admitted going into the kitchen and preparing a kettle to put on the stove.

They heard more footsteps approaching their door. Dan withdrew the pistol from his back pocket and stepped up to the door. He pulled the door open and shoved the pistol forward. Roger stood his hand up to knock on the door and Dan's pistol pushed up against his cheek. "Roger!" Dan said lowering the pistol.

"I take it that I did see who I thought I saw just run out of here." Roger said stepping into the flat.

"Yes. It has been quite an eventful morning." Lee said. "I'm getting ready to put the kettle on now, if you'd like to wait."

Roger pulled a pocket watch from his vest pocket and examined the time. "Yes, we have time for a cup of tea." He said seating himself on the crowded sofa.

Dan sat in the same chair he had fallen asleep in directly across from Roger. "You come for a visit or business?" Dan asked.

"Business," Roger said. "But we have at least an hour before our appointment. You should dress a bit less casual."

"Why?" Dan asked.

Lee came in from the kitchen. "What are we discussing?"

"The reason Roger was on the doorstep this morning." Dan responded.

"Quite," Roger said. "All that I am aware of I will gladly tell you."

Dan raised a questioning eyebrow as he took a cigar and match from the wooden box beside the chair. "Do you?" Dan asked Roger offering him the cigar.

Roger shook his head. Dan bit the tip off of the cigar and lit the match with the tip of his thumb. Careful to light the tip of the cigar evenly, Dan puffed on the cigar insuring that it burned properly. "So Roger, you were saying?"

"Yes," Roger said stiffening in his seat. "It has been requested that I bring both of you to a private audience."

"Who?" Dan asked enjoying the cigar.

"Her Majesty," Roger said.

The cigar hung forgotten from the corner of Dan's mouth. Lee was also taken aback. It had been over a year since last they had assisted the queen. "Guess I'll go put on a better shirt." Dan said putting the cigar out in the overflowing ashtray.

"Shave!" Lee called after him. "Do you know what business she has for us?"

"I was contacted as your regent warden and asked to pick you up this morning for an appointment with her Majesty in fifty-seven minutes." Roger explained consulting his watch, from the kitchen the kettle began to whistle.

2   The motorized carriage they found waiting outside of the building was impressive. Dan and Lee had never ridden in one before. Lee was amazed by the invention and looked the vehicle over inspecting certain aspects of the working. Roger stood behind them waiting for them to get into the carriage. The driver, who remained seated on a small bench at the rear of the carriage, wore a great scarf and goggles to prevent the soot from the vehicle's exhaust getting in his eyes and mouth. The bench seat was elevated so that he could see the street over the carriage. Lee was bending over inspecting the wheels. "Amazing!" He said standing up.

"What is?" Dan asked looking at the impressive wood exterior of the carriage.

"Instead of one wheel to guide in direction, the front wheels are attached to an axle of some sort with what appears to be control arms for independent movement." Lee explained.

"I see," Dan said but he did not. Mechanical items were Lee's area of expertise.

"Gentlemen, please." Roger said opening the door for them.

Dan and Lee stepped into the cabin and sat on the leather seats. The interior did not appear much different than the older horse drawn carriages. The driver's controls were also different than the velociter's. Rather than a lever between his legs there was a large wheel that allowed him to control the front wheels. There were two pairs of pedals at his feet rather than one. One pair for controlling forward or reverse motion of the carriage and the other controlled acceleration and deceleration. Checking to make sure that the road ahead of him was clear, the driver pressed the pedal for forward with his left foot and the acceleration pedal with his right foot.

The carriage started with a jump, causing its passengers to hold onto the handrail at the top of the cabin. Riding in silence, Lee mused over the workings of the carriage. Dan was more concerned with why they were being summoned by the queen herself. The last time the queen had asked for them, it had almost cost Dan and Lee their lives. It did however also lead to a very large reward for them as well. Nothing ventured nothing gained, Dan's father used to tell him.

The carriage arrived at the gates of Buckingham Palace. "Excuse me," Roger said stepping out of the carriage.

Approaching the gate, he showed something to the Captain of the Guard. Saluting, the captain ordered the gate to be opened. Dan and Lee could see the red coats and large black hats of the Queen's Guard as they stood watch. Several more were gathered behind small stone enclosures, with large six barreled guns mounted in place. Ever since the assassination attempt the guards had been rearmed and reinforced with newer methods of defense. Roger returned to the cabin and retook his seat as the carriage proceeded onto the grounds. Passing by the infantry that comprised the majority of the guard, they passed two other large machines. A Large cannon comprised the front of the machine while wheels and an engine brought up the rear. Behind the cannon was a seat for the operator. Dan and Lee marveled at the invention. "Mobile artillery," Roger said. "Apparently, it is the latest that our military has and her Majesty demanded they be added to her guard."

"Can't be too cautious." Dan stated.

"Indeed," Roger agreed, a sour look on his face.

The carriage came to a stop beside a set of doors on the side of the palace. Roger was the first out of the carriage. He opened the door and ushered Dan and Lee inside. As they walked through the wondrous halls, Dan and Lee could not help but marvel at the different works of art that they saw. Their normal visits with the queen did not take them through the palace so they had never seen most of it before. Roger stopped in front of a cherry colored wood door. He opened the door and held his hand out to enter. Dan and Lee entered and then turned around.

"Are you not coming with us?" Lee asked.

"My instructions were to lead you here and wait outside this door. Her Majesty will be waiting just beyond the next door." Roger closed the door separating himself from Dan and Lee.

Dan shrugged his shoulders and continued down the narrow hall to the next door. Lee was close behind. Dan reached the other door, turned the handle, and opened it. Stepping in he saw a lavishly decorated room, several small sofas were seated around a small table. Two silver pots of tea and a variety of biscuits were placed on the table. Looking around Lee and Dan entered the room and closed the door behind them. "Good morning," said Queen Victoria coming from around a curtain.

After the assassination attempt, she had needed emergency surgery to save her life. They had used brass and bolts to repair her. Her right arm had to be completely amputated, replaced with a brass and copper prosthetic. This had earned her the unwanted moniker of the Iron Maiden. Lee bowed before the queen. "Your Majesty," he said.

Dan slightly bowed his head. "Ma'am," was his response.

"Thank you both for coming," she said signaling that Lee could rise.

"It was our pleasure." Lee said.

"Please won't you join me for tea?" She asked.

The two men moved over to the sofa opposite her and waited for her to be seated. Once she had settled her matronly frame into the sofa, they sat. Lee served himself modestly after the queen had prepared her own cup of tea. "We have coffee, for your American tastes." The queen said indicating the silver pot on Dan's side of the biscuits.

"Thank you," he said pouring a steaming hot cup. He despised tea unless it was iced and brewed with sugar in it.

They sat for several minutes sipping their respective drinks. "I don't want to be rude, but can I ask why you called on us?" Dan said trying to sound as polite as possible.

"Certainly," the queen said. "Although, we are waiting for another guest who can explain the circumstances in detail. He will be able to answer your questions. I was merely asked to contact the best bounty hunters within our shores. Given your previous services for me, I could think of no other persons to contact."

Dan sat back and sipped at his coffee. It was good. Lee also waited as he sipped his tea. The queen herself barely touched her tea but sat pleasantly smiling at the men.

A tall gaunt figure entered the room from a different doorway. His beard was graying and his hair line was receding. Years of stress and worry had plagued him, but the men instantly recognized Prince Albert. Lee and Dan began to stand. With a wave of his hand Prince Albert stopped them. "I'm merely here to show in our guest." He said smiling.

A dwarf dressed in a specially tailored suit stepped past the prince and entered the room. "Sorry I'm late," the dwarf said, his tone gruff.

Prince Albert left closing the door behind him. The dwarf sat next to the queen looking at Dan and Lee. "Tea or coffee?" The queen offered.

"Coffee, if you don't have anything stronger." The dwarf said smiling. His great bushy beard moved when he spoke, his lips barely discernable through it.

Pouring the dwarf a cup, the queen daintily handed it to him. "Are these the men?" He asked.

Queen Victoria nodded. "Who are you?" Dan asked the dwarf.

"No question, he's the one from the other side of the ocean." The dwarf said. "Too bold to be English and he smells more like dirt than soot. Work on a farm?"

"I did, when I was younger." Dan said.

Lee watched the exchange curiously. "Have any weird dreams lately?" The dwarf asked smiling.

"I asked who you are?" Dan said repeating his question.

"So you did," the dwarf responded.

"Please," Queen Victoria said. "Gentlemen this is Ironhill Trungsden. I'll leave the rest of his story to him."

"As you wish," Ironhill said to the queen. "I sit on the Seelie Court. We have a situation that we need your help with."

"The Seelie Court?" Lee said his mouth gaping.

"Yeah," Ironhill said. "Glad you've heard of us."

"Of course we have. Thought it was all myth and legend. All we have heard is theory and rumor of the existence of the courts." Dan said.

"Who do you think sent those hounds after her majesty?" The dwarf said referring to the assassination attempt.

"Why?" Lee asked clutching the side of the sofa.

"We sent a delegation to discuss the tragic events that led to our mass discovery: the Limestone Massacre. Our kind has always tried to coexist peacefully with man so we continued that tradition. Our counterparts, the Unseelie Court, they would rather kill all humans off, can't quit fighting amongst themselves to do it." A low chuckle escaped Ironhill's mouth. "That infighting kept mankind safe. From what I hear the Unseelie don't like you two either, didn't you have some visitors this morning?"

"What do you know of it?" Dan asked narrowing his eyes.

"We heard things. Different animals told us of their passing through the forests and ways, skirting our domains, talking of avenging their fallen sister. I see they failed."

"They are part of the Unseelie Court?" Lee asked.

"All witches are whether they know it or not. Some werewolves, and vampires, bogles, a few goblin tribes, pixies, the more salacious pan's, all dark fey are a part of it but the other types that get brought in are there because they are the worst of their kind." All humor left the face of the dwarf. "Reality is, if they get their act together the world as you know it is doomed."

"Are the legends about the battle true?" Lee asked. "Upon the bridge?"

"Aye, they're true." Ironhill said his eyes glazed as he drifted to an ancient battlefield.

"I must apologize." Queen Victoria said. "I'm not as well versed in our local mythology as our guests."

"May I?" Lee asked Ironhill, who nodded his consent. "The two courts met on a bridge, neither willing to move aside for the other. It became a battle, but a curious thing happened, neither side ever came any closer to winning. They were too perfectly matched, at that point the council of both courts forged an agreement. They would never meet in open combat as they had and if factions of the courts were to fight it would be without the assistance of the other races of the court."

"It's the reason my people and the goblins still fight, we probably always will." Ironhill said. "But who knows, neither of our races share the immortality of elves and fairies."

"So how old are you?" Dan asked the dwarf.

"Almost three hundred years old." Ironhill said proudly.

Dan looked at Lee. Lee saw the look and knew he needed to ask the next question. "Why does the court need us sir?" Lee asked.

"In order to better maintain our realm and insure that we are not forgetful of the humans we share this land with, one human sits on the council. It gives us a human perspective in our actions. A child selected at birth by the council joins us at the age of seven and remains on the council for the remainder of their life." Ironhill said. "Our current human is dying; our next child is coming to age."

"How do we fit in?" Dan asked.

"If the human never makes it to their place on the court it will disrupt us. Take away the wedge that keeps us from being like the Unseelie." Ironhill took a deep breath. "You might as well know everything. Because Unseelie magic doesn't work on Seelie court members, those that actually take part and speak for their kind, the human is protected and our court does not pass into chaos. The wind has lately carried a foul thing upon it. The priests of the elves have determined what foul thing this is: The Council of the Black Forest has been contacted by the Unseelie Court."

"Black Forest?" Dan asked looking at Lee.

"In Germany?" Lee asked.

"The one and same, their version of the Unseelie Court resides there and is the council of the forest. We have reason to think the Unseelie have called out to the council members to take care of both the humans and other members of the Seelie Court."

"Other members would be appointed if that happened. What could the Unseelie gain?" Lee asked.

"If enough of us were ended, then the Unseelie could launch an attack, break the truce. With no clear leadership and the combined forces of the Unseelie and the Black Forest, the Seelie would be open and weak." Ironhill looked at his boots as they dangled over the edge of the sofa. "With one strike the Unseelie could wipe us out. After that even unorganized they would still attack your kind, probably wouldn't win but could do more damage than you'd like."

"Oh dear," Queen Victoria said putting her hand to her mouth.

"What do you need from us?" Dan asked.

"Most of the council have retreated amongst their own kind." Ironhill said. "Shortly after this I'll return to our stronghold where five hundred armored dwarves will stand between me and any assassins. We cannot protect the child though."

"Why not?" Lee asked.

"The child has to live among humans; to bring her in with us even for a short time would invalidate her for the council." Ironhill said. "It is too dangerous for us to protect her in her home and she cannot journey into the fey kingdoms without relinquishing a part of her humanity."

"What exactly did they send after the girl?" Lee asked retrieving a small notebook from his breast pocket.

"We don't know. As far as we can tell it is not some mischievous goblin or bogle. We think it is one of the beings known almost exclusively in that part of the world. Something will take the child away and allow her to be sacrificed, most likely not one of the child eating beasts from the dark land."

"Sacrificed?" Dan repeated.

"Yes with the right ceremony, all light magic can be suppressed for several days. We aren't sure this is what's happening we only think it's highly probable."

"Where is the child?" Lee asked making notes in the notebook.

"We aren't sure. The child can only be found once the current member passes." Ironhill cleared his throat. "All we know is that she's in the northern part of the country, near the Scottish border."

"Wonderful," Dan said.

"You've seen her haven't you?" Ironhill asked. "In your dream last night?"

"How do you know about my dream?" Dan asked standing up.

"Mr. Winston," Queen Victoria said sternly.

Dan looked at the woman and sat back down. "Once we knew who was being called to assist us, we had a dream sent to you." Ironhill explained. "It'll guide you to the girl and if we can identify the assassin we'll send that your way as well."

"I didn't see the little girl, only her hair." Dan said. "I also saw races fabled to be on the Seelie Court dead littered about me."

"Now you know why." Ironhill said.

"I don't like intruders rooting around in my head." Dan said stubbornly.

"We don't like having to ask humans for help, so I guess we're even." Ironhill retorted just as stubbornly. "Can we count on you two or not?"

"Of course you can," Lee asked. "I take it your Majesty is asking us as a matter of Queen and Country?"

"I am." Queen Victoria said standing from the sofa. "Success in this task will prevent the needless slaughter of the native inhabitants of our isle and also a future war that we do not wish to fight."

"As long as you're asking," Dan said. "I'll gladly do my part."

"Thank you," Queen Victoria said. "Now if you will excuse us, I need to discuss other matters with our guest."

"Certainly," Lee said bowing.

Dan and Lee left the room by the same door they had entered. They were headed toward the door where Roger was waiting. Almost at the door, they heard the report of rifles being fired. Opening the door, Roger fell through the doorway, his body was rigid and stiff. A gaunt pale figure dressed in black stood at Roger's feet. Lee turned and ran back down the hall, Dan right behind him. Bursting back into the room with the queen, they slammed the door behind them and pushed their bodies up against it. "What is the meaning of this?" The queen demanded turning away from the window where both she and Ironhill stood.

"Trouble," Dan said.

"Some form of undead." Lee explained. "Possibly a wight."

The door shoved forward, both men pushing with all their might against the door. Prince Albert rushed into the room from the other door, a curved saber in his hand. "You got anymore of those?" Dan asked.

"A pole arm is preferable," Lee called.

"Our gate is being attacked by undead fiends." Albert stated taking hold of Victoria's arm. "We must secure you."

"I'll not be rushed from my home." She said. Her regal manner provided her with courage. "It seems we have been breached, so this is our stand."

"More weapons now," Dan called as the door inched open again.

"A wight you think?" Ironhill said removing his suit coat.

"It paralyzed Roger, maybe drained him." Lee said. "Definitely not your run of the mill vampire or ghoul."

"Ironhill, can't you do something against this." Dan said.

"No, wights aren't part of any council; too solitary and single minded." Ironhill said rolling up his sleeves.

"Arms this way," Albert said leading Ironhill through the other door.

They returned. Albert carried his saber and a halberd. Ironhill carried a standard sword and a mace. "I'll keep the bludgeon if you don't mind." He told the group.

"Hand me the halberd." Lee said reaching out for it. Once he had it in his hand, he explained the plan to everyone. "The queen will stand in the back corner. When we move I'll try to keep him at distance with the tip of the halberd, you three need to take his head off."

"Seems easy enough," Dan said hefting the sword. The two and a half feet of steel gleamed in the light.

"It never is," Lee said. "Now."

Lee and Dan jumped away from the door but the wight did not try to enter. They exchanged puzzled glances. Motioning with his head, Lee told Dan to open the door. Steadying the halberd, Lee prepared to slam the pointed spike into the wight. Pulling the door open quickly, Dan jumped back into the room. Lee thrust the halberd into the hall. The wight, expecting it, allowed the stab to be made and then pushed back against it. The force of the push sent Lee off balance until he tripped over the table sending the tea pots and trays of biscuits onto the floor. Dan started to move forward to attach when the wight hurled a chair from beside the door into him, knocking him onto his back, stunned. Victoria seeing her attacker gasped and tried to move toward the door Albert had come from. The tall pale creature in a black funeral gown saw Victoria and moved toward her. Lee and Dan were both trying to recover their senses.

"Victoria!" Albert shouted as he plunged his saber into the attacker.

Turning quickly, the wight's fingertip brushed Albert's hand. His body went rigid and he fell to the floor. Ironhill rushed over the top of Albert and dealt a mighty blow to the middle of the wight's back. Bones cracked under the impact of the mace, but the wight turned and caught the mace as Ironhill tried for another blow. Ironhill held onto the mace as the wight threw it with him still attached across the room. Quickly now the wight raced and grabbed Victoria by the wrist. Nothing happened. Confusion crossed the wight's face, screaming Victoria freed her metal hand and struck the wight in the jaw sending it reeling back. She raced from the room. The wight tried to pursue her. Lee stuffed the halberd into the chest of the wight and using the floor for leverage lifted it slightly off the ground. Stretching its fingers as far as possible the wight could still not reach Lee. With a loud yell, Dan leaped from the nearest sofa, the sword held in both hands. One mighty downward stroke severed the head from the body. Still the body moved.

Ironhill standing on wobbly legs looked at the men and the impaled wight. "Take it apart." He called. "Only way to finish the job."

Dan and Lee exchanged looks around the wight. Dan shrugged and set about the gruesome task.

When he had finished the wight lay in ten different pieces on the floor. "You're going to need that stick to put him in a bag to take to Glorianna's dungeon," Dan said to Lee.

"That will not be necessary." Queen Victoria announced, returning with six of the guards who had been stationed outside. She immediately went to Albert's side. "Oh Albert, you brave fool."

"He'll be all right give him about an hour and then he'll be moving around. A little worn down for a day or two though." Ironhill said wiping his bloody brow with one of the cloth napkins on the table Lee had demolished when he fell.

"On the sofa," Victoria said as two of the guards lifted him from the floor to the nearest sofa.

"What happened out there?" Dan asked.

The queen gave a nod to the nearest guard. "Well sir, a gentleman came up and made as if he was going to ask a question. He touched one of the guards on the hand and he fell stiff as a board. That caught our attention, we of course surrounded him and that's when we believe this one entered. Twelve of these blighters attacked in total." The guard looked at his men. "All the others outside the gate have been taken care of."

"What of Roger?" Lee asked.

The queen waved her hand at two of the guards, who immediately left the room to check on the regent warden. They returned carrying his rigid form between them. Victoria motioned them toward the vacant sofa where they laid Roger down. "Should we wait on him?" Dan whispered to Lee shifting his eyes toward Roger's prone form.

"Nonsense," Queen Victoria said having regained her composure, after insuring that Albert was going to be okay. "The carriage is still waiting outside. It will take you back to your home. I trust that you can be packed and prepared for your journey."

"Thanks ma'am," Dan said. "We'll be on our way tonight."

As Lee and Dan walked down the hallway toward the door they had entered the palace through, small feet chased after them. Hearing the sound of hard soled shoes running on the slate floors, they turned and saw Ironhill coming their way. With puzzled looks they stopped and waited for him to reach them. He took a moment to speak as he tried to catch his breath. "Not used to running." He explained in between deep breaths.

"Not a lot of room under the mountains?" Dan asked.

Lee gave him a shocked look, his look softened when Ironhill laughed. "No, no there isn't." The dwarf responded. "Do not trust to what you know about the fey of this land, the Germanic agents aligned against us are most deadly and they do not abide by our rules. The necromancers that had to have set those wights on us are most likely from the Unseelie, but there's no way to be sure. The path will not be easy but trust to the dreams, they won't lead you wrong."

Dan nodded. "Thank you for all the help," Lee said.

Ironhill turned and walked away. "You're welcome," he called over his shoulder and then mumbled to himself.

The carriage bumped along the cobble stones street as it returned Lee and Dan to their home. "Interesting morning," Lee said looking out at the city as they sped past.

"Yup." Dan agreed. "Visited by witches, a collective wight attack, confirmation and employment of the Seelie Court, and we're most likely going to be attacked and possibly killed by German monsters. Interesting is definitely the term I'd use."

"We have books on German folklore. I assure you by the time we find our mystery assailants, we will know the manner of our foe and be more than capable of dealing with them." Lee said.

"Hoping we find them, before they find us." Dan said.

3   Once they had reached their flat they began to pack several trunks for the long trip, not knowing how long they would be gone. Ms. Edwards was in the midst of the chaos. "Do you know how long you will be away?" She asked.

"I'm afraid we don't." Lee told her, as he glanced over the spines of books before retrieving the volume he was looking for.

"This is a big deal, hopefully we won't be gone longer than our money's good for." Dan said winking at their landlady.

She blushed and gave him a disapproving look. "Mr. Winston," she said.

He gave a hearty laugh as he put one of the steamer trunks on his shoulder and carried it out the door to the velociter. "Pay up Lee." Dan called from the door.

Ms. Edwards gave a look from the doorway to Lee who was still taking volumes off the shelf. "What is he talking about?" She asked.

"We have already talked and would like to pay for the next year ahead of time, just in case our engagement takes us away that long." Lee said reaching into the top drawer of his desk. "Although I scarcely think we'll be away a month."

He retrieved a large bundle of pound notes wrapped with twine and handed them to his landlady. "This really is not necessary." She protested. "I will gladly keep the room until you return."

"We would not want you to be without the use of your room for no compensation. If we are gone for more than a year then you may feel free to await our return and then we will accommodate any lapsed rent payments, but until then please accept our advance." Lee said disarming her with a smile.

"All right, I'll accept it. But if you return before the twelve months is up I will return the remainder." She said turning to leave.

"If we return, I assure you we would like to remain your tenants so please keep it." Lee said as the older woman left the room and headed back to her quarters.

Coming back up the steps Dan stretched his back muscles. "She go for it?" Dan asked.

"Reluctantly." Lee stated placing the volumes on his desk inside a leather satchel.

"Well at least we won't be homeless." Dan said.

"Should we bring the Tin Man?" Lee asked.

Dan gave him a look that answered the question for him. "When do I ever think you shouldn't bring him?"

"Good point," Lee said. "I will go make sure he's prepared for travel. Where have you been putting our things?"

"Trunks by the engine, anything not watertight in the compartments." Dan responded.

Lee nodded as he headed out to the shed beside their parking structure. The Tin Man, as it was known, was kept behind locked doors. Despite the worn and weak look of the shed, it had been reinforced with steel plates to prevent anyone from breaking in. The lock was three inches wide and twice that long, Lee had to turn the key three times before the lock fully withdrew. Pulling back both doors revealed a trailer, something almost as tall as the shed was sitting under a rubber sheet to keep it dry in the event of travel. Taking a quick moment to walk around the trailer, Lee made sure that the ropes were tightly fastened and the rubber sheet firmly secured over the Tin Man. A quick inspection of the attachment and Lee was backing the velociter slowly toward the trailer. He felt a slight nudge and stopped the vehicle. Exiting the driver's seat, he saw that the attachment was perfectly aligned with the companion piece he had designed and attached to the velociter.

It was a cap that once lowered would fit perfectly onto the attachment's towing arm. With a few adjustments of two screws, the trailer containing the Tin Man was successfully hooked to the Velociter and ready for transportation.

Entering the room, Lee saw Dan putting on his gun belt with a pistol on each side. Lee watched as he finished buckling the belt and then he took a bowie knife and placed it in his boot, covering the handle with his pant's leg. "You should think about carrying," Dan said. "And not just the rifle."

Dan slipped his overcoat on and checked in the mirror they kept in the corner. Seeing that his pistols were not noticeable, he gave a quick nod to his reflection. Lee made sure that the leather rifle cover was secured so the Winchester would not fall out. Thinking about the advice Dan had just given him, he walked to his room and retrieved the folding pocket knife, which he had procured in America and a revolver similar to Dan's. The knife he put in his pants' pocket and the pistol he put in a special holster he had made. The holster slid over his shoulders and fastened onto his trousers, tucking the pistol conveniently under his arm. He also checked his reflection the small bulge under his arm was noticeable, but no one would be expecting it to be a pistol.

"Ready?" Dan asked.

Lee nodded. Dan hoisted the last steamer trunk onto his shoulder and started toward the door. Slinging the Winchester over his shoulder, Lee picked up the satchel with the books and left the room; shutting and locking the door behind him. "Goodbye, Ms. Edwards," Lee called as he passed her door.

Outside he saw Dan tying down the last trunk. Dan made his way over to the passenger seat. "Drive." Lee called.

Dan gave him a puzzled look. "Didn't think you liked my driving?"

"I don't." Lee stated. "But I have to read and I detest your reading skills more than your driving."

"Just because I don't have a pretty voice," Dan said putting on a horrid British accent.

"I cannot believe you have been in the country this long and you still cannot come close to a passable imitation." Lee said.

"Shut up and get in," Dan said walking around to the driver's side.

Placing the Winchester beside the seat, Lee climbed into the passenger door and fastened himself in with the small lap band. Pulling back the hem of the coat so he could get to his pistol if he needed to, Dan sat down and stared at the velociter controls for a moment. "Where did you pack the shotgun?" Lee asked.

"Compartment on your side, wanted it close if I needed it." Dan replied.

With a jerk and screech, the velociter jumped forward the weight of the Tin Man and the trailer the only thing keeping it from zipping through the streets. "Easy," Lee cautioned. "The trailer is not made for quick turns."

"Okay," Dan said adjusting the lever to relieve some of the energy building within the boiler. "Amazing what a little water and whiskey can do."

"Yes, miracle of the modern world." Lee said rolling his eyes.

Dan was referring to the mixture of water and whiskey that allowed the boiler to generate enough energy to move all the necessary parts of the engine. "Why was coal a bad idea?" Dan asked.

"You'd have to constantly shovel coal into the engine. This way you put half a bottle of whiskey and just let the rain fill the boiler, and it will operate for days, plus the air is cleaner without all the coal smoke." Lee said.

"Yeah, just look at the beautiful London sky." Dan said. "Let me know when you see it."

"Imagine if everyone with a velociter added to the problem." Lee said. "Plus you'd have to shovel the coal. I'd think you would be grateful to not have any additional chores."

As the velociter left London headed north toward the Scottish border, Dan and Lee noticed the change around them. The closer they had come to the outskirts of London the fewer velociters and mechanical carriages they saw to the point that the last mile was completely empty of them, with people relying on horse drawn wagons for transportation or walking to the commerce centers of the city.

Once free of the confines of the city, the cobblestone portion of the road ended and it became hard packed dirt cutting through the grass and trees of the land. The further from London they went the clearer the sky became until they could see the sun passing beyond the horizon. The orange rays touched on the dark clouds rolling in from the English

Channel. As they saw the sun sinking low and the rain approaching, Dan stopped and lit the lamps beside the compartment. The lamps would light the way ahead of them and keep anyone from wandering into their path. Lee stayed in the compartment and continued reading as he had done during the entire length of their trip. "Well," Dan said climbing back into the driver's seat.

"Once it gets too dark for me to read, I will be more than happy to continue driving while you rest." Lee informed him. Dan gave a curt nod as his response. "I've also found several candidates that fit the description of our possible assassin."

"Anything good?" Dan asked.

"One is known simply as the piper." Lee said referring to the notebook that he had been writing in. "It is a musician who with his flute or other musical instrument will lead an entire village's children away never to be seen again."

"Witch?"

"Doubtful, I'm more willing to wager it is a glamour of some sort." Lee said flipping a page in his notebook. "There are several child stealing beasts; our best hope though is that they do not know who their target is anymore than we do. Ironhill did say that they could not locate their next human."

"Doesn't mean the dark side hasn't figured out a way to," Dan said. "Whole thing makes me nervous."

Lee agreed with Dan. The velociter continued on the dirt road as the storm clouds rolled to meet them.

It had grown dark over an hour ago, with both the storm clouds and the setting of the sun. Lee had taken over as the driver of the velociter, while Dan got as comfortable as he could on the seat and laid his head back. He really wanted a cigar but in the velociter the smoke would merely annoy Lee, so instead Dan decided to try and get some sleep. Lee could barely hear the noise of Dan's snoring over the sound of the velociter on the uneven road they were on. It had been several hours since they had seen another vehicle. Lee was comforted by the confines of London the familiar sights and sounds of the city. Never would he be as calm as Dan in the wide open spaces of the world. Still Lee did not think on that as he saw distant lights, not sure if it was a manor house, small village or another velociter. Still the possibility of people made him ease a bit. Dan slept on while Lee dealt with his anxieties.

The field was just as it had been in the last dream. "Again?" Dan called across the open plain.

He heard the voice from the same place as the previous night. "Help!"

Dan wasted no time and took off at a full run toward the glimpses of red hair that he saw over the wheat. Any clue as to where this was would be most welcome. There was a forest of gnarled old trees not too far beyond the border of the field. Turning and looking beside him he saw a small stone wall and a village. On the far side of the village away from the field a great stone steeple rose into the air. It was black and in disrepair. Dan was not sure but it could have been a church or possibly an old lord's residence. Looking in the other direction he saw only open field, something prevented him from looking behind him. It was a dream and in dreams not everything is done for a reason; Dan accepted this and continued running toward the girl.

A great shadow fell across the field. Dan looked but did not see anything in the sky. The shadow never moved it only grew smaller. This puzzled Dan, when a great stone statue fell to the ground before him, it startled him so much that he fell backwards. The statue was of a great beast that he had never seen before. The ground under him shook several more times and still the child called for help. Rising he looked about and saw several other statues of different beasts; they were not familiar to him and did not appear to be solid. The shapes continued to change and distort until glowing eyes appeared in all of them and he could see they were all looking at him.

Looking beside him was Ironhill's dead body. The corpse turned toward him. "The path is besought by obstacles. This is your path." The corpse said as it crumbled into dust.

"God, I hate this." Dan said standing up.

The animal from the first statue was moving off of the dais it had been on and came near Dan. A low inhuman sound, worse than a goblin's laugh, came from the moving shadows.

Putting his fists up Dan screamed at the beast. "Well what are you waiting for? Come and get it!"

Lee jolted at the violent outburst from his sleeping partner. Hitting the control stick with his leg, the velociter turned off of the path and bumped along the road for several seconds until Lee could direct it back to the path and stop the vehicle. Dan sat with his eyes wide open and his fists in front of him as if he were in a brawl. "Are you okay?" Lee asked, his own heart calming.

"Another dream." Dan explained. "Why couldn't they have given them to you?"

"We will ask them if we get the chance. What was this dream of?" Lee asked retrieving his notebook and pen.

Dan proceeded to tell Lee the entire dream, which ended when he was jarred from his sleep by the velociter's bumpy ride getting off the path. Lee made sure to copy every detail Dan gave. "So the statues kept changing shape?" Lee asked.

"Yeah, I think the dwarf knows there are different agents out there, not to mention the Unseelie court members, but he doesn't know what or who. This was his way of giving us what information he has." Dan said tilting his head and popping the vertebrae of his neck. "Next time I see Ironhill remind me to lay a beating on him."

"Duly noted," Lee said putting away the notebook. "On the bright side, I think we'll be to that village in a few hours."

Dan followed Lee's finger. It was pointed toward several lights in the distance. "How do you know it's a village?"

"The lights haven't moved and it's too big to be another velociter. Most manor houses would be sleeping currently. But a village would still be open for some local tavern or perhaps a common house." Lee explained. "Also according to the map we aren't too far from Berkenshire."

Dan stayed awake for the remainder of the ride as the lights grew closer until he was also sure it was a village. Both Lee and Dan could hear the nearby thrum of the turbines from a nearby but unseen power station. It was most likely buried and would explain why they could not see any lights from it. Ahead of them loomed a walled city with large wooden gates. Lee pulled the velociter to a stop. Dan looked out through the window of the velociter before opening the door and stepping out into the night air. Two large lanterns hung by the wooden gate. "Hello," Dan called.

A small panel in the door was pulled back and an older man put his face in the gap. "Who goes?" He asked.

"We go," Dan said studying the old man, "sent by the queen from London."

"Sure you were," the old man said returning Dan's studious gaze. "And just who are you?"

"Dan Winston, my associate is Lee Baum. Now will you open or not?" Dan demanded.

"You're a yank." The old man said.

"And proud of it."

"What business are you in?" The old man said staring at Lee inside the velociter.

"We're exterminators of the strange and weird by name but we handle most any problem outside the normal realm of things." Dan said.

"Bless me soul!" The man exclaimed and vanished from the panel.

Dan turned and gave Lee a confused look. Then the gates opened. There were several men standing inside the gate. The old man, another man a bit older but wearing the trappings of minor nobility, a young strapping man with the badge of a constable, and a few people who may have been curious townspeople. The small street that comprised the main avenue of the town was lined with powered street lamps and most buildings had the telltale glow of being powered as well. "I told you Queen Victoria would hear our plea." The nobleman said. He stepped through the gate and shook Dan's hand vigorously. "I am Rodney, the mayor of this town."

Dan gave a nod. "Nice to meet you Rodney."

"We are so glad you came, we have been having the most awful trouble with the beast." Rodney continued.

"Beast?" Dan asked.

"Yes, surely the queen gave you all the details."

"No, she just told us you good people needed help." Dan said smiling.

"Certainly, please come in. We don't have proper accommodations for your . . ." Rodney looked at the velociter trying to determine what word to use. "Transportation, but you can store it in the barn behind the tavern." Rodney said smiling.

Rodney gave Dan directions to the stable. "Good news," Dan said to Lee as he returned to his seat in the velociter. "Apparently, we've got a job."

Lee arched his eyebrow at the statement. "Apart from the one we currently have from the queen?"

"These good folks think that we're here to help them deal with some beast." Dan said.

"What beast?" Lee asked.

"Didn't get the details," Dan said smiling. "But they told me where to park and we can talk about it at the tavern, where they'll prepare a room for us."

Lee did not return Dan's smile. He grumbled as Dan directed him to the stable. It was a very old building and had seen better days. There was a large hole in the roof and it seemed that there were more cobwebs than hay bales in the hayloft. A teenage boy held the door open as Lee drove the velociter inside. Checking to make sure there were no horses near the stalls, Lee carefully backed the Tin Man on his trailer into the vacant stall and shut down the velociter. He made sure to remove the ignition switch to prevent anyone from taking it. The teenager had a head full of curly brown hair, a small chalk board hung around his neck. Waving the boy got their attention, Dan and Lee looked at him. He scrawled "thank you" in big letters across the chalkboard. "For what?" Dan asked.

Using his sleeve to erase the chalk, the teenager wrote "for getting rid of the monster." He looked up with a big smile on his face as he finished writing.

Lee and Dan returned the youth's smile. Dan, careful to make sure that the shotgun was wrapped, took it and a small bundle of clothes from the steamer trunk. Lee carried the Winchester still in its cover and his satchel with the books, stuffing a change of clothes into it after removing them from one of the other steamer trunks. Motioning for the duo to follow him, they followed the teenager from the stable across a large empty lot where charred remains of a building loomed up from the ground. After crossing the remains of the house, they found themselves at the local tavern a wooden sign above the door told them the tavern was called the Thieves' Den. The picture showed several rogues sharing a drink gathered around a table. "My kind of place," Dan said over his shoulder to Lee.

"Indeed," Lee agreed frowning.

Stepping in they saw that the tavern was well lit but not many people were within its confines. Rodney was sitting around a table with the local clergy and the constable. The bartender a big burly man with a great big bushy beard was drinking from a large tankard. When he placed it back on the bar, the frothy remains of the beer that he had been enjoying were present in his beard, encircling his mouth. Rodney stood when he saw Lee and Dan. "Gentlemen," he greeted coming towards them. "Thank you so much for joining us."

Dan and Lee put on their best business smiles. "Our pleasure," Lee said shaking Rodney's hand. "Before we begin might you tell us where we can place our items?"

"Of course," Rodney said. "Edmund show them to their room."

Shaking his head the teenager ran to the two men and led them up the stairs to the third door on the right. He opened the door and passed by them on his way back down the stairs. The room was large with two separate beds, a small table and a tub and a chamber pot in an adjoining room. A large window graced the wall and gave a decent view over the wall and into the dark of the forest on the border of the village. "Nice room," Dan said.

"Very nice." Lee said admiring the view. "Well no time to admire it now, we should find out what beast we're to be slaying."

They came down the stairs and found the teenager, Edmund, sitting on a small stool by the fireplace. The men were still seated at their table. The bartender had moved away somewhere that they could not see. They approached the table with the men. "Room to your liking?" Asked the barkeep coming from a doorway behind the bar, most likely the kitchen they assumed.

"Quite," Lee said. The barkeep beamed with pride as he smiled.

"Gentlemen," Rodney said once again. "This is Vicar Wallace and this is our constable Gregory George."

Dan and Lee took the empty seats at the end of the table. Raising his hand to get the attention of the barkeep, Dan signaled for a drink. Nodding the barkeep turned to fill a mug. Lee not caring for anything took his notebook from inside his jacket and opened it to a blank page. "I really must apologize for our ignorance of your problem, but it is always best to get the word from the people directly." He said smiling.

"Never know how fouled up it'll be if we get it some other way." Dan stated taking his drink from the barkeep, who turned and made his way back to the bar.

Dan smiled as he drank greedily. Lee did his best to hide his embarrassment at his partner. "So if we might, what can you tell us?" Lee asked.

Dan finished the mug in one continuous drink and placed it on the table in front of him. His thirst quenched, he listened attentively to the details being given. "It began only ten days ago," Rodney started. "At first you tell yourself it's a local animal or person, but then the attacks became more calculated, defeating our best defenses."

"We have always had the wall and the gate but we did not keep it locked and guarded as we do now, not until the killings began. The wall was climbed and people taken back over it in the dead of night. I do not know how it is being done, not with what we've seen." Gregory started. "The first few we found within the streets, then inside their beds, then after we barred the door and posted the guard. The ones we've found have been found outside the wall."

"And you're sure that they were inside when the gate was barred?" Lee asked.

"Positive." Gregory confirmed nodding. "We've instituted a house by house check to insure that everyone is home after we bar the gate."

"What was done to the victims?" Dan asked.

"Different things, the first ones were killed cleanly, the next were wounded more so than the first ones. The ones we've found outside the wall have been savaged and pieces of them missing. Only one thing was noticeable about all of them; no blood." Gregory said.

"No blood?" Lee asked. "As in they did not bleed or there was no blood in their bodies or at the scene of the attack?"

"We could not find any blood anywhere in the bodies, or on the bed sheets, nor on the grass around them. None of it."

"The devil came for them," Vicar Wallace said. "This power we've found to make things run and lights without fire is an abomination to God and he is punishing us by setting loose the fallen angel. He walks through the walls of our security and plucks those dwelling by the abominations."

"Thank you Vicar," Rodney said coldly.

Dan slapped the older clergyman on the back. "I like him," Dan said smiling.

"Mock me if you want, but I've seen him." Vicar Wallace said. "He came singing, his ears rose to a point, and he left not a print where he stepped."

"Where did you see him?" The constable asked surprised by the news.

"He was in the parish, waiting for me. His words were like ice in my veins, but he told me as long as we lived by such ungodly ways he would prowl our streets until none of us were left." Vicar Wallace said.

"Why didn't you tell us about this before?" Gregory demanded. "Do you know the people we could have saved?"

"None of them," Dan said. "You aren't dealing with Lucifer himself, just an animal that likes to toy with its food. Sorry Vicar, you've been had."

"What do you think?" Lee asked his partner.

"Most likely what you're thinking," Dan said.

"Please don't keep us in the dark, what is happening here?" Rodney implored the men.

"If we tell you it won't do you any good, suffice it to say that we'll be more than happy to deal with this predicament." Dan said.

"One or two," Lee said.

"Two, three maximum." Dan said.

The three locals watched the exchange between the two men, puzzled at their conversation.

"Well then, in three nights or sooner we will have solved your problem." Lee said closing his notebook and standing. Dan stood with him and they started back toward the stairs.

"What should we do?" Rodney asked.

"Go to your homes bolt all the doors and windows and just wait." Dan instructed.

"It really is the best advice we can give." Lee said following Dan upstairs.

The constable, mayor, and vicar sat at the table exchanging puzzled looks. "I suppose we should do as they say," Rodney said.

"You go ahead," Gregory said standing up. "I can't just act like nothings out there."

"Son, listen to reason. These men are trained hunters. They will bring down the beast if possible. If you continue tempting God you will find yourself a victim. Spend the night with me in prayer." Vicar Wallace offered.

"I've no need for prayer." Gregory said leaving the tavern and going into the darkness.

"Young fool," Rodney said.

"He has lost much," the Vicar said. "We should know that young blood does not cool so easily."

Closing the door and locking it behind them, Lee and Dan went about preparing for the evening ahead of them. "I tell you if I had any doubts, they went away when the holy man described the devil to us." Dan said.

"Do you think this is related to your dreams?" Lee asked. "Does this mean we are on the right path?"

"I think so. This is the first obstacle, I suppose. It began ten days ago and escalated this quickly. Definitely not normal behavior and the timing seems off. So the Unseelie Court found out that the Seelie are going to try and get someone to their target before they do. Since they know it won't be members of the court itself the Unseelie send out minions to try and deter us." Dan said. "Good plan."

"I would much rather prefer they just surrender their plans and give up." Lee said sourly.

"Me to, but we'll have to take what we got." Dan said lying down on the bed.

"Open the window?" Lee asked.

"Naw, then it'll know it's a trap." Dan said placing one revolver in his hand and laying it on top of his leg.

Lee detached the shotgun from the pack and disconnected the hose. He stood in the bathroom door. "Are you sure you would not rather switch roles?" Lee asked.

"No, I'll play bait. When you hear me shoot come quick but don't shoot me." Dan said placing his hand on the light control by the bed. "Don't go to sleep." Dan cautioned turning off the lights.

"I swear it's like you think I haven't been doing this with you for a while," Lee said going into the attached restroom.

4   Dan lay in the dark on the bed pretending to snore, his eyes open and alert. Lee sat on the edge of the small tub, the shotgun resting across his knees. They had been in their locations for some time. Dan did not move, Lee stood and stretched his back occasionally. The goal was to present an easy target for their prey. So far nothing had happened, nor had they heard any sounds of disturbance in the village. After several hours passed, Dan heard the latch on the window being slid back allowing the window to be opened. Most of the streetlights had been shut off hours ago, but the moon provided enough light that Dan could see the silhouette of something crouched on the windowsill. Dan continued to make the snoring sounds. He knew not to scare the prey just yet. The figure on the windowsill stepped silently onto the hardwood floor.

      Dan flipped the switch turning on the lights and sat up aiming the pistol at the target. It was a lithe figure dressed in black leather clothing, a gentle featured face, and eyes colored so dark they appeared black. The skin was pale almost translucent, with a slight blue hue to the edges. Long dark hair adorned the head with tall ears rising to a point. Taking in the intruder in a quick glance, Dan squeezed the trigger and fired several times. His attacker was quick and slipped out of the way of the bullets. "Lee," Dan yelled.

      While the evil fiend dodged Dan's bullets, he never saw Lee slip from the bathroom and fire the shotgun. The buckshot tore into the side of the beast slamming it into the wall. "Delvin?" Lee asked.

      Dan reloaded his pistol. "Yeah," he confirmed.

      Lee aimed the shotgun once more at the beast as it turned to face them. It let out a long hiss, its face contorted in demonic rage, baring sharp long canines. Before Lee could pull the trigger again, the delvin had dove through the open window into the night. Lee tossed the shotgun to Dan, who caught it and turned it toward the open window. Running to his bedside, Lee retrieved his Winchester rifle and attached a small round piece of glass to the barrel. He secured the small clamp on the rear of the glass and hurried to the window. Quickly he leaned over and back in to make sure that there was nothing waiting on him. Scouring the city with his naked eye, Lee looked for their intruder. Something moved through the shadows, Lee placed the stock of the Winchester against his shoulder and sighted down the rifle, using the glass attachment to magnify his vision. "Lee?" Dan said from behind him.

"Go." Lee stated and heard the sound of Dan's boots as they went down the hallway.

Lee tried to follow the figure as it made its way through the empty streets. It was a hard effort given the lack of light through most of the village. He caught a glimpse of movement in the moonlight and followed the figure. It barely stood out, a darker black against the shadows. Lee had fought these monsters before and knew how to find them but it was still difficult especially at this distance. It helped that Lee knew the final destination of the target: the wall. Judging by the current heading that Lee had tracked, he narrowed the possible section of wall to a twenty foot section near the forest. Dan was running through the street toward the wall, his boots thumping through the dirt, occasionally slowing. Lee knew he was checking around blind corners to make sure that he was not being ambushed.

Something began to clamber up the wall, exactly in the center of the section of wall where Lee had expected it. Taking careful aim, Lee slowed his breathing, taking in a short breath and exhaling as he squeezed the trigger. The shot rang out in the night, and the bullet ran true. The dark spot on the wall screeched and fell back to the ground. Despite his urge to run into the street to help Dan confirm the kill, Lee remained where he was making sure that there were no additional targets. Something began climbing the wall again, slower and more cautious. Lee took aim. He was not sure how the target he had hit was able to continue climbing. It was definitely the same size and moved as if injured, but it continued climbing. Waiting until it mounted the top of the wall and prepared to leap off; Lee took another shot this time aiming for the head. The body began to leap down when the bullet struck and Lee saw his target somersault off the wall into the forest.

Lee removed the glass piece from the rifle barrel and headed out the door to meet Dan at the wall. As he ran through the darkened streets, he saw a figure leaning over something in an alleyway. Leveling the rifle at the leaning figure, Lee steadied his breathing. "Who goes there?" Lee challenged the shadowy figure.

"Who do you think?" Dan replied. "I left the matches in my coat, you got any?"

Lee felt in his pockets and found the familiar rectangular shape. He retrieved it from his breast pocket and handed it to Dan. Dan struck the match and it flared to life. Using the flame, he lit the lamp hanging on his belt. "I'd love one of these fellas that didn't need fire to work." He said blowing out the match.

"I've been working on something," Lee said absently as he scanned the surrounding area. "I put two into our escapee."

"Did they stop him?" Dan asked.

"First one didn't, second one I'm not sure." Lee said.

Dan turned and his lantern illuminated the body that he had been leaning over. It was the constable, a terrible gash ran down the side of his throat. "He got a little bit of food before I got here," Dan said.

The constable's coat had been pressed against the wound to staunch the flow of blood. "We should get him to a doctor," Lee said scanning the signs in front of the different buildings.

"The tavern, they can get the doctor for him," Dan said getting set to hoist Gregory by his arms. "Get the feet."

Lee did his best to carry the man's legs while maintaining the Winchester in his hands. After struggling with him, they knocked on the door to the barkeep's quarters and had him send for the doctor. Edmund, the mute teenager, ran from the building to find the doctor. The barkeep replaced Gregory's jacket with one of the bar cloths and put a pot of water over the fire to boil. The doctor, a younger bespectacled man, came rushing in carrying his black leather bag; Edmund leading the way. "What happened?" The doctor asked.

"The same thing that got the others, tried to get him." Dan said placing a long piece of straw into the fire. When the tip caught fire, he used it to light his cigar and then discarded the straw.

Dan and Lee sat at a table far away from the doctor, his patient, the barkeep, and Edmund. "We should go after it," Lee whispered.

"You know as well as I do," Dan said exhaling the blue smoke. "These things are worse in the dark, and it's wounded, that's double deadly."

"I know but if we wait," Lee started.

"Yeah, yeah, I know but we can track it in the daylight, it won't be on the move and also it's wounded so it'll leave a nice trail. Out there we're sitting ducks. Can't see as well, hear as well, or move nearly as quietly. I say we wait 'til morning and then take our chances." Dan said.

Lee grumbled his agreement. He knew Dan was right, but Lee hated leaving a job undone, normally two shots and the thing was finished but this seemed to be a different type of circumstance. While Dan was still finishing his cigar, Lee went to the room. He closed the window, placed a few warding items across the sill, and picked up the few pieces of debris from the floor. Finally, he lay down in the bed. Its billowy comfort was just what he needed after riding in the velociter most of the day and all the excitement. This was their first day on their journey and Lee could only wander how much worse it would get before it was done.

By the time Dan had made his way up to the room, Lee was fast asleep still in his shoes on top of the blankets. Dan grinned and shook his head. He finally pulled his boots off and lay down in his own bed. It did feel nice. Looking at the window he saw the warding articles and was able to relax.

When they awoke, voices could be heard coming from downstairs in the tavern. Dan and Lee looked at each other. "Constable's going to make it," Dan said from the bed.

Lee rolled out of bed and went into the bathroom. Shaving and bathing, he changed into a fresh pair of clothes and went back into the room. "Dan," he said. Dan opened one eye and looked at him. "We don't want the trail getting cold, do we?"

"No," Dan agreed sitting up mumbling under his breath.

Splashing some water on his face and changing clothes, Dan grabbed the shotgun leaving the pack in the room. Together they went down the stairs into the main room of the tavern. It was filled with people, most of the town by Lee's estimation. Everyone got quiet as the two hunters came amidst them. "Good morning," Lee said smiling at the people. A few returned his smile, most did not.

"Got any coffee?" Dan asked. The barkeep shook his head. "Figures," Dan said heading toward the door.

"Excuse me gentlemen," Rodney said from the middle of the group of citizens. Lee and Dan turned and faced the local government representative. "We were wondering how the constable was attacked?"

"We found him outside after the attack had occurred." Lee said. "It is our belief that as the creature was fleeing the constable got in its path and was attacked."

"Which means, he didn't go home and lock himself in like we told him to," Dan said.

"Understandably so, but we were under the impression you were here to handle this problem." Rodney stated, a few of the braver citizens agreed.

Dan fixed them with a stare and they quieted down and refused to look up from the floor. "You want us to fix this then stay out of our way and let us do our job. That's why your constable got tore up, he didn't listen. We'll take care of this but we won't be responsible when you people refuse to listen to us." Dan stormed out of the tavern, Lee followed close behind.

"The nerve of some people," Lee said.

"I know, not like we attacked him or said we'll make sure no one else gets attacked. Stupid people, they're everywhere." Dan said as they marched through the town toward the gate on the other side of the village.

Once outside the gate, Lee led Dan along the wall to the place where he had shot the delvin. There was a clearly crushed place in the grass where something had landed, and also a blood spray. "Well you got him all right," Dan said squatting down to examine the blood trail. "It leads toward the woods, no real surprise there."

Dan stood and began to follow the tracks and blood drops. Despite how light the delvin could walk it still left evidence, it was just harder to find. Once they were among the trees, it was easier to spot the blood. Following it into the forest, Dan and Lee were aware of how quiet their surroundings were. "No birds. It is too warm for them to have migrated." Lee observed just so the only sound was not their footsteps across the soft earth floor.

"Yeah," Dan agreed keeping his eyes to the ground seeking the next blood drop. "You know well as I, they don't like being near these unnatural monsters."

The quiet solitude of the forest closed in around them. Lee felt the presence of the forest, it differed greatly from the city. Within the confines of the city, man was the creator; here within the forest they were the intruders: they were not welcome here. The smell of loam and the rotting leaves under the large boughs of oak and pine added a scent of decay that made the forest more foreboding than it would have been during the height of spring.

The forest was in its annual cycle of dying, which was what made Lee so uncomfortable. Dan knew the forest, had grown up in them but these English forests were different than the friendly woods of Tennessee. They always seemed to have old souls blooming for a few months out of the year spending most of their time dead or dying.

Tennessee had trees similar to England but the evergreens lived up to their name keeping a reminder that the world was not always bleak and the trees bloomed and had their cover for almost half the year. Not to mention that the sun always seemed to shine so much more in Tennessee than it did in England. Despite his familiarity with woodlands, even Dan could not get comfortable in the ones found in England, especially knowing what was waiting here for them.

They made their way to a large oak standing wider and taller than the other trees. Dan followed the trail and walked completely around the tree before coming back to the original starting point. He looked up and climbed the first few branches to make sure that the delvin had not climbed up the tree. There were no other signs; they stopped at the base where the roots dug into the earth. Hopping off the branch and landing on the ground, he lowered the shotgun toward a knot in the tree. "Here," was all Dan said as he indicated with the shotgun.

Lee nodded and laid the Winchester against a nearby tree. Inspecting the knot and the roots protruding from the ground, Lee searched for the way to open the delvin's resting place. Withdrawing his hand quickly, Lee found what he was looking for; a cold dead spot on the tree. "Here," he said standing and retrieving the Winchester.

"Sure?" Dan asked pulling the Bowie knife from his boot.

"Positive," Lee said making sure a round was chambered in the rifle.

With two mighty strokes of the Bowie, Dan cut through the root that stood up from the ground before disappearing into the dark soil. Once the root was severed, the ground fell away like cascading water. Within the revealed space was the delvin, eyes open. It was adorned with a large wound in one cheek exiting the other and another wound in the chest. Its eyes roamed from side to side seeing Dan and Lee. "Howdy," Dan said placing the Bowie knife back in his boot. "We know you can't move or really do much, but we do know that you can at least talk. I suggest you do so."

"Why are you here?" Lee asked.

The delvin sat there not saying a word merely glaring with unmitigated rage at its captors. "All right out into the sun you go," Dan said grabbing the collar of the delvin's shirt.

"No," it hissed. "I am here, you know why."

Dan kicked the beast. "We want to hear you say it."

"I am the first of many to block your path," it said. "I am the first; I am also the lowliest of those that will block your path."

"Given how easy you were, I assume we're supposed to be scared." Dan said.

The delvin laughed; a low sound absent of warmth and happiness. "You are fools. Nothing will stop what has been started. The worlds of light and man will fall before us."

"What is the next obstacle and where will we find it?" Lee asked.

"I do not know what awaits you," the delvin said.

Dan pulled the Bowie out once more and leaned down. He drew back to strike and cut the creature's hand off. "Lies!" Dan accused the delvin.

"No, my masters merely told me where to await you. I am but a pawn as are you. I will tell you where next death is awaiting you." The delvin gave a ghastly smile with the cheeks destroyed and most of the back teeth blown to bits by the bullet. "Continue north and there death waits for your next encounter."

"Anything else," Dan asked Lee.

"What has been sent for the Seelie Court member?" Lee asked.

"Kill me. I will not betray our victory over your kind." The delvin said.

"Fine," Dan said striking the head from the body with one blow from the Bowie. "Give me a hand."

Lee bent and lifted under one arm as Dan lifted under the other. Together they drug the body into a bright patch of sunlight. It did not burst into flames as vampires do, it merely turned into mist and wafted into the sky. "I like the ones that burn better," Dan said.

"Why?" Lee asked.

"I know they're dead," Dan said walking back to the head. He tossed it into a sack he had brought and headed back toward the village.

Once back at the tavern they found most of the townspeople still gathered. Lee and Dan looked at them. "We have succeeded. You will be plagued no longer." Lee said comforting the frightened people.

A large cheer went up from the crowd and some went back to their homes while others stayed to celebrate the hunters with mugs of ale. Dan found Rodney at the bar with a mug in his hand. "Rodney," Dan said pulling the mayor aside. "I need someone to carry this with a message for me."

While Rodney went to find the messenger, Dan had tied the top of the bag and written a note that he had placed into the bag.

Rodney returned with a young man. "Best rider in the town." Rodney said leaving Dan with the young man.

"Can you read?" Dan asked.

"Yes sir," the messenger said.

"Good, take this sack to this man at this location. If you can't find it ask for Scotland Yard, it's the small building beside it. Understood?"

The messenger took the scrap of paper and read it, then he nodded. "I won't fail you sir." The young man said. "I'll leave immediately."

Dan gave him four pounds for his journey and went to the bar as the young man left on his horse, headed for London.

As the night grew darker, the villagers did not feel the fear they had felt at the darkening shadows. Dan sat with the vicar, Rodney and a few other local men. Lee sat at a separate table with several of the locals, predominantly available young women. Dan had tried to strike up a conversation with them but the women quickly abandoned him for the table where Lee sat sipping a glass of wine.

"So what was the foul thing?" Vicar Wallace asked.

"A delvin," Dan answered.

"A what?" One of the men at the table asked.

"You've heard of elves?" Dan asked. The men at the table all nodded their heads. "Good, well a vampire is an undead human that drinks blood from the living. A delvin is an elf that has gone dark; they eat flesh and drink blood. Now your common elf eats only vegetables, berries stuff like that. The delvin will not touch anything like that they only want meat, very rare meat."

"Why are they so different?" Rodney asked.

"Well according to the stories, they were originally elves just like any other but they were warped by dark magic and trapped. They resorted to eating one of their own to push back the hunger growing in them. Ever since they've been different, sunlight destroys them they sleep in the ground. If they attack another elf, he may become one or he may not, they say it depends on what lies within the heart of the elf." Dan smiled. "But that's all just myth and legend."

"The church," Vicar Wallace started. "How did he enter the church, vampires can't?"

"Elves and delvin have different rules than you or I. They don't play by the same rules or believe in the same things as we do. Vampires have to be invited in, can't enter a church, and can't cross running water. Delvin can do all of those things but always live near the roots of trees and always within a forest. Just a difference in the species I suppose." Dan explained.

There was a short burst of giggles from the table nearby. Dan looked over at Lee who was charming all of the ladies at his table. The conversation at Dan's table shifted more toward crops and farming as the men began to talk amongst themselves, excluding Dan from most of the conversation. It did not bother Dan.

Lee was enjoying the company at the table, even though it was a little out of his element. He was not used to entertaining so many young ladies at one time. Yet he felt it would be rude to leave them at the table while Dan was still entertaining his guests. Finally, after having told every anecdote and amusing story that was appropriate for mixed company, Lee began to inquire of the ladies.

Lee knew that they would all be more than willing to talk about themselves, so he let them. By the time that the ladies were preparing to go home, Lee had learned of their families, their educations, and most of them had told him of their dowries. Seeing them off into the night, Lee turned and saw Dan sitting with a few of the remaining men. They were not talking with him rather, Dan seemed to be sitting with them to waste time. Nodding to his friend, Lee went upstairs. He could hear the familiar sound of Dan's boots climbing the stairs not far behind him. Lee entered the room and waited. Dan entered a few strides behind him. Lee closed the door.

"Any interesting conversation?" Lee asked.

"Lots, I learned about the crops and cattle around here, which had the best soil and all manner of useless stuff." Dan said sitting down to take off his boots. "You?"

"I think most of the young ladies at my table were expecting to be whisked off to London tonight." Lee said smiling to himself. "It's quite flattering."

"I bet," Dan said. "So tomorrow we'll pull out and keep heading north?"

"I can think of no better direction to go. Do you think it was telling us the truth?" Lee asked.

"Hard to say, never can trust them but we know we have to head toward the border so I don't see why not." Dan said. "I don't see why it would have sent us away from danger."

"Too true," Lee agreed. "They do seem to have something of a hatred for us."

"It's mutual I'm sure." Dan said lying back on the bed.

The morning sun woke them both as it shone into the room. Dan was groggy from all the ale he had drank the previous evening. Lee was up and ready to face the day as was usually his fashion. Looking out the window at the woods on the edge of the forest, he saw birds fluttering above the trees. It was the sign he needed to know without a doubt that the problem had been dealt with completely. "The birds are back," Lee informed Dan.

Dan covered his head with the pillow, ignoring Lee. Choosing to leave rather than annoy Dan further, Lee went downstairs. The barkeep made him two eggs and a rather large piece of sausage. Lee was finishing the last of the food when Dan came trudging downstairs. The barkeep gave him a cup of black liquid that was thick. "Coffee," the barkeep said smiling.

"Thanks," Dan said weakly returning the smile.

He took a sip of the coffee and fought back the urge to spit it out. "Good brew," Dan said to the barkeep that was beaming with pride.

The barkeep returned with a plate of food for Dan as well. He left the two men to talk. "How is it really?" Lee asked indicating the cup of coffee.

Dan looked around to make sure the barkeep was not nearby. "This is some of the worst swill I've ever had," Dan confided to his friend. "So what's our next move?" He asked scooping a large portion of eggs into his mouth.

"I see no reason to stay here any longer, as I tried to tell you this morning. The birds are back in the forest so all should be fine. If we head north there are several villages along our path. We can stop and ask there if they've seen anything that corresponds to your dream. Speaking of which did you have another one last night?"

"I did," Dan confirmed. "Same as the night before except the first statue was destroyed, so first one down I suppose."

"That is good news," Lee said standing from the table. "I will go pack our things and we can be on our way within the hour."

Dan just nodded his head as he ate the food in front of him and tentatively drank the drink the barkeep had called coffee.

5   The velociter made its way through the countryside, the sun shining through the perpetual clouds that hovered over the British Isles. Something large and gray was moving across the sky. Dan tapped Lee on the shoulder. "Is that what I think it is?" He asked.

"It appears to be one of the new airships." Lee observed squinting at the object. "I heard they were looking into using them for commercial travel and of course military uses."

"What can the military use those for?" Dan said almost driving the velociter off the road as he watched the large dirigible.

"The Prussians used them to conquer the Western half of Germany. Dropped large explosive units, our military referred to them as bombs, onto key locations and of course, the Germans only had their large artillery to respond. Not very accurate and of course even when they would make a direct hit you suddenly had an explosive ball of helium plummeting to the ground." Lee said remembering the article he had read. "Since then many of the better organized countries have started investing in both the airship technology and more accurate weapons to combat them."

"When can we get one?" Dan asked having to swerve back onto the road again.

"Will you please watch the road," Lee chided. "As for when we can manage to procure one, not anytime soon. They cost more than all the bounties we have so far collected and frankly we don't need one. You do realize that we have not had any issue with high flying creatures."

"What about dragons?" Dan asked.

"No one has seen a dragon in centuries."

"They're still out there. Just hibernating," Dan said.

"Hibernating?" Lee asked amused at Dan's assumption.

"Yeah, bears back home do it during the winter. Take a nice long nap. Maybe dragons do the same thing, but we don't know when their spring'll be here."

"You are only putting forth this theory because you want to find their hordes of treasure," Lee said.

"If we did, we could buy an airship." Dan said.

Lee tracked the airship for a few more moments then returned to his reading. "I will tell you this," Lee said looking up from his book. "The German fey have many of the same weaknesses that ours do but they seem to be of a much more malicious nature."

"So we'll just be malicious right back at them," Dan said watching the road ahead of them. "Cobblestones ahead."

Lee looked and saw the road was converting from the packed dirt path to an actual cobblestone road. The velociter jolted as it hit the cobblestones. "Back to the subject at hand. These German fey are not just more malicious, they are actually from everything I'm seeing more wicked and violent from most of our counterparts." Lee said. "Their troll for instance . . ."

"Trolls, they eat goats and cows turn to stone in the sunlight, occasionally live under bridges and inside old wells, I know about trolls." Dan interrupted.

"Not these, goats and cows are sometimes their food. They prefer children. According to what I've read, they will lie in wait under a child's bed or climb in through an unlatched window and spirit children away into the night. Sunlight turns them to stone but no one knows where they make their residence." Lee said.

"Do they like the riddles?" Dan asked.

"Doesn't say," Lee said.

"Good, I hate their stupid riddles."

"Their goblins are a little bit more vicious and they have a creature called a gremlin, which wreaks havoc with machinery."

"Sounds like Black Powder Clan to me," Dan said.

"No, they don't use technology they just like to mess it up. Strange, they seem to be mainly mischievous with disastrous results." Lee went back to his reading while Dan drove the velociter.

After several hours of travel, Dan began to slow the velociter. Lee looked up from his reading and saw why Dan was stopping. Pulling off of the road, Dan stopped and exited the vehicle. He stretched listening as his vertebrae popped. Lee also opened his door and got out. The Winchester was in his hands as he scanned the periphery. They stood at the end of an abandoned path which circled in front of an old manor. Fire had damaged much of the stone façade and the beams could be seen through holes in the roof, like the ribs of a corpse protruding from under a funeral shroud. "This place was not listed on the map," Lee said double checking the map.

Dan was walking closer to the structure down what appeared to be an overgrown carriage path. Lee watched as Dan stopped and kneeled in the overgrown grass. Standing up, Dan held up an old wooden sign. The letters were faded and Lee could not make them out. "Can you read it?" He called to Dan.

"Yeah, it says Soulderbrook Manor." Dan said dropping the sign and heading back to the velociter.

"Are you sure?" Lee asked. "I didn't think . . ."

"I didn't either," Dan said cutting him off.

Dan pulled the pack with the reattached shotgun onto his back. "What are you doing?" Lee asked. "You know the stories."

"Yeah," Dan said coming to stand beside Lee. "Can't help but believe this may be the second obstacle."

"Think about this," Lee started. "Given what we know if only a fraction of them are true, we are in no way prepared to deal with this."

"Listen to wise counsel, hunter." A serpentine voice called from within the mansion. "Death awaits you here."

"Lee, do we have anything that can burn the house?" Dan asked.

"It appears fire has already been employed besides we don't have the means to take the stone apart."

"Tin man?" Dan asked.

"Same as the farm house, we need to check the floors but I'm willing to bet it's going to be too brittle to support him." Lee said. "We're here and if you think we can clear it out before nightfall, then we'll go, but I am going to go ahead and say I advise against this."

Dan's shoulders slumped. "Not now, but when this is over we come back, prepared for it." Dan said unbuckling the pack on his back.

"Agreed," Lee said. "This will require a massive amount of research and we may need to bring in a few extra hands or a small squad of Royal Marines."

The serpentine voice laughed as Dan and Lee climbed back into the velociter. "Leave hunters unless you wish your bones to join the others within these walls."

Retreating like this gnawed at Dan, but he realized that to go into Soulderbrook Manor unprepared would be the last thing he would ever do. "I guess this means the stories are true," Dan said once they were safely on the road headed away from Soulderbrook.

"I can only assume so. Do you know how many hunters allegedly went hunting for Soulderbrook? Most use it as a joke when they are leaving the trade, but now that I've seen it." Lee was quiet. "You know Turpin went after it."

"Tough Tom Turpin," Dan said.

"The one and the same, he left one night with his three assistants all well trained and well armed. No one ever saw them again after they left London." Lee said. "Do you think?"

"Like you said, if a fraction of it's true, who knows?" Dan said.

Both of them grew quiet, Lee picked up his book to continue reading. Lee could sense the frustration that Dan felt at leaving the Manor house behind. "We had to," Lee said.

"I know," Dan agreed trying to forget the taunting voice.

"We will come back and tend to it. Our jobs are always completed, I do not think we will start leaving things half done, do you?"

"No," Dan said smiling a little.

They continued north, until the sun set. There were no lights ahead of them that they could see as they did with Berkenshire. Lighting the lamps on the front of the velociter, Lee took over the responsibility of driving, allowing Dan to rest in the passenger seat.

This time his dream was different, he was not in the field. Instead he was in a cave with torchlight reflecting off of the walls. Ironhill sat in his traditional dwarf armor a chainmail coat ran under a broad breastplate. He wore iron bracers on his arms and a battleaxe hung by his side, a vicious war hammer sat against his chair. "Sit," he said to Dan.

"Why the change?" Dan asked.

"You passed that accursed place today, which was wise on your part to keep going." Ironhill said. "It wasn't one of your obstacles. We don't know what the next one will be, but we've been fighting defensively here. The elves are the only ones that have not been attacked; fortunately none of us have fallen. I would like to be hopeful that all of us can withstand indefinitely, but I'm a realist, nobody wins them all." Ironhill said with a weary voice. "You are doing good work, and making great progress but the path is still very difficult ahead of you. Do not take any unnecessary chances but you have to be quick about your business when you come to it. We are keeping watch on your progress and will convey to the proper people any bounties that you acquire, but no more nights in the pub. Once the obstacles done, move on, it's the only way you'll make it in time."

"All right," Dan said. "Really wish you fellas would fight your own battles."

"We are," Ironhill said. "If we fall we're done for, if the child falls humans will fall. Seems only right a human fights that battle, doesn't it?"

"I hate being used." Dan said.

"You'll have to deal with it," Ironhill said. "See you soon."

Dan woke to find Lee looking at the map, the velociter stood still in the middle of the dark night. Lee glanced at his friend. "Glad to see you didn't wake up swinging." He said.

"Yeah, different dream this time," Dan said. "The manor wasn't our next obstacle. Why are we stopped?"

"Fork in the road," Lee said. "Both head north and lead to two separate villages. Any suggestions?"

"What are the names of the villages?"

"The one to our right is the village of Carney, and to our left lies the village of Falls."

"That's the one," Dan said remembering Ironhill's words. "I'm positive it's Falls. Ironhill used that word several times. It must have been a hint."

"Good," Lee said folding the map back up and putting it between their two seats.

Lee turned onto the left branch of the fork and they drove along in the dark, clouds covering the moon. The only lights were those of the lamps attached to the front of the velociter. In the distance no lights shined to signal that they were headed toward a village or any other structure.

Dan looked out the window, there wasn't much to see. Clouds obscured the moonlight. *Just as well* Dan thought to himself, *nothing out there but trees and grass.* He changed his mind when he saw something move in the darkness. Pressing his forehead to the window, Dan looked carefully into the darkness. He cupped his hands around his head to block out the light from inside the velociter. Once again, he could swear that something was keeping pace with them. "You okay?" Lee asked.

"Maybe," Dan said trying to find the moving object. "I think we're being followed."

"How?" Lee said looking around trying to see if there was another velociter nearby.

"Something very fast, running beside us." Dan said. "It's tough to tell what, too damn dark."

Lee maintained the velociter's speed. "You don't think we picked up something at the fork?"

"Don't know, seems like the best time if something was waiting for us."

"Should we stop and investigate?" Lee asked.

"We go out there and we're going to be at a disadvantage. Even with the lamps and our rifles, it's too dark. Thing could get behind us before we knew what happened." Dan said continuing his vigil at the window. "Where's my belt lantern?"

"Under the seat I believe," Lee said rummaging under the seat. He pulled out the familiar square object.

"Thanks," Dan said lighting the wick of the lantern.

They continued riding in silence. "Aha!" Dan shouted shining the lantern's beam out the window.

Lee turned his head in time to catch a quick glimpse. Whatever was following them was large, hairy, and had teeth, lots of teeth. It turned quickly and disappeared out of the range of the lantern's light. "What was that?" Lee asked, speeding the velociter along.

"If I had to guess, I'd say it's a big wolf. It had a saddle on its back." Dan replied. He looked back into the darkness. "I think the rider was quick enough to duck behind that big thing. Any ideas?"

"I know there are some of the underground and woodland creatures that raise large creatures to ride." Lee said. "I didn't get a good enough look to identify it. Did you?"

"I think so." Dan said. "It's definitely been living in the woods, hair was matted and I saw tufts of grass in its coat."

"You don't suppose it could be a werewolf do you?"

"Never seen one go on all fours and be that large, I think this is something new. Might be our first German visitor," Dan said. "He'll keep his distance for rest of the night. How much farther?"

"Hopefully only a couple of hours." Lee responded. "Where's your shotgun?"

"In the compartment, your Winchester?"

"Right here," Lee said handing the rifle to Dan.

Dan set it between them so either of them could easily reach it. He slid one of the revolvers from its holster around his waist and held it in his hand, scanning the darkness. Opening the front cover of the lantern, he blew out the flame to conserve the kerosene within the fuel case.

The minutes crept slowly by, Dan continued looking at the darkness sure that what they had seen was still following them. Lee continued following the road before them. He made sure to watch for any traps, if they were stranded this late at night far from any shelter, they would be perfect prey. Both men had a suspicion that had they been on horseback the beast they saw would have attacked but was wary of the vehicle they traveled in.

Lee strained his eyes to see ahead of them. "Something's wrong," Lee said.

"You see it?" Dan asked.

"Therein lies our problem, I don't see it." Lee said. "We should be able to see a lantern by a gate, a light in a building, something to indicate Falls, but look it's completely dark."

Dan turned away from the window and looked ahead of them into the night. There were not any lights coming from anything ahead of them. "Maybe we've missed a turn somewhere," Dan offered.

"According to the map, this road goes in a fairly straight route directly to the village. There are no turns indicated and no adjacent roads." Lee said. "I don't like this."

"Neither do I, but keep going and we'll see what we can see when the sun comes up." Dan said.

Lee continued on while Dan kept his eyes alert and focused on the darkness engulfing their small vehicle and its lanterns. Finally, they passed a sign that indicated that Falls was only several miles ahead. Still the road in front of them was dark and no lights showed where the village might be. "We'll be in the gates in about ten minutes," Lee said.

"Why do all these little villages have walls and gates?" Dan asked.

"To keep the animals from the forest out, originally they were used to keep out invading armies and allow them some protection." Lee explained.

Dan made a noncommittal grunt and continued peering into the night, his thumb continued pulling back and relaxing the hammer of the pistol. The unconscious manner that Dan was working the hammer on the pistol made Lee nervous but he had never seen Dan accidentally fire his weapons so he would not say anything about it.

A dark shadow rose up, standing out slightly in the darkness. "That our village?" Dan asked.

"Should be," Lee responded.

When the lanterns on the front of the velociter were in range to illuminate the wall and gate, Lee stopped the velociter suddenly. Dan turned from the window and stared straight ahead. The large wooden gate that at one time had protected the village of Falls was splintered and lay in pieces within the gateway. Arrows of thick black wood and bone were embedded in the rock walls surrounding the gateway. The town was dark; the only source of sound and light was the velociter. Dan opened his door and glanced around their vehicle before dropping out of the door and retrieving the shotgun and its pneumatic pack from the compartment under the cabin. Quickly he climbed back into the passenger seat and strapped on the pack. It cramped him in the already small quarters of the velociter, but he would rather be uncomfortable than ill equipped to deal with anything waiting within.

"What should we do?" Lee asked.

"We don't have much choice," Dan said. "We know there's something that followed us so there's probably more behind us. We don't know that anything is still in the town. Might also find some survivors, I've never heard of anything killing entire villages."

"Neither have I, but these are not our normal prey." Lee replied glancing at the darkened structures lining the streets.

"I need to get into the trunk behind us by the boiler," Dan said.

Lee picked up the Winchester and made sure the safety was off. With a nod, both men jumped from the velociter and met at the back. Lee stood on the body of the vehicle in front of the boiler, keeping a watch in all directions as best he could, while Dan cut the rope holding the nearest trunk and flipped open the top. He held up three small waxen red sticks. "Dynamite!" Lee exclaimed.

"Never know when you might need it." Dan said smiling.

The two men went back to the cabin of the velociter checking around them the entire time. "You get the feeling we're being watched?" Dan asked as he closed the door.

"I do," Lee said. "Judging by those arrows, I'd say they can easily pick us off."

"Maybe not, could be they aren't any good at shooting from indoors." Dan said.

A light appeared from the trees to their right a large tree on fire was being pushed toward them. "Move!" Dan ordered.

Lee sped the velociter and the trailer out of the way but the tree blocked their exit through the other gate. Opening the door and jumping out, Dan looked at the log and could not see anything to shoot. He could hear something running outside the wall, it sounded like armor clanging together, and there were also sounds of movement coming from within the dark structures lining the street. Taking his lantern and lighting it, he clipped it onto his belt. "What are you doing?" Lee asked through the open passenger door.

"Getting some answers." Dan said stepping up to the nearest structure.

According to the sign by the door, it was a doctor's office. There were bloodied hand prints along the wall, some were human and others looked like grotesque deformed human hands. Kicking in the door, Dan used the shotgun to scan the room and make sure there were no enemies within. There were several overturned chairs and smears on the wall, a small counter sat near the wall a closed door behind it. A bowler hat sat on the counter. It looked similar to the one that the Black Powder goblins had shot off of his head. Lifting the hat, Dan looked at it. He placed it on his head. It fit.

The closed door burst in and a large black cleaver came crashing down into the counter. Dan stumbled back trying to grip the shotgun to fire it. The lantern glinted off of crude black armor. Dan saw the face of his attacker; its eyes glowed faintly yellow, two tusks protruded from the corners of its mouth, and its dark green skin was pocked with scars. The monster stood much like a gorilla with arms dangling close to its knees and was almost as large. The massive hand gripping the leather wrapped handle wrenched the cleaver free of the counter. Finding his footing, Dan fired the shotgun into the beast's barrel chest. The armor crumpled before the shotgun pellets and the beast fell to the floor. The cleaver lay on the floor beside the body. Dan stood over the beast and caught a whiff of its musk.

He gagged and stumbled towards the door. "Christ, how did I not smell you earlier?"

Hearing the sound of clinking metal Dan turned around. The beast was standing shaking its head. Seeing Dan it swung a massive arm catching him in the jaw. Dan went reeling, tasting blood in his mouth. He spit the blood on the floor and grabbed the hat that had fallen from his head. Using its arms to propel it much like a gorilla, the beast dashed toward the cleaver. Dan fired again this time taking the beast in the side of the head. A gaping wound appeared in the dark green skin, and a brackish smelling yellow liquid oozed from the wound. The beast this time lay dead. Just to be sure, Dan used the cleaver to stab where he assumed the beast's heart would be. Hooking his hand through one of the leather straps on the armor, he dragged the carcass out in front of the velociter. Opening the door, Lee stood and looked at the dead body on the ground.

"We need to go now." Lee said.

"What is it, first?" Dan asked.

"Orc," Lee responded.

"What's that?"

"Magically fused goblin with a demon, occasionally ride giant wolves called wargs." Lee said. "Now get in we need to go."

Lee shut his door. Dan left the carcass and headed for the passenger door. Arrows began to strike the passenger door of the velociter. Diving through the door he had kicked in, Dan landed with a grunt. "Go!" He called to Lee.

The arrows falling onto the velociter convinced Lee to drive through the streets, trying to reach the other end of the village. Looking around Dan could not see any other attackers in his immediate vicinity. Hurrying, he looked through the door his attacker had burst through. It appeared to be the room where the doctor saw his patients. A small staircase in the corner led upstairs. Hearing the sounds of movement from outside, Dan climbed the stairs. He came to another shut door at the top of them. Taking a deep breath, he shoved the door in with his shoulder and found a bedroom; a small table, bed and nightstand were the only things in the room. Closing the door, Dan piled the sparse furniture against the door. Standing beside the window, he quickly darted his head around the window frame and ducked it back. He saw many dark shapes moving through the darkened streets. The wind picked up and moved the clouds away from the moon. Quickly, Dan extinguished the flame in the lantern and slid the window open. A cackle rose in the sky. Looking, Dan saw two witches riding their broomsticks across the woods headed for the village.

"Hunter we have found you," one of the witches called.

"Peg, Meg, I'll kill you this time." Dan mumbled under his breath as he stepped onto the wood tiled roof of the doctor's office.

He looked about not seeing any enemies in the windows or nearby rooftops. There was a lot of movement from the street below, and he could hear the sound of heavy steps coming from the stairs. The barricade he had set up would not keep the orcs out for long. Several of the large wolves, similar to the one they had seen earlier were in the street being ridden by smaller orcs. *Most likely headed after Lee,* Dan thought as he continued his walk across the rooftop.

Leaping to the next rooftop, Dan saw a small black barbed arrowhead protruding from an open window. He approached the window from the side. Calming his nerves, he darted his hand in and grabbed the first thing he felt. With a quick pull, the orc was flung out of the window to the street below where its surprised cry was silenced by a heavy thud. Several voices began chattering in the street. Dan assumed they were speaking German but wasn't sure, all he knew was that it wasn't English. A few arrows sprang up from the street and bounced off of the window sill and tiles of the roof around him. Dan looked into the room and seeing nothing climbed in. The arrows continued falling. Snatching up a nearby candle, Dan struck a match on the bottom of his boots and lit the candle. The faint light revealed a child's room, in the corner Dan saw where the orcs had been using it as a latrine. Putting the shotgun in its place beside the pack, he took one of his pistols and opened the bedroom door. Sounds came up from the floor beneath him. The weak light of the candle did not reveal any immediate threats. Directly across the small hall was another door, Dan quickly crossed the hall and entered. A window was in the middle of the far wall, in the center of the room was a bed. Walking past it, Dan saw the blood splatters and pieces of bone. Disgusted, he tossed the candle onto the bed watching as the flame spread to the mattress and covers.

Looking out the window, he saw no dangers and climbed onto the opposite side of the roof. The alleyway between this house and the next was small. Leaping, Dan landed as softly as he could on the adjoining roof and began to make his way across the rooftops. At one point he stopped and saw that the fire he had started on the bed had begun to lick out the window and through the roof. There were shouts from the orcs, Dan smiled to himself. "Love a good distraction," he said as he continued climbing across the roofs.

A screech arose from behind him, turning he saw an orc holding a crude axe begin to stand. It had crawled out of the one of the small windows in the top floor of the building he was on. A war cry rose from the orc's lips and it began to charge. Leveling the pistol, Dan squeezed off a single shot into the orc's face. The grotesque beast fell onto its back and rolled off the roof to the street below. Cries of alarm went up and Dan saw other arms scrambling to get out of the windows. Not waiting to see how many of them were in the small village, Dan quickened his pace across the rooftops. He stopped and fell backwards as he came to a much larger gap between the houses. There was no movement coming from the large building across that gap. Not sure if he could make the leap, Dan backed up several feet and ran toward the edge, leaping at the last possible moment. As he started to descend, he realized he was not going to clear the gap. The edge of the roof slammed into his chest. Dan grabbed for any kind of purchase that he could find. The pack on his back threw his body off balance and he fell. His feet hit solid ground and he stood on a small balcony outside of the windows. Pushing in the window, he climbed into the room. Closing the window behind him, Dan moved deeper into the room. From the rooftop he had leapt from he heard the orcs speaking, waiting a few moments he relaxed as he heard their feet running back the way they had come.

Looking around, there was enough light coming through the windows from the moon to allow him to see that there were several doors in the room as well as several beds. Listening at the doors, Dan tried to decide his easiest way out. One of the doors was quiet except for the distant sound of clanking metal, the middle door was completely silent. Opening it, Dan saw a small storage space. The last door was quiet except for a small sob and an answering word in the orc's language. The sob didn't sound orc, it sounded like it came from a human. Retrieving the bowie knife from his boot, Dan holstered the pistol and gripped the handle of the door. A shadow glided across the moon, and Dan knew it was the witches seeking him out as well. Pulling open the door Dan saw a small amount of light coming from the end of the hallway. Dan crept down the hallway until he came to the source of the light.

6   Lee was conducting the velociter through the empty streets, hoping that Dan was still alive. Orcs were not known for taking prisoners or for being simple kills, of course neither was Dan. Something large darted out in front of the velociter. Rather than steer away from it, Lee maintained his course through the street. The velociter struck the giant warg that had been ridden in his path. There was a sickening crunch and the warg howled into the night. Arrows continued to pepper the cab, but they seemed to be coming in smaller doses. "They set a trap for us." Lee stated amazed.

Orcs were known for being fierce and powerful but not known for being overly coordinated. This troubled Lee, but he would have to think about it later, for now he had to make it outside of the gates of the city. Several orcs ran from cover to cross in front of the velociter. Lee aimed directly for these scurrying targets, occasionally he was rewarded by crushing one of them under the wheels of the velociter and the trailer, most of the time he would only manage to graze one of them. Using the mirrors on the side of the cabin, Lee could see several of the smaller orcs riding on wargs trying to overtake him. The narrow streets prevented them from getting the better of him. One of them did try to ride around his side. With a simple turn of the stick, Lee smeared both warg and rider across the front of a building where they fell dead.

The others held back after watching their comrade fall beneath the large machine. Some of them pulled down different alleys trying to get ahead of Lee. He merely adjusted the controls to speed the velociter along its way. Something stationary was laid across the street. Lee could not be sure but he thought it was a table. His guess was not far from being accurate. A small hay cart still filled with hay had been put across the street to block his path. Lighting a magnesium flare, Lee lowered his window. He tossed the flare forward into the cart, the hay caught fire. When Lee hit the cart with the velociter, flaming debris was sent onto the nearby houses and across the street. The wargs pursuing him stopped and pulled back at the flames. The harsh whips of their riders convinced them to continue on. One of the wargs rolled onto its back and crushed the orc atop it. Free of its rider, the warg turned and ate the broken screaming body of its former master.

Lee thankful for the small reprieve from the chase focused on the path ahead of him as he secured his window back into place. The orcs that had led their wargs around were now gathered in front of him. The one in the center was brandishing a crossbow. Aiming at Lee, it fired. Dodging his head to the side, Lee avoided the arrow as it crashed through the windshield and lodged into the head rest of his seat. Without wavering from his course Lee continued on, the three orcs in his path stood their ground. Right before impact, the two on the sides rode out of his path. The one in the middle with the crossbow did not and was trampled under the heavy carriage of the velociter. Both rider and warg were dead.

Lee could see the rear gate of the city not far ahead of him. Pulling the arrow free from the headrest, he continued on his way coercing every iota of speed from the velociter. These gates had also been splintered. Lee did not like that but he would have to take his chances. Driving out of the gate, Lee stopped the velociter and exited placing the butt of the Winchester to his shoulder. The remaining riders followed him, joined by the two that had fled from their trampled crossbow toting companion. Taking careful aim, Lee shot the first mount. It fell to the ground, pitching its rider forward where he landed and his neck snapped from the force of the impact. The other wargs fell as easily. Their riders however were not dispatched so simply as their cohorts. Lee did not allow them the chance to rise and attack him. Each was dealt with by a single bullet to the head. One of the wargs was trying to stand. Lee saw the blood coming from the shoulder near the head. It hobbled from the street down a nearby alley. Quickly scanning the area around the gate while reloading the rifle, Lee made sure that there were no other immediate threats.

It was time to take the Tin Man off the trailer. Removing the rubber covering, Lee loosened the fasteners on the straps and began to crank the small turbine that powered the battery within the mobile unit. Once the meter on the battery was in the green, Lee attached the cable that ran from the controlling unit to the back of the Tin Man. The large treads rolled forward carrying the Tin Man down the ramp onto the dirt road outside of the village. Lee looked at the long cable that ran from the control unit to the mechanical man. The Tin Man had a large torso shape that two people could stand in comfortably while being protected from outside attack, the two arms could be operated by the passenger as a battering ram to remove obstacles, normally doors and walls, and a large head shaped piece with a mirrored visor that was connected to another set of mirrors to allow any passengers to view upcoming targets. Hidden within the large round torso was a miniature three barreled artillery cannon, spring mounted and operated. The barrel would push back into the recessed spring portion to prevent the recoil from damaging the protective shell. This could also be operated by the passenger. Rather than legs, Lee had created two large treaded tracks that allowed the Tin Man to move.

Lee began to wrap the long cable up until it fit behind the protective sheeting of the Tin Man's back and shoulders. Climbing into the secure confines, he set his Winchester on the hooks normally occupied by Dan's shotgun. Using the telescope in the eyes, Lee began to move the Tin Man through the street back toward where Dan had last been. This was a new experience for Lee, he had never ridden on the Tin Man before; he had always controlled it from outside the battle zone.

Dan stood at the end of the hallway looking into the cramped quarters before him. A little girl sat sobbing. Her face dirty, tears had cleaned the portions of her face where they had traveled down. The little golden locks of hair sodden and matted with all manner of foul material. Standing near her, speaking to her was an orc. Judging by the build and curvature of the hips, Dan guessed it was a female. Human skulls were tied together around her neck. Dan grew angry as he saw the different sizes of the skulls. The orc quit speaking and sniffed the air, smelling the scent of the man. As she was turning, Dan threw himself at her and tackled her. A fierce blow to the head made his vision blur and threw off his balance. Being female did not make them any weaker than their male counterparts.

Despite the dizzying effect of the blow, Dan held tight to the scrap of cloth the orc wore and began stabbing down into the body mass of the beast. His blows were furious and the orc cried several times before stopping. Three more stabs with his knife convinced Dan that the beast was truly dead. Wiping the blade on the fur covered body of the beast, Dan put the knife back into his boot and made his way over to the little girl. "Hey there, what's your name?" Dan asked. The girl struggled against her bonds to get away from him. "No need for that, I'm here to help." Dan said trying to comfort the frightened girl.

"They'll eat you like the others," the girl said squeezing her eyes shut.

"No, they won't." Dan said firmly.

He untied the girl, not using his knife for fear of cutting her. She still would not move. "Can you stand up?" The girl just nodded her head. "Okay, well you're going to have to if you want to get out of here."

The girl stood up and swayed, unsure of her legs. Footsteps began to sound from the floor below them. "She was their chief," the girl announced staring at her dead captor.

"Do you know a way out of here?" Dan asked.

The little girl went to the wall and pulled away a small piece of canvas that hid a panel. "This goes to the attic," she said.

"Good enough," Dan said lighting his lantern.

He pushed in the panel and picked the little girl up in his arms. Climbing through the hole in the wall, Dan pushed the panel back into place and looked around their surroundings. There were no windows or any other opening for his light to be seen. Several old dusty crates were in the room. He climbed out of the small recess in the floor that the panel had opened into and set the girl down. Grunting, Dan forced one of the large crates into the recess in the floor. It thudded into place and blocked that entrance to the orcs. "Any other ways up here?"

"The door over there," the little girl said pointing.

Dan saw a regular sized door in the wall. He went to work piling as many crates as he could in front of the door. "That'll buy us some time," Dan said admiring the barricade he had built. He sat on the dusty floor and removed his new hat. "Come here," he said motioning to the little girl.

Reluctantly the child came to him and sat down near him. Dan hoisted the child up and sat her in his lap. "Now what's your name?" He asked.

"Elizabeth," the girl responded.

"Pretty name," Dan said. "Do you know if anybody else is being held like you were?"

"No," Elizabeth said. "They're all gone."

"How do you know?"

"They ate them," she responded. "Every last one of them, tried to make me eat them."

Elizabeth buried her face into his chest and began weeping again. "Elizabeth, this is important. Do you know why they were keeping you tied up?"

"One of them said it was for my power, they wanted it."

"Power?"

"Dad said I was a visionary. I could see stuff before it happened."

"Well, can you see how I get out of here?" Dan asked as something heavy crashed against the door.

"I've never seen anything after this day," Elizabeth confessed. "We all die."

"No, we don't." Dan said standing her up as he stood up. "We're getting out of here. My friend's out there too, and we're not going to let anything happen to you."

"We can't get out of here, there are too many of them. This is where they rest during the day, and this is where they eat. I heard the screams."

"Listen to me," Dan said. "Before this night is through they'll be screaming." Dan said winking at the little girl.

Dan stepped to the roof and found a loose board. He began pushing on it. The muscles in his neck and shoulders burned with the effort. Finally, he was rewarded as the board pulled away from the beams and he was able to create an opening. Throwing his shoulder into the board beneath the opening, he widened the gap enough so that he could get out. Taking off the pack, Dan sat it in front of Elizabeth. "Stay here," he said as he went toward the barricade.

The door was opened a little more than an inch wide. Removing one of the sticks of dynamite from his pants' pocket, Dan cut the fuse to burn for only a minute. Using the lantern to light it, he dropped the stick through the crack in the door. The orcs on the other side began to throw themselves into the door more furiously. Dan ran and pushed his pack through the opening onto the roof of the building, then climbed out the hole. Reaching back into the attic, he pulled Elizabeth from the house. Putting the pack back on, Dan saw the nearest rooftop and leaped to it with Elizabeth tightly clinging to him. He was able to get to the other side of the building, before the dynamite went off. The upper corner of the building blew up, scattering orc remains and flaming rubble outward across the village. The house that he had started a fire in earlier was completely engulfed. He could see a different fire burning in the main thoroughfare of the town. Carrying Elizabeth, he began leaping from rooftop to rooftop headed toward the fire that he assumed Lee had set.

A cackle rose from above him. Meg and Peg had seen him and were approaching. Elizabeth tightened her grip around his neck. Dan ran as fast as he could across the slanted roofs. His foot slipped and he fell onto his back and slid down the roof, landing on a lower roof closer to the street. A bolt of energy came from the sky and the roof beneath him fell away. Dan fell to the stone floor, stood up, and carried Elizabeth away from the gaping hole in the ceiling. The witches cursed from their broomsticks at Dan's fortune. Dan found himself in a small garden. He licked his thumb and forefinger and used them to extinguish the lantern's light. Finding the door to the adjoining house, Dan entered. Elizabeth's legs were propped across Dan's right forearm; in his right hand was one of his revolvers.

Lee saw the flicker of energy and in the quick illumination saw the two sisters they had spared days before. They were riding on their brooms seeking revenge. "Focus on the problem at hand," Lee said to himself.

From their location, the Tin Man was an ineffective weapon. The artillery could not be aimed accurately enough to hit such a small target and they were too high, the barrels could not be adjusted to aim that high. *Something to consider in the next version,* Lee thought to himself.

He ignored the floating problem above them and focused on the small groups of orc warriors that were scurrying away from him. One orc, that was taller than the rest, approached the Tin Man. Lee watched in fascination as the beast cautiously lumbered forward and then struck a blow square to the center of the body. The metallic ringing sound echoed within the confines of the Tin Man. Covering his ears and steadying himself, Lee looked back out and saw the orc returning; it had retreated after its strike. The beast drew back the large dull cleaver it held in its hand and prepared to strike at the face. "I think not," Lee said engaging the piston in the arm.

The large metallic fist shot out and returned to its place. The orc was propelled down the street its head nothing more than crushed pulp. A satisfied smile crossed Lee's face when he saw the orcs in his nearby vicinity run from the main street trying to escape him. Lee continued to roll into the center of town, hoping to find Dan soon.

Dan held Elizabeth as the witches that had been following him began to fly low to the ground flying past the window of the house he was hiding in. They searched for him. "I smell a child," Meg proclaimed to her sister.

"As do I dear sister," Peg agreed. "Perhaps the hunter is going to offer us a snack."

Both of the witches cackled and Dan could see the flowers in the neighboring house's window box wither and die. He ground his teeth to try and block out the sound. The child in his arms covered her ears with her hands. Dan decided to try going up to see if he could get a shot at one of the witches. Climbing the stairs he did not encounter any orcs, they were most likely on the street trying to find him as well. From the window facing the alleyway he could see the corner of the main street through town. He saw the two old hags riding the gnarled wood of their broomsticks. A warg leaped from a nearby alleyway and snatched Peg off of her broom. The warg tossed about the old woman's carcass rending her. Meg rose higher into the sky, an anguished rage peppering her scream. A bolt of energy left her fingertips and the warg's skin and fur disappeared. The beast whimpered and died. An alarm rose from the streets.

"That's right hunt something else," Dan said making his way back down toward to the ground floor.

A fury of black barbed arrows left the streets and windows of the village. Meg laughed at the projectiles. "Nruter," she cried in the damned witchspeak.

Dan heard it and then heard the cries of the orc archers as their arrows turned and shot back into them. No archer that fired an arrow survived the arrow's return. Outraged screams filled the streets as the orcs found something else to kill. Watching from the shadows within the house, Dan saw several of the orcs rush past the front of the structure. Their footsteps and clanging armor dying away as they continued on, he waited another minute and opened the door. The alleyway was empty. He turned back toward the main street. The destroyed body of Peg lay on the ground oozing black blood and maggots. "Don't look," Dan said pushing Elizabeth's face against his chest.

This spelled trouble for Dan and Lee. When they had killed the first of the sisters her magical powers had split between Peg and Meg. Now with Peg dead, all of the magical powers the sisters had shared were now Meg's to command. Dan would deal with her later; right now his priority was getting to Lee and getting Elizabeth out of town. Turning the corner onto the main street, Dan walked past several of the building fronts stopping once to pick up a small bottle of whiskey and put it into his back pocket. A large contingent of orcs came spewing out into the street not too far in front of him. He could hear Meg cackling as she chased after them. Ducking into the nearest doorway, Dan set Elizabeth down.

"Okay Elizabeth, I'm going to need you to walk for a little bit. Hold on tight," Dan instructed placing her hand on his belt.

Elizabeth gripped the belt until her knuckles were white, her tiny frame shook, and her eyes were wide. "It's going to be okay," Dan said winking at the girl. "Just step when I step okay?"

The little girl nodded, her confidence still nonexistent that she was going to survive the ordeal. Dan holstered the pistol and retrieved the shotgun from across his back. Taking deep calming breaths, he stepped back into the street. There was more of the yellowish ooze on the ground sitting amongst pieces of the black armor. Dan could wager an educated guess what had happened: Meg, drunk with her newfound powers, was tormenting the orcs. When monsters fought, Dan did not care which one came out on top just as long as some of them died, this was no exception. With Elizabeth holding tightly to his belt, Dan skirted the edges of the buildings trying to stay out of direct sight of anything that might be flying above him. The clatter of orc feet and armor were echoing down different parts of the city, below that clamor Dan could make out the familiar sounds of the Tin Man. He smiled.

His pace quickened, but he made sure to check every alleyway for any surprises. Just as they were coming around a bend in the road, they saw the fiery hay cart that Lee had ignited. It had caught onto several of the buildings and provided plenty of fire to illuminate the street. "We need to run by this quickly." Dan told Elizabeth.

The two of them hurried past, Elizabeth running as fast as her feet would carry her, Dan keeping a slow enough pace that the child could maintain it. As they were in front of the flaming buildings, hugging the front of the adjoining structure to avoid the flames and any falling debris, Meg made her appearance, blowing a large hole in the building in front of them. "You sought to escape me, thinking I would give up my power in your home and never try again." Meg cackled into the night.

Orcs huddled in the shadows. Dan could smell them over the burning building. They had come to fear Meg and knew it was better to stay out of her path. "Meg, sorry about your sister, but I've got more important things to deal with at the moment." Dan said looking for a way out.

"The child?" Meg asked. Dan nodded. "Oh well, once I've relieved you of your breath and possibly your bones, I'll be sure to relieve the child of the sweet meat on her bones."

Dan shifted the shotgun to face at Meg. The witch cackled once again. "You sure like to laugh don't you?" Dan asked.

"You know that toy will not harm me," Meg smiled revealing the rotting remains of the few teeth still in her mouth.

"Yeah, I do." Dan said. He smiled and lowered the shotgun slightly.

He pulled the trigger and his shot missed Meg, but it blew the front part of her broom to splinters. Meg screamed as the splinters tore into her flesh and the broom flew out of control directly into the burning house. "That won't stop her either, hurry." Dan said to Elizabeth. He loaded a fresh shell into the shotgun's magazine and started to run down the street.

The orcs seeing that Meg had been dealt with turned back to the target at hand and started to stir from their hiding places to attack Dan. Seeing the mobilizing hordes, Dan reached back and pulled the cord on the pack. The piston began to pump and Dan was ready for them. Ahead he saw a small group of orcs mobilizing in the street. They were too far away for the shotgun to be effective. Resting the barrel of the shotgun on his shoulder, he pulled one of his pistols and fired off all six shots, he killed four of the six orcs he had shot at and hit all six of them. Putting the pistol back into the holster, he prepared to fire the shotgun. A familiar whistle came from behind the orcs and Dan stopped running and knelt down covering Elizabeth with his body. An explosion sent the orcs flying, some of them in pieces and others on fire. A large crater stood in the middle of the road, where the orcs had been standing. Dan saw the Tin Man on the far side of the crater just past a fountain.

Dan put the shotgun back in its place on the pack and scooped up Elizabeth. He ran for all he was worth, hearing the sounds of the orcs behind him. There was a dent in the center of the Tin Man's body and one of the fists was covered in gore, Dan ignored it and ran to the rear.

The compartment door swung open and Lee stood holding his hand out. Grasping the offered hand, Dan was hoisted up. With Dan carrying the girl and wearing the pack, the compartment would not close. "Hold on," Dan said sitting the girl down so that she was standing against the side. Dan shrugged out of the pack and sat it between his legs.

The compartment closed but it was a tight fit as Dan and Lee were brushing elbows and shoulders with one another. Elizabeth was pressed against the wall and could barely move. "I'll drive, make sure we aren't followed." Lee instructed.

Dan nodded and moved the small strip of metal that allowed him to see where he was firing the three artillery cannons. "How many shells?"

"Four a piece and I've used the center cannon once." Lee said rotating the Tin Man's head to face backwards.

Dan looked out at the small village around them. The orcs having turned down the alleys after the first explosion had begun to gain their courage again. Tilting the cannon slightly up, Dan fired the far right cannon and sent a shell streaking through the night impacting at the corner of one of the buildings. The explosion threw the orcs across the street and sent stone from the building down on top of them. Turning, Dan fired the left cannon at the downed remnants of the orcs. They tried escaping but were caught by the blast. Looking through the slot above the cannons, Dan did not see any other movement coming from the streets. "They may have learned their lesson," Dan said.

Arrows began to bounce off of the Tin Man's thick armored walls. "Perhaps not," Lee said concentrating on steering the vehicle back to the gate.

Dan saw several archers clustered in windows of some of the houses. Adjusting the cannons, he fired at all of their locations. He could not be sure if they had been killed in the resulting explosions, but the arrows stopped coming. No other attacks came, but Dan could see the orcs gathering in the shadows behind them. He sent one more shell in their direction, knowing they were out of range. It detonated and they retreated back into the alleyways.

The Tin Man passed through the gates of the city and Lee steered it up onto the trailer. He opened the door and the evening air gave them a chill compared to the warmth inside the Tin Man. "Everyone out," Lee said taking his Winchester from the wall and stepping out.

Sweeping the perimeter with Winchester at the ready, he turned back toward the compartment once he was sure there was no immediate danger. "Come along little one," he said offering his hand to Elizabeth.

The child tentatively took his hand. Lee ushered her out of the Tin Man and lifting her up stepped off the trailer and sat her in between the driver and passenger seats of the velociter. Closing the door, he returned to the trailer as Dan was closing up the chest cannons and jumping down, pack in hand. "Help me cover it," Lee said grabbing the ropes.

Dan and Lee tied it down and covered it with the rubber sheeting as best they could while maintaining their watch toward the village streets. "Here," Dan said tossing Lee the bottle of whiskey.

"Good idea," Lee said.

The orcs were now coming down the street. Seeing the men outside of the Tin Man, they were brave once more. Lee went to the engine system of the velociter and poured the whiskey in the proper opening. "Dan!" Lee called.

"A minute," Dan said in response.

Lee heard the piston on the pack begin to cycle. Aiming at the approaching crowd, Dan squeezed the trigger and held on. Sweeping the barrel from one side to the other, Dan was able to wound most of the orcs that had dared come after them, and the others were hesitant given the display they had just witnessed. Climbing into the driver seat, Lee watched as Dan ran past the passenger door and opened the lamp compartment. Something began to spark. Shaking his head, Lee knew it was a stick of dynamite. Using the already lit fuse to light another, Dan hurled the first stick toward the wounded mass of orcs. Some of them scurried away from it but most were curious by the funny sparking stick. The last stick Dan tossed against the stone wall of the gateway. Quickly he climbed into the velociter. "Go!" He ordered.

Lee sped the velociter as quickly as he could away from the explosives. The first stick detonated destroying the curious orcs who had come out to investigate the sparking stick. The other stick destroyed a portion of the wall, causing some pieces to destroy the buildings against the wall and the rest tumbled across the path through the gateway creating a clumsy obstacle for any orcs that would try to follow them. Once the explosives had went off, Dan asked Lee to stop the velociter. Lee complied stopping the vehicle. Dan stowed the shotgun and pack in the compartment under the cabin.

Something came out of the darkness and struck Dan. Lee heard Dan grunt and then heard the sound of something falling to the ground. "Dan," he said turning toward the open passenger door.

One of the orcs leaped into the cabin, a small axe in his hand. Elizabeth screamed. The orc looked at the child and then back to Lee. It was all the time Lee needed. The revolver he wore in the shoulder holster was out in his hands. The orc started to scream and then Lee squeezed the trigger. The orc fell dead a hole in the center of its head. Pushing the large dead monster, Lee forced it out of the compartment. Tenderly, he lifted the hysterical Elizabeth out from between the seats. Looking all about, he stepped out of the velociter and did not see any other threats. Still he kept his guard up. Making his way to the other side of the velociter, he saw Dan on the ground. A large knot rising on the back of his head, Lee knelt and checked for a pulse. Finding one, he went back to looking for any other attackers. There were none to be seen. "I need you to stay with Mr. Winston. Just for a moment I have to attend to something." Lee said. Elizabeth nodded her understanding. "Watch out for anything and if you see anything scream."

Going to the trunks, Lee found some of his work rags. Stifling back a gag, he cleaned the orc's blood and brain matter from the velociter. Once he had wiped up everything he could get with the rag, he poured some of the water onto the spot and scrubbed again. The rags he threw into the grass beside the road. Lifting Dan up and carrying him to the velociter was the hard part. By the time, Lee had managed it Dan was starting to rouse. Lee escorted the child back to the driver's side and had made a small cushion for her from their already worn clothes. "I beg your pardon, but I don't believe I know your name?" Lee said.

"I'm Elizabeth," she said. "Your friend saved me from those monsters."

"That I did," Dan said, his speech slurred. "Right fine job if I do say so myself."

Elizabeth drew in a sharp breath. "I can see! I can see!" She exclaimed.

"What are you talking about?" Lee asked not sure what to make of the child's outburst.

"Visionary," Dan said.

"Couldn't you always see?" Lee asked.

"Told you we weren't going to die back there," Dan said smiling.

Lee realized what she was talking about. Those with the ability to divine future events, commonly known as visionaries, could not see beyond the day of their death. "Yes you did sir. Thank you." Elizabeth kissed Dan on his cheek. "Thank you so much."

Dan opened the storage contained under the seat and retrieved a bundle wrapped in folded cloth. "Enjoy," Dan said handing the bundle to the child.

Elizabeth opened the cloth containing the bundle and found it was an apple, a wedge of cheese and a large portion of bread. "Give her some water," Dan said.

Lee retrieved a canteen by his seat and handed it to the little girl. Tears streamed down her face as she ate the apple. She took a few bites of the bread and a few from the cheese before she was full, that did not stop her from drinking almost all of the water in the canteen. Contented and full, the child curled into a small ball between the seats and began to snore. "We should be able to make it to the next village by tomorrow evening," Lee said.

"Good," Dan said his faculties finally returning. "Hopefully we can find a place for her. Almost thought she was the one we were looking for, but then I saw the hair."

Lee took a glance at the sleeping child between them. "Good thing we arrived when we did," Lee said. "Do you think she can tell us where we need to go?"

"Don't know." Dan admitted. "But we can ask when she's rested."

7   Dan found himself once more in the field. No obstacles lay in his path. The statues had been reduced to rubble. Ironhill stood near the largest pile of rubble. "Well done," the dwarf said. "A group of those blighters tried attacking us. They learned it was an unwise choice." The dwarf let out a hearty laugh.

"So what's the next clue," Dan said. "I assume I fell asleep."

"Aye," Ironhill confirmed. "Can't say I blame you; I would've to."

"Okay," Dan said looking around. He saw the familiar red hair rising above the wheat in the field.

This time there was a dark blot on the horizon headed toward the girl. "That's what you'll be facing," Ironhill said pointing toward it.

"What is it?"

"Not sure, but it'll find the girl. Find her and make sure she dies." Ironhill looked at Dan. "Unless you get to her first."

Dan started to take a step toward the red hair running through the wheat and stumbled over some loose pieces of rubble. "Just because the big problems have been removed, don't forget about stumbling stones." Ironhill warned.

"I hate all this cryptic nonsense," Dan said standing upright.

The dark blot continued gaining on the girl, and Dan could hear the sound of horse hooves trampling on the ground. Again, he looked about for any signs that would help him identify his location. He saw the wall and the stone steeple. Straining he saw a sign near the gate, it was green and had two large points rising off of it. The words were blurry but the shape of the sign was unique. "We're counting on you," Ironhill said. "So is she."

Dan looked back and the little girl was gone, a bright sprout of red hair was jutting from the side of the black figure as it retreated back over the horizon.

Sitting bolt upright, Dan came awake and saw the bright sun shining down on them. "How long?" He asked, taking a drink of water, trying to wash the taste of sleep out of his mouth.

"A good while," Lee said. "Not as long as some."

Dan looked between them and saw Elizabeth, still sleeping soundly on the pile of clothes. "Stop, I need to stretch my legs." Dan said trying to stretch inside the cab of the velociter.

Lee pulled the velociter off of the road into a grassy patch. Stepping out, Dan lifted his arms above his head and heard his neck and back pop. Taking several steps around the velociter, he saw Lee on the other side examining the map. "I tell you, you boys must be born with a steel rod in your back to sit that long comfortably." Dan said.

"Yes I believe they call it good posture," Lee retorted, never looking away from the map. "Comes from not dragging your knuckles around when you walk."

"A caveman joke," Dan said.

"Sorry, it has been a long night." Lee said.

A scream came from the interior of the velociter. Both Lee and Dan ran the distance to the cab and peered in. Elizabeth was sitting upright looking about, relief washed over her face when she saw Lee and Dan. "I thought you'd left me." She admitted blushing.

"Not out here," Dan said. "We'll find you a nice place to stay first."

"Oh," she said. "I thought . . ."

"Oh dear," Lee said. "We would under normal circumstances take you with us, but we are currently involved in matters beyond our control and it would be far too dangerous to take a child with us."

"I understand," Elizabeth said, but her face told them she did not.

"I'll let you in on the secret." Dan said. "We're searching for another little girl that's going to be killed by monsters if we don't get to her first. I know you may think this sounds like a load of bollocks as you people say." Elizabeth giggled at the vulgar word. "Queen Victoria herself asked us to go on this mission."

"The queen," Elizabeth said her mouth gaping. "You've met the queen?"

"Several times, you know about the attack on her right?" Dan asked.

The little girl nodded her head. "Then surely you know how her attackers were brought to justice," Lee continued the story. "That my dear child was our doing."

"You're the great inventor and you're the American?" Elizabeth asked. Her idea of them most likely inflamed by all the different rumors that had spread since that particular case.

"I don't know about great," Lee said modestly.

"I'm the American, but you can call me Dan." He winked at the girl. "Let's keep it just between us."

"Certainly," Elizabeth said nodding vigorously.

After assuring her they were not going to abandon her, they walked around behind the velociter. "Dan, where did you get that hat?" Lee said. "I've been meaning to ask you about it and just had not gotten the right opportunity."

"Found it back yonder." He said pointing his thumb in the direction they had come. "Found it in that doctor's office."

"You took a hat from a dead man?" Lee asked flabbergasted.

"No, it was just sitting on a desk."

"But the owner is most likely deceased." Lee could not believe the audacity of Dan.

"Look I needed a new hat, haven't had time to get one. Besides the owner of this one isn't going to miss it one way or the other." Dan said.

Lee considered the logic that Dan was employing and realized that it was true. Dan would never steal from a corpse, Lee knew that and at the time, Dan probably did not realize that everyone in the village was dead, with the exception of Elizabeth. "You're right, my apologies." Lee said.

"You ain't got to apologize all the time. For crying out loud we're partners, when's the last time I apologized for breaking something or falling asleep in the chair and knocking over your papers." Dan said.

"You're right, never." Lee said. Reaching up, Lee used the tips of his fingers to knock the bowler hat from Dan's head. It fell to the ground.

"Hey," Dan said.

"I'm not sorry for that. You drive for a while, I need some rest." Lee said making his way to the passenger door.

Dan picked up the bowler hat and brushed it off with his sleeve, he grinned from ear to ear as he made his way back to the driver's seat. Lee was resting with his head against the rear of the compartment and his eyes shut. "How much further to the next village?" Dan asked.

"Most likely tomorrow morning, it was further away than I anticipated." Lee answered.

Dan pulled the velociter back onto the road and continued on the path as Lee drifted off to sleep. Elizabeth drifted in and out of consciousness as they traveled along.

Lee was jostled awake as the velociter bounced across the clumsy wooden bridge over the Trent River. "Where are we?" He asked still groggy.

"I saw a sign a little ways back said Nottingham was only about forty miles to the west of us." Dan said. "I trust I was supposed to keep on the same road."

"Yes, why?" Lee asked.

"Passed several crossroads and just assumed you'd have told me if I needed to turn before you took your nap."

Elizabeth was awake again and sitting quietly between the two men. Lee noticed the sinking sun. "Since we aren't going to make Blackmoore until tomorrow morning. Where should we stop?" Lee asked.

"I don't think we should sleep in the velociter," Dan said.

"Is that the name of your carriage?" Elizabeth asked.

"Yes," Lee said. "If we see an inn we should stop."

"Sure thing," Dan said continuing on the road ahead of them.

Lee stayed awake and thrilled Elizabeth with tales of their adventures, told from an English perspective. Dan thought he was leaving out the best parts and would occasionally interrupt and tell his side of the story.

Eventually night fell and the stars gave some light to see by, but not so much that they did not need to light the lanterns on the front of the velociter.

"I don't think we're going to find an inn." Dan stated.

"I fear you may be right." Lee agreed. "See what you can find and we'll take shelter where we can."

Several miles down the road Dan spotted a small cottage. Its roof was still intact, despite the worn walls and busted windows. A great gaping hole was in the door near the floor. "I'll go check it out," Dan said gathering his lantern from under the seat.

Lee and Elizabeth watched as the lantern's beam of light cut through the shadows on the lawn. Finally, Dan entered the house and they could see the light shining through the windows. A few minutes later, Dan came walking back to the velociter. "I think it'll be fine for tonight," Dan said. "Grab the gear Lee."

Carrying their equipment inside, Lee saw that the cottage had one room. An old cast iron stove sat in the corner, the wood pile beside it rotted. Large cobwebs hung in the corners of the ceiling and the fireplace was permanently black with soot. A large mold covered mattress, on a frame that did not look trustworthy, and several pieces of furniture lay in different levels of disrepair. "I don't think we'll have to worry about the proprietor," Lee said sourly.

"Me either," Dan said. "Makes it perfect. We should still take shifts watching the place. You take first."

"Certainly, you go get the firewood while I finish bringing in the equipment." Lee said.

Dan stepped out the front door and went around the side of the house, his lantern clipped to his belt. Lee made his way back to the velociter by the warm glow of the front lamps. He hefted the pneumatic pack and the leather satchel filled with his books. "Ready?" He asked Elizabeth.

She hesitated and then nodded. Turning back to the cottage, Lee saw what she was so hesitant about. The cabin was foreboding in the night, the trees around it preventing the starlight from fully shining on it. Turning the lamp from the velociter until it was loose, Lee picked it up and carried it in front of them. "Now this is not as bad," he said.

Elizabeth slipped her hand inside his and he led her to the cottage.

Dan scoured around behind the cottage until he found a small tree that had fallen during a recent storm. The wood was dry. "This'll burn nicely," he said to himself.

Taking the small hatchet he had found behind the house, he began to cut the tree into smaller portions that he could carry back with him. A twig nearby snapped. Drawing one of his revolvers, Dan focused the lantern onto the area the sound had come from. A grey fox stood stunned by the light. "Get," Dan said throwing an acorn at the animal. It scurried away.

Having finished cutting the tree, Dan hoisted four of the pieces and carried them around the cottage and dropped them beside the front door. Lee opened the door and looked at the logs. Smiling, Dan handed him the hatchet. "I'll go get the rest."

Dan heard the sounds of Lee chopping the pieces into smaller portions to fit in the fireplace and the stove. Gathering the last pieces, Dan returned around front. Despite the quiet, Dan felt that he was not alone. He thought that something was watching him. He found half of the tree segments missing. The hatchet stuck in the one nearest the door. Taking the hatchet, Dan cut the rest of the pieces and carried them inside.

Opening the door, he could see the blazing lights of the fire and smell the fresh cut wood burning. Lee was stoking the flames in the fireplace. A kettle had already been set on top of the stove. "We got any food?" Dan asked, setting the wood beside the fireplace.

"Some bread, a little bit more cheese and some dried beef. We should be able to get more supplies in Blackmoore." Lee said standing up.

Turning back toward the rest of the cottage, Dan saw the bed roll he had brought was laid out on the floor, beside it was Lee's. Elizabeth sat on top of it, smiling at Dan. "No place like home," Dan said.

"Quite," Lee said grimacing at the dingy surroundings. The kettle began to whistle. "Tea anyone?" Dan's expression soured.

"Yes, please." Elizabeth said excited. "I can't remember the last time I had tea."

A smaller kettle from behind the stovepipe also began to whistle. "That one is for your coffee." Lee said.

"Thanks," Dan said slapping Lee on the shoulder.

Settling down the three of them sat down and sipped their drinks. Once their cups were empty, Lee pulled the sturdiest chair near the door and sat down, his Winchester laid across his knees. Elizabeth curled up inside of Lee's bed roll. Dan slept on top of his bed roll, still wearing his pistols and boots, the shotgun reassuringly beside him. It did not take long before Dan was snoring.

Sitting motionlessly in the cabin, Lee maintained his watch out the front window. He had blocked the other windows with some of the furniture from the room, but he had left this one open so that he could keep an eye on the velociter and the Tin Man. The time passed quickly and nothing happened. As the time to switch shifts came, Lee thought he heard something scratching at the door. He eased out of the chair and looked out the window. He could not see anything near the door and the scratching stopped. "Must've been the wind," Lee mused to himself.

Checking his watch, he went to wake Dan. It did not take much. As soon as Lee laid a hand on his friend's shoulder, Dan opened his eyes, hands resting on the pistols at his side. "Time already?" He asked.

Lee just nodded his head. Dan sat up wiping the sleep from his eyes. He reached beside him and grabbed the empty cup. Going to the stove he retrieved the kettle he had used for his coffee and poured more of the hot black liquid into the cup. Yawning, he took a sip and sat in the chair. He left the shotgun beside his bedroll and kept one hand on one of his revolvers.

Settling down on top of Dan's bedroll, Lee fell asleep almost immediately. Looking out the same window that Lee had looked out; Dan tilted back the chair and watched, sipping his coffee. The night was quiet, but not the quiet that came from a menacing presence, this quiet was good it was the quiet that came when the animals of the forest were settling down for the evening. Only a lone owl sounded. It was times like this that Dan was reminded of his home. Of course when the small green creature flung itself through the window, Dan forgot his nostalgic musings. His body reacted automatically, swatting the small green figure out of the air into the wall and retrieving his pistol all in one fluid motion.

Dan heard the familiar sound of Lee working the lever action on the Winchester behind him. The small green being tried to stand and fell back down. Stepping closer to the creature on the floor, Dan took one step to the side so Lee had a clear shot. The barrel of Dan's pistol never strayed from the prone form on the ground. "It's a goblin." Dan proclaimed puzzled.

Lee shrugged his shoulders and went to the window. He could not see any other goblins in the area. "Clear," he said closing the half destroyed shutters on the window.

Dan picked up the goblin by the scruff of its shirt, the creature was still unconscious. Using his index finger, Dan poked the creature in the side repeatedly. After the fourth poke, the goblin swiped at Dan's finger. Opening his eyes, the goblin screamed and tried to pull free of Dan's hand. "Hold still," Dan ordered shaking the creature.

"What is that?" Elizabeth asked from the bedroll where she pulled the cloth tight around her.

"Nothing to be worried about," Lee said.

"Why do you look familiar?" Dan asked the goblin.

"You killed my clan," the goblin said. "I'm the last of them."

Looking over the goblin carefully, Dan drew back. "You're that goblin I kicked in the farmhouse."

The goblin lowered his head and looked at the floor. "Yes."

"Why don't you wander along and join another clan?" Lee asked.

"They no want me. Think I a coward, ran off to leave others to die, but I not. He kicked me hard. Can only join clan after kill you." The goblin said wrapping an arm around his ribs.

"You were going to shoot me," Dan said. "Besides I gave your boys a chance. They didn't want to take it."

"Humans always come and take away goblin homes. First it the dwarves and sprites, now humans." The goblin accused.

"Okay, I tried to reason with your chief. They built that blunderbuss and it blew up on them," Dan did not tell the goblin that he helped the explosion occur. "Besides that was a farm, not a goblin structure at all."

"Still home," the goblin said swinging a balled up fist at Dan. The swing missed and the goblin twisted at the end of Dan's fingers. "My clan gone, now I no have place."

"Dan, we might be able to make something useful of him." Lee said.

Dan raised an eyebrow. "You think so?" He asked examining the goblin once again.

"I'll leave it to you," Lee said. He placed the Winchester on his shoulder and crouched beside the fireplace drawing in the ashes with a twig.

"Did your clan sit on the Court?" Dan asked.

"Court no like the Black Powder Clans. Only Claw Clan sits on Court." The goblin said.

"Fair enough, I have a proposition for you." Dan said, the goblin gave him a distrusting look. "Before we begin what's your name?"

"Boom," the goblin said.

"Your real name, or I toss you into the fireplace." Dan said swinging the goblin in the direction of the flames.

"No!" The goblin exclaimed shaking, tears falling from his eyes. "Brackish Thumtum."

"Very well, Brackish," Dan said sitting Brackish on the floor. "You want someplace to belong, a new clan as it were. I think we can accommodate that."

"A new clan. Black Powder?" Brackish asked. "You know others."

"Not exactly," Dan said. "We know your kind and the rules you live by. Lee and I would be your new clan. How does that suite you, then you wouldn't have to try and kill us?"

"You kill my clan I avenge them, bathe in you blood," Brackish said spitting at Dan's boot.

"Well that's going to be a problem," Dan said spitting at Brackish, who had to jump aside to avoid it.

"Then leave me track after you or kill me as my clanmates," Brackish said.

"Fine, first things first: I only killed them that tried to kill me. Most of them died when the big cannon they built blew up." Dan said again. "Way I hear it, you cannot break clan ties. That true?"

"Clan is binding," Brackish said. "I avenge to join a new clan."

"Lee?" Dan asked.

"I'm finished," Lee said rising from his crouch.

Dan scooped Brackish up by the back of the neck again and walked over to the fireplace. A goblin rune had been drawn in the ashes. Grabbing his knife from his boot, Dan handed it to Lee. Lee cut the tip of his thumb, with a slight hiss through his teeth, and squeezed a few drops into the center of the rune. Brackish was struggling and protesting trying to free himself from Dan's clutches. Holding tightly to Brackish, Dan held his other hand out toward Lee. Lee made a small cut across the top of Dan's thumb. Following Lee's example, Dan squeezed several drops into the rune and then placed his thumb in his mouth. Prying at Dan's hand, Brackish screamed and wailed. "Hold him will you?" Lee asked.

Dan took his thumb from his mouth and used his other hand to grasp one of Brackish's smaller arms. Lee took the knife and made a cut across the top of the goblin's thumb. The goblin screamed in panic at the sight, then Dan forced the open cut over the rune where several drops of the light green blood fell joining with Lee and Dan's blood. The goblin stopped fighting and hung limp in Dan's hand. "Now that's better," Dan said.

He let go of the goblin. "Well Brackish, how do you like your new clan?" Lee asked. They had forced the goblin into the clan, but by doing so had forced him to quit attempting to kill them and now they would not be forced to kill him either. Brackish looked around his face sullen. "This not clan," he said dejectedly.

"Check the symbol," Lee said. "It is one of your clan binding symbols."

Brackish looked closely at the signal studying every angle of it. Then a giant smile crossed his face. "Clan, a new clan!" He exclaimed. The goblin was happy again. Dan and Lee were both aware that within the confines of goblin society, the individual is worthless without a clan. Now Lee and Dan had solved the problem and gained themselves a new assistant.

"Glad that got settled," Dan said. "How'd you find us?"

"This fell from you." Brackish held up one of their business cards, their address printed plainly underneath their names. "I went and saw the witches run. I followed you watching as you."

"Where did you hide? I know you did not keep up on foot." Lee said coming to stand near Brackish.

"Underneath your carriage. Enough place I could sleep and ride."

"Do you know what we are looking for?" Dan asked.

The goblin shook his head.

"Good," Dan said. "Here's the deal since you're a new member of this clan. First of all you don't try to kill us ever again or any other human unless they try to kill you first. Second you'll keep an eye on our flat while we're away."

The goblin looked at the two men his face curious. "Do not kill you?"

"I don't think you can, but just to make us feel better. Although if I think you're lying I'll go ahead and put you headfirst into the stove." Dan said.

"I no try to kill, you clan now. Clan is binding." Brackish said, Dan knew that the goblin would not lie to them after joining their clan. "What I do at flat?"

"You will introduce yourself to Ms. Edwards, the woman that owns the building in which we live, and you will make yourself useful to her in any capacity that she decides. Your other duty will include insuring that no other creature enter our flat, we of course have precautions against some but not all. Do I make myself clear?" Lee asked clasping his hands behind his back.

The goblin nodded. "Oh, and no laughing," Dan added.

The goblin stared curiously at Dan, but nodded his agreement to the term. Producing a small length of silver colored wax, Lee used a burning piece of kindling from the stove to heat the wax and dripped a portion onto the back of the business card. Using his ring, Lee pressed his own personal seal into the wax. He handed the card back to Brackish. "You will give her this card and tell her what your orders are,"

Lee glared sternly at Brackish. "We will send word to make sure you have followed through on your oath to us."

"Brackish Thumtum, we know your name. Your kind knows better than most that names are power." Dan said winking at the goblin.

Brackish visibly paled. "I do as bid."

"You should probably get going. It's going to be a long walk." Dan said smiling as he opened the door.

Brackish stepped out into the night, his shoulders slumped in defeat. He turned south in the direction they had come and began jogging off into the night. "Think he'll make it?" Lee asked.

Dan shrugged. "Don't really care."

Dan returned to the chair and opened the shutters, making sure that nothing else was going to spring in on them. Lee laid back down on the bedroll. Elizabeth had dozed back off to sleep at some point during their discussions with Brackish.

They rose shortly before dawn. Dan used the last of the coffee and tea to douse the fires in the stove and fireplace. As the sun rose in the east, the velociter was on its way toward Blackmoore. Both Lee and Dan had checked under the velociter to make sure they did not have any other unwanted riders. It was not long before they passed a horse drawn cart. A grizzled old bearded man sitting upon it. "First person we've seen outside of the villages," Lee commented.

"Underhill did say there weren't any other obstacles." Dan said. "Plus Blackmoore has several close neighbors."

They crossed several other intersecting roads that led to smaller villages all within twenty miles of Blackmoore. "They may have a messaging system," Dan said.

"Yes." Lee agreed. "We can go ahead and send a message to Ms. Edwards."

"Yeah, and let's send one to Roger. Tell him to get several groups up to Falls and finish anything we left. We'll make sure they go in during the day, and have heavy weapons with them."

"Top idea," Lee said. "Elizabeth, they'll most likely have someone here that can help you. I'd actually like to get you back to London and have you meet our regent warden."

Her eyes brightened. "London?" She exclaimed. "I've always wanted to go to London. Papa once went to London and he told me about all the wonders he saw."

The mention of her family erased the joy she had felt and tears brimmed to her eyes. Dan looked at Lee and motioned toward the girl with his head. Since Dan was driving, Lee understood the message. He picked up the child and put her in his lap and held her to his shoulder letting her cry. Her little hands gripped tightly to the lapels of his long coat as she wept for her family.

The closer they drew to Blackmoore the heavier the roads became with traffic both coming and going. Theirs was no longer the only velociter on the road and several more carts were being pushed by large work horses from the local farmers.

8   After another hour, they saw the city of Blackmoore. It did not have a wall surrounding it, but like London just began with buildings growing more numerous and closer together. Blackmoore even had some of the industrial factories that spouted great clouds of smoke from their giant chimneys. Fortunately these were not as numerous as in London, so that the air quality was better. It was still noticeably worse after their days in the open country. Elizabeth was no longer sad but sat in Lee's lap pointing at all the strange new things she was seeing. Most of them were technological marvels while others were simply street performers juggling and doing handstands.

A rather stocky constable stood on one of the street corners swarmed in people, trying to direct the flow of traffic in the street. Dan pulled up beside him and stopped. "Hey," Dan called out the window.

The constable did a quick look at him. "What can I do for you?" The constable asked, a hint of a Scottish accent in his voice.

"Need a place to stay with a shower," Dan said.

"Three streets down turn left, two streets over go right. Big place called the Elizabethan House." The constable said, stopping traffic so people could cross the street.

"Thanks," Dan said tipping his hat toward the constable and proceeding down the street.

They passed a self powered carriage station. Lee took special note of its location, expecting that would be the best route to get Elizabeth back to London. Following the constable's directions through the crowded streets, Dan saw the sign for the Elizabethan House. It had a large picture of Queen Elizabeth out front. It had a classically English façade with large windows covering the front. A sign marked velociter with an arrow pointing to a small ramp leading under the hotel caught

Dan's eye and he turned into it. The velociter made its way down the ramp into a larger cavernous room that had once been a cellar. There were many stalls for velociters to park. Finding an empty slot against the back wall, Dan parked the vehicle and exited. "Wait here," he said. "I'll go get someone to bring up the trunks."

A few minutes later two bell hops came out to the velociter with a luggage trolley, Dan followed behind them. They stared at the covered Tin Man. "Sir, you'll have to park that in a separate space." The older of the two bellhops said to Dan.

"Yeah, just load up the luggage and take my friends up to the room." Dan said opening the driver side door.

The two men smiled and went about retrieving the trunks from the velociter. "You'd best wrap that rifle. I'll be leaving the shotgun where it is. Take little Elizabeth here upstairs and see that she gets a nice bath, we've got someone coming by with a package soon for her."

"A package," she said clasping her hands in front of her.

Dan gave her a wink as Lee tossed him the leather cover for the Winchester. Avoiding the eyes of the bellhops, Dan slid the rifle into the cover and handed it back across the compartment to Lee, who ushered Elizabeth around the velociter as they waited for the bellhops to complete their task and show them to the room.

After Dan had parked the Tin Man in the space across from the velociter he made his way up to the room on the third floor. Lee's boots were sitting beside the door for cleaning. Opening the door he saw Lee sitting in a high backed chair one of his books in front of him. Dan pulled off his boots and put them beside Lee's and then shut the door.

He heard Elizabeth giggling from the bathroom and another female voice. Raising an eyebrow, Dan pointed toward the door.

"I was able to convince one of the maids to assist her in bathing and dressing." Lee smiled. "She said that Elizabeth is up to her neck in bubbles."

"Good," Dan said. "I tell you that ain't any way for a child to be found."

Lee nodded his agreement. "Our clothes, with the exception of the ones you are wearing, have also been taken down to be laundered. Did you find out anything useful?"

"Actually yeah, there's a message center not far from here and we can have one of the hotel staff send it for us. Also Blackmoore's large enough that it has its own regent warden's office."

"I was unaware of such, Nottingham was the nearest that I knew of." Lee said.

"Apparently, it just opened up last month." Dan cleared his throat. "Seems James Brogan moved into the neighborhood and started making it necessary."

"Brogan, the Scot?" Lee asked.

"Yeah," Dan said.

"I wonder if it's true that he carries a large sword with him at all times."

"Did last time I met him." Dan said tossing his newly procured hat onto a nearby desk.

"When did you meet him?"

"Shortly after I got to your wonderful country, he didn't like me. Can't say I liked him either."

Lee groaned. "I suppose you responded with your usual charm."

"No, but we almost had it out." Dan said. "Big fella, I remember that."

The bathroom door opened and the maid stepped out. "She'll be out momentarily," the maid said. "Is there anything else?"

"No, thank you so much." Lee said.

The maid curtsied and left the room closing the door firmly behind her.

While the two men waited on Elizabeth to come out there was a knock at their door, it was one of the bellhops with a box tied with brown twine under his arm. Dan took the package, shut the door, and cut the twine. The bathroom door opened once again and Elizabeth stepped out, swallowed up by the adult robe she had put on. "Perfect timing," Dan said.

He stopped in his tracks as he and Lee took their first real look at the Elizabeth that had been buried under the dirt and grime. She had a perfect round angelic face and bright blonde hair. She smiled at the men. "I didn't have anything else when the lady took my clothes," she explained regarding the bathrobe.

Dan held the box out toward her. "You do now," he said as she took the box and lifted the lid.

"It's lovely," she said jumping up and hugging Dan about the neck.

Lee stifled the chuckle that rose in his throat as he saw Dan, the man of eternal action who did not flinch in the face of any danger, squirm uncomfortably in the grip of a child. Elizabeth broke her hold on his neck and ran to the dressing room next to the bathroom. The box tucked carefully in her arms.

"Never thought I would see the day," Lee started.

"Not another word," Dan said, pointing threateningly.

Lee raised his hands defensively and chuckled softly.

"When you send the message to Roger, tell him about Elizabeth. We'll tell him when she'll arrive once we know." Dan said.

The dressing room door opened and Elizabeth stepped out in the light blue lace dress that Dan had ordered through the front desk. "Wonderful," Lee said standing up.

"Absolutely," Dan agreed.

She looked as a child should look, not the broken spirit that Dan had found in the village of Falls. "Lee get to work on those messages, I have some errands to run. Where are my brown boots?"

"You packed them in one of your trunks," Lee said going to the writing desk.

Looking through his trunks Dan found the boots sitting underneath the dynamite. Dan put on his brown boots that were more worn than the black boots sitting in the hall. The brown boots had made the journey across the Atlantic from Tennessee. Dan had bought the black pair when he arrived in England where everyone wore black shoes, seemed only right to try and blend in. He liked the feel of the old boots.

Lee had written the messages for Ms. Edwards and Roger. Having completed the task at hand, he went and took a shower in the bathroom. Exiting the shower, he saw Dan sitting in the high back chair that Lee had earlier been sitting in. "Bout time," Dan said pushing past Lee into the bathroom.

Once Dan finished showering, he exited the bathroom and found music playing in the room. Lee was teaching Elizabeth how to waltz.

141

Dan could not tell where the music was coming from. The dancing duo stopped when Dan entered the room. Lee walked over to a small box on the table and turned a switch on the side shutting down the music. "Where'd the music come from?" Dan asked confused.

"Apparently, it is previously recorded on wax cylinders and then they play it in the lobby during the day and using vibrational frequencies these ingenious devices can play the music as it is playing in the lobby." Lee explained. "I had heard about such technology being used but did not realize it was already being adapted for commercial purposes."

"You two wouldn't be hungry would you?" Dan asked.

"Most definitely sir," Elizabeth said.

"Where did you have in mind?" Lee asked.

"The restaurant downstairs seemed nice. They also have coffee."

Dan finished dressing and led Lee and Elizabeth downstairs. The restaurant was occupied by only a few couples. Most of them glanced at Dan and Lee as they entered. A host in a black suit showed them to a table near the rear of the restaurant as Dan had requested. Sitting at the table with the fine china and crystal glasses, Elizabeth looked at the menu but did not know what half of the items were. "Excuse me?" She said to Lee and Dan.

Both men looked at her attentively. "I don't know what most of this is." She stated.

"I will be more than happy to order for you," Lee said. "Would you like tea, water, or milk with your meal?"

"Tea please," Elizabeth said.

When a waiter in a black vest with a pencil thin mustache came to their table, Dan and Lee could tell before the man spoke that he was French. His strange accent seemed to amuse Elizabeth. They both ordered a steak with potatoes and Dan ordered carrots, Lee asparagus. Lee ordered a braised pheasant for Elizabeth with mashed potatoes and broccoli. Dan looked at the front entrance during their entire time in the restaurant. After the dishes had been cleared away and Dan finished his coffee, they paid the check. Lee and Elizabeth were headed back toward the main lobby when Lee noticed that Dan was not following them. Placing a hand on Elizabeth's shoulder stopping her, Lee turned to his partner. "Dan?" He asked.

"Go upstairs," Dan said. "I'll be along shortly."

Lee looked back toward the door and saw a tall red headed man with thick corded muscles and a full bushy beard on his face. The hilt of a sword was visible over his shoulder. "Winston," the mountainous man said in a thick Scottish accent.

"Brogan," Dan said coolly stepping forward to meet the man.

"Come along Elizabeth," Lee said taking the child upstairs.

It was not long before Dan joined them in the room. He stretched and smiled as he entered the room. "What happened?" Elizabeth asked.

"Apparently, the staff of this fine establishment had a strong premonition that there was going to be trouble. Seems they have a method for getting contacts to other buildings within the city. Not long after you left several constables came in and escorted Brogan out." Dan said sitting down in the chair beside the door.

"How did he know you were here?" Lee asked.

"I may have been seen by associates of his when I went about my errands." Dan said.

"What did you do?" Lee asked.

"One of them made an unappreciated comment, and I taught him the value of manners." Dan said folding his hands on his lap.

"Wonderful," Lee said frowning.

"It will be fine." Dan said. "We now have more important things to discuss. Did you write those messages?"

"I did, although I did not finish the one for Roger." Lee said.

"Now you can, tell him Wednesday afternoon at four sharp." Dan said.

"That's two days?" Lee said. "Are you sure?"

"Positive," Dan said. "She'll have the entire ride to herself so that she can be left alone. Roger should meet her at the depot when she arrives." Dan turned to Elizabeth. "When you meet Roger, he is the one that sends us after these monsters, tell him what happened in Falls. Okay?"

Elizabeth nodded her head. "I don't want to leave," she said the first tear spilling down her cheek.

"I know, but like we've told you we have to go save another little girl." Dan said. "Besides we'll see you again once we get back to London. Won't we Lee?"

"Indeed," Lee said standing and showing the letter to Elizabeth. "As you can see, I've told our friend Roger to keep every detail of your housing so that we can locate you when our business on this journey is concluded."

Elizabeth looked at the words written in Lee's tidy script. She turned from the letter to the two men that had rescued her. "Okay," she agreed finally.

Dan and Lee walked her to the station, stopping to personally deliver the messages to the clerk at the message office. They would be steam propelled in a leather lined brass cylinder through an underground tube to Nottingham, where an overnight carrier would deliver it to the London messaging office in the morning. At the station, Elizabeth hugged Dan and Lee as they placed her into the carriage, with a small case containing several other dresses that Dan had ordered when he placed the order for the first dress. They watched as the coach powered up the engines and pulled away from the curb headed out of Blackmoore and toward London.

A large hand clapped down on Dan's shoulder and spun him around. He barely had time to duck as the massive fist passed through the space his head had occupied a moment before. Lee turned as well. Two men caught him by the arms and pulled him away from Dan. "Stop this at once," he protested.

"You don't want to get caught up in that," one of the men said.

"I do not intend to, but you will unhand me." Lee demanded.

"All right," the other man said dropping Lee onto his back.

Lee hopped to his feet and faced the two men. "I don't believe I've had the pleasure of your acquaintance."

"We work for Brogan, the big bloke. That tosser hurt one of me mates and Brogan don't take kindly to that." One of the men said. He was missing his two front teeth, the other one had a crooked nose most likely where it had been broken and never properly set.

Lee looked as Dan dodged the strong blows that Brogan was throwing at him. "Do you want to calm down and talk about this?" Dan said sidestepping another massive blow. "Guess not?"

Dan kicked Brogan's knee out from under him and brought his right hand straight up into the giant Scot's solar plexus taking the breath out of him. The two men that had restrained Lee started to run toward their fallen employer. Lee grabbed the back of no teeth's shirt and pulled him to the ground, where his head made solid contact with the brick sidewalk. "Why you," crooked nose said drawing back to throw a punch.

Lee brought both of his hands up and struck the man on the chin with one hand, when the man's head was knocked back he hit the man's throat with his other hand. Crooked nose stumbled away clutching his throat. No teeth started to stand up when Lee sent his elbow crashing down on top of the man's head, sending him back to the bricks. Turning back toward the original cause of the excitement, Lee saw Dan kneeling next to Brogan, talking.

"Everything okay?" Lee asked Dan.

"Yeah, just a misunderstanding." Dan said smiling. "Isn't that right Brogan?"

The downed giant just nodded still catching his breath. "Had to explain the situation and what happened?" Dan looked at the two men that had pulled Lee away. "I see you did all right for yourself."

Lee straightened the cuffs of his sleeves. "I did fine." He said. "Did you inform Mr. Brogan of our adventures in Falls?"

Brogan looked up at Lee and then to Dan, curiosity clearly etched onto his face. "Not yet, it might be something to discuss with your regent warden to get some help." Dan said. "You know somewhere we can talk?"

After Brogan had regained his breath and sent his men home, he led Lee and Dan into a nearby tavern. It was called the Goblin's Nest and had a wooden sign above the door, a picture of a goblin sitting on an egg carved into the wood. Walking through the patrons, Dan and Lee noticed that most of them had some form of weapons. Sitting at a booth near the rear of the pub away from the crowd at the bar, Brogan held out his hand to the bench opposite him. Lee and Dan took the seats. Brogan held up his hand with three fingers raised. Dan started to speak and Brogan held up his hand to silence him. A slender girl carrying three pints of ale set came to the table and set the pints in front of the men. "Thank ye, lass." Brogan said slapping her on the backside.

The girl giggled as she left the table. "So all hunters," Dan said motioning with his thumb toward the crowd.

"What gave them away?" Brogan said taking a large drink from the mug.

"Weapons," Lee said.

"Also they had that air about them. You know what I'm talking about," Dan said.

"Indeed I do." Brogan said. "That's how I knew you when I first saw you. So what's this business about Falls?"

Lee and Dan told them their tale. "We've sent word to our regent warden in London to send several groups out to attack in the daylight."

"Don't think he'd mind if we beat them to it do you?" Brogan asked finishing the mug.

"He wouldn't but they would and you know it," Dan said. "Of course we've already been there, so do what you think best. Trust me though you don't want to go alone."

"That bad," Brogan said.

Dan took a drink from his mug. "Yeah, if that witch hadn't interfered when she did. Well let's just say it would have been a lot tougher. And these things are probably as strong or stronger than you and they like cleavers and bows, I may have seen an axe or two."

"Daylight would most likely be the best time to attack, they seemed to be more of a nocturnal creature and may even be somewhat blinded by intense light, like the sun. Also I believe they have a breed of dire wolf known in Germany as a warg that they use as mounts and possibly protectors during the day. You can kill them easily enough but they are quite formidable and I would not recommend close quarters combat with one of them." Lee added.

Brogan smiled. "He doesn't know me does he?"

"We all know the stories," Dan said. "I'd listen to Lee if I were you. I saw one take a witch off of her broom and tear her apart in under five seconds."

Brogan let out a low whistle. "That is impressive," he said. "How many do you think are left?"

Dan just shrugged. "Hard to say, we don't know how many were there to begin with." Lee said. "It seems they are watching the roads leading into the village though. We were followed by one of their riders. So if you decide to do this make sure you take precautions."

"I will. Thanks." Brogan said getting up from the table.

Dan put a hand on his arm as he passed and stopped him. "Don't take horses either," Dan warned.

Brogan nodded and pulled free of Dan's grasp.

When Dan and Lee entered the hotel a man was sitting waiting for them in the corner of the lobby. He was older, well-dressed, and appeared to be too big for his suit. The man waddled over to Dan and Lee. "Gentlemen," he said tipping his hat to reveal a large bald spot. "May I have a word with you?"

"Certainly," Lee said motioning back to the chair that the man had just left.

All three of them sat in the lobby corner. "I'm Daniel Thorne, the regent superior for this area," he said pausing for the men to be impressed, when neither of them were he continued. "We received word that you had been spotted in our town and we were wondering as to your intentions."

"Well Daniel, much as I'd love to tell you all about why we're here, I can't." Dan said.

"How dare you?" Daniel said shocked by Dan's response.

"Sir," Lee said in a soothing tone. "Unfortunately, we cannot inform you of our purposes or intentions but if you contact her Majesty or our regent warden Roger at the London office, they can confirm that we are well within our bounds to be here."

"The Queen eh?" Daniel said raising a suspicious eyebrow at both men. "I'll just see about that."

"You mind telling us why you're harassing two fully licensed hunters, who had no location restrictions on our practices in country?" Dan asked.

"Well, as you know we have a large population of hunters in town and we would like to prevent any trouble with them. The famous hunter . . ."

"Brogan," Dan said interrupting the man. "We know, just had a pint with him."

Daniel's round face shook as he sputtered trying to get out his next word. "If I might suggest, you contact either Queen Victoria or our regent warden and take up this discussion with them. We are in no violations of any policy." Lee said helping the warden supervisor out of his chair and toward the front door of the lobby.

They watched as the rotund form of Daniel Thorne waddled out of the building and into the street. "That was interesting," Dan said.

"To say the least," Lee agreed.

After having returned to their room, Dan and Lee spent the evening going over Lee's maps trying to determine which village they should head to next. After a fruitless evening Dan went to unpack his sharpening stone, he had often found that he could think better when he was sharpening the knife and lost himself in the rhythm of it. A small piece of stationary fell out of his pack. He picked it up and unfolded it. "Hey," he said handing the parchment to Lee.

Lee took the parchment and read it, then turned back toward the map in front of him. "I do believe she has set us on a course," Lee said handing the note back.

Written on the paper in tiny neat letters was a message: *Head north toward Carlisle, Elizabeth.*

"She must have done that when I was showering." Lee said.

"Well now we know which way at least initially we need to go." Dan said.

Their clothes, cleaned and pressed were hanging in the wardrobe and their shined boots sat on the floor. Dan looked at their clothes and then Lee and he made out their timetable. It appeared they would be able to be on their way toward Carlisle shortly after the sun rose.

Drifting off to sleep that night, Dan was prepared for his dream meeting with Ironhill. Once more in the field with little changing, except the black figure was closer and more defined. "I see you've got your heading," Ironhill said.

Dan looked at the dwarf in his armor. It was more tarnished than when he first saw him in it. "What have you got to report?" Dan asked.

"More attempts on us, so far we're holding." Ironhill looked at him. "The pixies were not as fortunate, a redcap took their chieftain with a spear. The heirs were safely moved elsewhere, and the gnome lords are in need of reinforcements."

"So send reinforcements." Dan said. "You seem to be in good shape."

"No need, the foxes, owls, ferrets, and badgers will be upon their attackers soon. Gnomes have powerful allies." Ironhill said.

"Anything else," Dan said paying closer attention to the figure approaching the child.

"Just that the little girl you saved may be the key to you saving this little girl." Ironhill said. "So far you've done fine work, but fine work is not all that's required. You'll very likely risk your soul before this is done with."

"Figured my life was enough," Dan said flippantly.

"Everyone gets a life and it starts and ends, but your soul. That's the bit that started before you were formed and keeps going after you're body rots. I assure you, it's more valuable to you than you realize." Ironhill warned. "It's about time for you to be waking up."

Dan sat up as the clock by the bed chimed the hour.

9   They were able to find an open market before sunrise and restock their supplies, allowing them to get through the middle of the city before most people were out about their business. The only real traffic on the road were the farmers bringing their wares into town to start selling once the city was good and awake. As they drove out of the city, the buildings began dwindling into farms and forests. "I never did think that England had so many trees." Dan remarked.

"They didn't. Once the fey joined us, Jack O'Green set about planting them for his people." Lee explained.

"Makes you wonder," Dan said.

"Wonder what?" Lee asked opening his book to begin reading once again.

"If all this progress and the fey coming out is a good thing. Look at those black powder goblins, using technology to make their own way. Just doesn't seem right." Dan said.

"It seems no different to me than the Indians of your homeland taking up rifles against the cavalry." Lee said.

"I guess it ain't much different." Dan said, steering the velociter around a small herd of sheep that were on the edge of the road. "World just seems to be spinning faster than it used to."

As best they had charted, if they drove through the night they would reach Carlisle in less than two nights. The horizon was clear and they passed through several villages as they went, stopping and asking for news from Carlisle and from the villages themselves to see if they were having any type of unnatural trouble. The area seemed clear of supernatural threats, both domestic and imported. Shortly after midday on the first day of their journey the skies clouded over and let loose a torrential rain. Dan had ventured out into the maelstrom to light the lamps on the front of the velociter. It was not an easy task with the wind howling and the rain falling in giant sheets.

His long coat was the only thing that prevented him from being drenched through to the bone. His boots were wet with water piled in them. Lee gave an annoyed look at Dan as he removed his boots and socks before continuing on their journey. The storm made travel hard, with portions of the road turning to mud and the lamps providing little light against the darkness overhead. "I don't think this is natural," Lee finally said.

"Why not?" Dan asked.

"Stop driving and look." Dan stopped the velociter and looked out the window where Lee was pointing.

Lightning flashed in the distance and the clouds formed the silhouette of a figure. Three more flashes and the figure was still there. "What are we dealing with Lee?" Dan asked trying to spur the velociter onward.

"If I had to guess," Lee started flipping through one of the books he had already read. "I'd say it was a Son of Donar."

"How do I kill it?"

"You don't, not now. Once you're out of the storm you can challenge it and battle it without the use of its weather power."

Dan kept trying to get the velociter moving, but the vehicle's wheels continued to turn in the mud. "What happens if we can't get out from under the storm?" Dan asked.

"We'll most likely die from some form of weather related injury." Lee stated keeping an eye on the silhouette in the clouds.

Finally the wheels reached rock under the mud and lurched forward dragging the heavy trailer with the Tin Man behind them. The storm raged around them, the wind sounding like the screams of the damned. After several miles of driving through the storm, they could clearly see the line where it ended. The sun was shining and the ground outside of the cloud was completely dry. Dan raced for it, as the velociter slipped and fought for purchase on the muddied road. As soon as sunlight reached the cabin of the velociter, Dan swerved into the grass and jumped from the compartment. He tossed his hat and coat onto the seat. "All right, I challenge you . . ."

"Son of Donar," Lee said.

"Son of Donar to a fight man to whatever you are." Dan called into the sky as he stood barefoot in the middle of the road.

The storm immediately quit and the clouds dissipated into a clear blue sky and a solitary figure drifted down to the ground in front of Dan. It was not what either he or Lee were expecting. The figure was a blond man with high cheek bones and blue eyes. He was also wrapped in a funeral shroud and had started to decompose. Cataracts had started to cover the blue of his eyes. "Lee, is this right?" Dan called.

"No," Lee said seeing the thing before them. "They're living beings."

"You have challenged me," the undead creature said in a tone no louder than a whisper. "Vanquish me again and free me from the torment of this curse."

Dan raised his pistol to the figure's head. "Sorry, fella." Dan squeezed the trigger repeatedly sending three bullets into the head of the weather demi-god.

The dead body fell to the ground, crumpling in its funeral shroud. "What in the hell's going on?" Dan asked looking at Lee. "What curse was he talking about?"

"I'm not sure. Remember what Ironhill said about the wights." Lee glanced around.

"A necromancer."

"Right," Lee confirmed. "A very powerful one at that, they were able to control not only the wights, no small task in itself, but also raise an alleged demi-god from the dead and force it to do their bidding. This may be local talent or one of our foreign adversaries. Next time you see Ironhill you should ask him."

"Yeah," Dan said stepping back to the vehicle. He poured the rainwater from his boots and set them on the Tin Man's trailer to dry in the sun.

Climbing into the velociter, Dan and Lee headed back on their path as they approached the next village on their way toward Carlisle.

They passed through several villages learning of no supernatural troubles, until passing through an inn situated on the road not near any village; but a place for weary travelers. The inside of the inn was welcoming, a small bar and tables were set near the fireplace where currently a big pot of stew was cooking. A small old man wearing thick spectacles came out front to greet them. "Stay the night?" He asked.

"No thank you," Lee said. "Could we trouble you for two bowls of soup?"

"Two?" The old man asked looking at Lee standing by himself.

Having put on his boots, Dan entered and the man smiled and went to the large pot hanging over the fireplace. Dan and Lee made their way to a table and sat down with two bowls of beef stew laid out in front of them. The old man brought them some bread to eat with the soup. "Excuse me sir," Lee said. "Can you tell us if there is anything strange in these parts?"

The man looked at them curiously. He took the glasses from his nose and began cleaning them with a rag from his pocket. "We've got a bogle under the bridge up the road." The man said. "It leaves most folks alone as long as they throw food at it."

"Same road that heads north of here?" Dan said.

"Yes, just several miles up, road forks. Right is quicker but fewer people take it because of the bogle." The man said. "If you do not feed it, it'll ask you word puzzles."

"Thank you," Lee said.

Standing at the fork, Lee and Dan looked down both paths, to the left was a looping pass that seemed to skirt the forest and arc around to the west. The path on the right went directly through the forest. Unlike most forests this one was full of toadstools and willows overhanging the path. "I understand why they take the left." Dan said. "What do you think?"

"Bridge trolls are not usually friendly creatures but I do believe we can get information out of it, if we were to persuade it." Lee said.

Dan smiled. "Lee my friend, that's music I can dance to." With that, Dan turned the velociter onto the right path and headed toward the bridge.

The forest was foreboding and was clearly a place devoid of the touch of the lighter fey. It was not long before they saw the bridge ahead of them. It was a covered bridge that had fallen into some disrepair over the years. Most likely, they quit repairing it when the troll moved under it. A hairy man sized creature loped up the sides from the creek bed below and stood in front of the mouth of the bridge. Dan stopped the velociter and jumped out.

"I guard this bridge, feed me or answer my riddles three." The troll said.

Dan shot it in the leg. The troll fell to the ground with a thump and began wailing. "We've got three riddles for you instead?" Dan said standing near the creature.

Its crooked teeth were stained with the raw meat and fish that it sustained itself on and the smell was awful. Dan chose to stand upwind of it. "First riddle," Dan said.

"No, cannot pass the bridge unless you feed me or answer my riddles three." The troll said again.

"I'll feed you another bullet," Dan said pulling the hammer back on his revolver.

"I cannot answer your riddles, you must answer mine." The troll let out a different cry this time and more cries echoed from the woods.

"I do believe he has friends," Lee said retrieving his Winchester and Dan's shotgun from the velociter.

Dan holstered the pistol. "What are your riddles?" He asked.

The troll darted its black tongue out and licked its lips. "I have many eyes but cannot see," the troll said looking attentively at Dan.

"Potato," Dan said looking to make sure that the trolls that had surrounded them were remaining in the woods.

"I am silent as a cat and stalk all about me, you will never see me approaching but you will succumb to me," the troll said.

Dan looked over at Lee. Lee returned the look and shrugged his shoulders. The two men were both thinking of possible answers knowing that if they were to answer incorrectly the troll herd would be upon them. The troll stayed in the middle of the road, giggling at the trouble the riddle was giving the men. Hesitantly, resting his hand on the grip of his pistols Dan answered. "Sleep."

The slight smile faded from the troll's face and his brethren maintained their position in the woods. "What is your last riddle?" Dan asked.

"I run North to South but flow South to North, what am I?" The troll said staring at the men before him.

Dan's face betrayed the reality that he had no idea what the answer was. This was not the normal type of question they asked. It was clearly a river but which river, Dan could not even begin to guess. "The Nile River," Lee said from beside Dan.

The troll began to jump up and down, angry at having been beaten by these men. The trolls surrounding them in the forest began to disappear back into the wooded depths. Walking to the rear of the velociter, Dan came back carrying a rolled coil of rope. "Well," he said to the troll.

"You have answered my riddles and are free to pass," the troll said limping to the side of the bridge.

Lee stowed the shotgun and started to climb into the velociter when he heard the troll make a surprised sound and then call for its fellow trolls again. Dan was running to the velociter and climbing in. Lee matched his pace and climbed in quickly. The coil of rope was around the troll and the velociter sped away across the bridge as the trolls poured out of the forest into the roadway. "What are you doing?" Lee asked.

"Well, I lassoed the troll." Dan said. "Thought we might get some answers."

"So now we've left him," Lee said.

"No, we've brought him with us." Dan said looking at the troll being drug behind them.

Lee saw the figure behind them. "How?"

"I tied the other end of the rope to the back of the velociter when I went and got it." Dan said. "I imagine that when we stop he'll be in a better mood to talk."

"What about the other trolls?"

"Why do you think, I'm not staying there? I'm fairly certain those trolls won't go far past that bridge." Dan said. "Even if they do, they can't keep up with us. I don't think."

Lee watched as the trolls swarmed across the bridge and then did not go much further than the other side of it, staring after their captured fellow.

Driving out of the forest, Dan stopped the velociter as the road rose up on a hill overlooking an old church. Stepping out with Lee following, Winchester at the ready, Dan walked around to the back and cut the rope free of the velociter, but not the troll. "Now it's time for you to answer our questions," Dan said.

"No, that is not the way it is done. You must answer me." The troll said.

"We did, then we passed the bridge. Now you will answer our questions." Dan saw the troll glance at the church and then look away.

"If you don't answer our questions, we'll take a stroll on the hallowed ground you see right there."

The troll began to shake with fear. "No," the troll begged.

"You don't want to do it, then answer our questions." Dan said. "We answered yours but now you don't have your bridge with you."

The troll looked around in all the other directions and realized there were no bridges around. Reluctantly, the troll realized the situation that he was in. "What are your riddles?" The troll asked.

"We do not have any riddles, we merely need information." Lee said.

Exchanging glances, Dan knew that while he interrogated the troll that Lee would make sure they were free of any interruptions. Dan knelt beside the troll as Lee climbed on the trailer of the Tin Man and kept a watchful eye. "We know that there are groups of fey that are from some where else, how are they getting here?"

"Through the stone ring," the troll said.

"What stone ring?" Dan asked.

"The stone ring," the troll repeated.

"Do you know why they are here?"

"To break the court," the troll said laughing.

"Where are they headed?" Dan asked fighting the urge to kick the troll.

The troll quit laughing and did not answer immediately. "I do not know," it said lowering its head.

"Final question," Dan said. "What do you do when people can't answer the three riddles?"

"Eat them," the troll said tilting its head to get a better look at Dan.

Without a word, Dan grabbed the coiled rope and began to spin pulling the troll on its feet and around him in a circle. Dan let go as the troll was at the edge of the hill. The troll fell and rolled down the hill, bumping up against the churchyard wall. The wall was old and weak the bulk of the troll coupled with the momentum that it had built up allowed the troll to break through the wall and land in the churchyard. No sound came from the troll as its body turned to stone. Retrieving a pry bar from the Tin Man's trailer, Dan walked down the hill careful not to fall. Hefting the pry bar high above his head, he shattered the troll's calcified remains. He carried the rope back up the hill when he returned.

Lee was sitting on the rear of the Tin Man's trailer as Dan came up the hill. Dan's face was red with exertion and his shoulders hurt from the powerful swings he'd taken with the pry bar. "Should we continue toward Carlisle?" Lee asked.

"I suppose," Dan said looking back at the pile of rubble that had been the troll. "I was hoping he'd be more help."

"He knew more than I expected." Lee said standing up.

"I imagine most of those on the Unseelie will know of the plan if only in the vaguest sense." Dan said stowing the pry bar. "You drive this time."

Lee went around the trailer to the driver's side of the velociter and climbed in. Dan took one last look around at the foreboding forest behind them, and the abandoned church with the fresh pile of rocks in its yard. The countryside looked peaceful, but Dan had learned almost anything can look peaceful until you look hard enough.

The velociter found smooth roads and before long the sound of the car was lulling Dan into sleep. This time he was ready for Ironhill.

"What necromancer could raise a German weather demi-god and command him?" Dan blurted out as soon as he saw Ironhill.

"I don't know," Ironhill responded. "We'll have some of our agents see if they can locate the necromancer you seek? So the son of Donar was dead?

"Yeah, fairly fresh at that, didn't even put up a fight when I challenged." Dan said. "Asked me to free him from his curse."

"Most peculiar," Ironhill said as the familiar screams of help began.

"Also, it may not be one of ours, could it be one of theirs?"

"I'll see if we can pinpoint the source of the magic," Ironhill said turning back toward the cries.

"Does the stone ring mean anything?" Dan asked.

"Not to me, why?"

"We interrogated a troll and it said that the German fey were coming over through the stone ring," Dan explained. "You're sure?"

"Yes, now pay attention." Ironhill said pointing toward the sounds of the cries.

Turning, Dan's eyes widened as he saw a rider in black chasing after the red headed child. He and Lee were in the field running after the girl while firing behind them at the rider. A black saber slashed out from the rider's hand and cut across Dan's back, he fell to his knees and then Lee's head went sailing over the wheat as his body fell to the earth. "What are you trying to say?" Dan said grabbing Ironhill and shaking him. "Is this hopeless?"

"Not at all, but you must realize your usual methods of shooting and blowing everything up will not work on this one." Ironhill cautioned. "You'll have to be smarter and remember that sometimes the natural walls are stronger."

Dan woke up as the velociter was moving along, the night sky was cloudy. "Anything new?" Lee asked.

"Yeah, a lot of cryptic nonsense," Dan said. "I saw us die."

"What?" Lee gasped.

Dan proceeded to tell Lee what had happened in the dream. "The natural walls are stronger?" Lee repeated.

"That's what he said," Dan confirmed. "I figured you'd know what it meant."

"I'd have to see the place before I could make a remotely accurate guess." Lee said. "Although it is something worth keeping in mind."

"I suppose." Dan said. "Still wish they'd just tell us flat out what we need to know."

"As do I," Lee said. "We're coming to a village up ahead."

Dan looked out and saw a village in the distance. The warm welcoming lights of the village made Dan wish for a bed, but he knew that the time was drawing short and they could not afford the rest. "What village is it?" Dan asked.

"I don't know, I couldn't find it on any of the maps," Lee said.

"Go around it," Dan said.

"The road goes right through it," Lee said.

"Find a cart path around it," Dan said.

Lee and Dan both stared at the village ahead of them. "It doesn't feel right," Lee said. "You feel it to don't you?"

"Yeah," Dan agreed.

Lee started to turn off of the road to cut through a field when a large fireball tore through the middle of the village. People came pouring out of the gates scared and some even on fire. Dan reached for the door handle to get out. "Don't," Lee cautioned.

"We have to help these people," Dan said.

"No," Lee said throwing himself across Dan to keep the door closed.

"What's wrong with you?" Dan said trying to shove Lee back.

The village continued to burn and the people that were on fire had fallen to the ground. Those that had panicked into the night were nowhere to be seen. "Dan, look. Where are all the panicking people? This is just part of the trap." Lee said.

Dan was looking around, no longer reaching for the door handle. Lee took the opportunity and sped the velociter across the field. As the vehicle rounded the side of the village, the village started to shimmer, like heat rising from the body of a furnace. Then with a loud pop the village vanished, taking with it the burning bodies that had been scattered around the gate. In the center where the village had been stood a dark featured woman. She let loose an angry screech at the men. Then while both Dan and Lee were watching, giant wings spread from her back and she shot up into the sky and out of sight. "Glamour." Dan said. "Sorry Lee."

"I wanted to help to but it seemed odd to me that it happened at the exact moment we were going to go around." Lee stated, explaining his hesitancy to rush from the velociter. "I don't know if that was one of ours or theirs, seemed like a standard spellcaster."

"Yeah, that's what worries me. Why would one of our light fey be helping them? It had to have been one of theirs." Dan said.

"It seems that you are gathering more questions from Ironhill than he has answers for you," Lee said. Looking into the sky, Lee tried to find their escaped illusionist.

"That does seem to be the way it goes. I guess we can get back on the road now, but let's not take any chances. Anything out of place, I say we avoid it." Dan said.

"Agreed," Lee said nodding his head.

10   The morning found Dan driving the velociter through the small farms and around the carts pulled by their workhorses while Lee slept in the seat next to him. They had encountered no other problems since the village illusion the night before. Dan hit a very bad hole in the road and Lee was jarred awake. "Where are we?" He inquired.

"Several dozen miles from Carson, we should reach it about midday," Dan said swerving around another horse pulled cart.

"What are we expecting to find there?" Lee asked.

"I'm not sure, I'm hoping we can find out if we need to go all the way to Carlisle. Elizabeth's note just said to go north towards Carlisle." Dan said reminding Lee. "It never said we had to go the whole way or if we had to go further."

"Have you seen anything that corresponds with your dream?" Lee asked looking at the countryside sprawled around them.

"Nothing yet, but I'm keeping my eyes open and it seems that some of these farmers are growing wheat, so we know we're at least getting closer as far as the crops go." Dan said. "Let's just keep looking for the building with the ruined steeple."

The afternoon saw them coming upon a small village with a low stone wall encircling it. It was a far cry from the other walls they had seen. Wheat fields surrounded the road to the village. Dan stopped the velociter and walked out into the field. Lee watched him marking his place in the book that he was reading. A forest stood in the distance across the field. Searching the rooftops, Dan saw a blackened steeple in disrepair. Lee watched surprised as Dan ran back to the velociter. "This may be it, we need to go into the village," Dan said closing the door and spurring the velociter up the road.

"What did you see?" Lee asked holding on as the velociter bumped along.

Dan pointed across the rooftops to the steeple. Following his finger, Lee saw the rising obelisk. "And you're sure?"

"I have to see one thing and I'll be positive." Dan said.

The carts that were on the road were easy enough for Dan to swerve around. Fortunately, there were no people in his path. "Slow down," Lee cautioned.

Dan begrudgingly slowed the velociter to manageable speed and maneuvered into the village. He was looking about at the signs on the buildings. Paying only minimal attention to the people in the street and those staring at the velociter, many of them seeing one for the first time, Dan sought the sign he had seen in his dream. "There," Dan said almost turning the velociter into a crowd of people.

Lee grabbed the stick and righted their course. "Dan, show me later. First please let's park the vehicle." Lee pleaded.

Dan looked about him having forgotten where he was. "Sure thing Lee," he said blushing. "Sorry about that, lost my head."

"Quite all right, but you have to be careful." Lee chided him.

"I know," Dan said steering toward the nearest inn. "What do you think?"

Lee looked at the small squat two story building. It was old and Lee was not confident that it did not leak when it rained. "I suppose," he said. "Hopefully they have a stable to park the velociter."

Once Dan had parked the velociter, Lee carried the bags he felt were needed up to the room. The inn was small and the room was musty but it was sufficient for their needs. Opening the window at the foot of the bed, Lee hoped the room would air and not be as musty. Dan entered shortly after carrying the shotgun and one of the steamer trunks. He dropped the steamer trunk onto the floor and set the shotgun and its pack on top of the trunk. "You ready," Dan said turning to go back to the door.

Lee grabbed him by the shoulder. A confused look crossed Dan's face as Lee pushed the long coat into his hands. "So we don't surprise people or draw any unwanted attention," Lee said looking at the uncovered pistols at Dan's sides.

"Right," Dan said putting on the coat and making sure that the pistols were covered.

Dan led Lee down the street less than a mile from the inn. He stopped and pointed at the sign in front of a pub. "What about it?" Lee asked.

The sign was round and had two points reaching up from the round portion. It was a green sign that announced the place as the horned snake. "This is the sign I saw in my dream. I couldn't make out the words but the shape of the sign is impossible to mistake." Dan explained.

"Without having seen the name we can't be sure that this is the place," Lee said.

"The steeple, the wheat field, the sign, and the forest are a lot of coincidences don't you think?" Dan said.

"I'll agree it is very likely this is the place." Lee said. "I still don't think it's wise for us to assume this is the place and give up our search."

"I'll bet you five pounds this is our place," Dan said spitting in his hand and holding it out towards Lee.

"I'll bet with you but I'm not shaking that hand," Lee said walking into the horned snake pub.

The interior of the pub was the same as most pubs, a few lights hung from the ceiling casting a dim light on the patrons while chairs and tables took up most of the floor space. It was still early in the day and most of the men were working, most likely in the fields. There was a group of old men gathered around the bar telling tales and drinking pints. Dan and Lee stood close enough to hear the stories they were telling. Like most old men they were talking about their misadventures from when they were young. Ordering a pint, Dan caught the attention of the man nearest them. "Pull up a stool laddie." The old man said. "You look like you've got a story to tell."

"Several," Dan replied.

"Oh and a Yank at that, well Yank give us your best yarn." The old man said as his friends quieted down to hear Dan.

Dan sat on the stool, Lee choosing to sit at a nearby table, listening as Dan told tall tales from his home in Tennessee. The old men laughed and slapped Dan on the back as he made some of them lose their breath from laughing so hard. "That's some funny stories friend," one of the old men said to him wiping a tear from his eye. "What brings you to our little village?"

"My friend and I are exterminators of a sort. We think someone here may be in danger." Dan said.

The men stopped laughing.

"You one of those men hunt bogles and the like?" A man asked. Dan nodded.

"What do you think, Seamus?" One of the men asked.

"About what?" A man with graying hair that still had a reddish tint on the tips responded.

"They might help that granddaughter of yours, the ones been bewitched." The man replied.

"I doubt it," Seamus said sliding off his barstool and heading for the door.

Dan laid several pounds on the bar. "Next rounds on me," he proclaimed to cheers from the remaining men.

While they placed their orders, Dan and Lee followed Seamus out onto the street. "What do you think?" Lee asked.

"I'll know once we see the girl." Dan said keeping his eye on the cap atop of Seamus' bobbing head.

Seamus made his way out of the city and began to walk through one of the field's. Dan and Lee exchanged concerned glances. The field had no one else in it, so that it would be obvious they were following Seamus. However it might be the only way they could locate the girl. Dan stepped into the field first, followed by Lee. The old man they were following turned back toward them.

"I don't want your help and I don't need your help." Seamus said, his Irish heritage making itself known in his speech. "Now get on with you or I'll be clouting the lot of you."

Seamus assumed a boxer's stance and started making his way around Dan and Lee.

"Is he serious?" Lee asked.

"Looks like," Dan responded. "Seamus, we aren't here to hurt your granddaughter."

"Quite the opposite, we have been sent to protect her from a very real and very dangerous threat." Lee said.

"What do you know of it?" The concerned grandfather asked.

"We know that your granddaughter, if she's the child we're looking for, is to sit on the Seelie Court to represent humanity in their affairs." Lee said. "We know this because we were sent here by an emissary of the court and Queen Victoria."

Seamus laughed at Lee. "You two are as crazed as anyone if you expect me to be believin' that the old iron maiden knows of me granddaughter." Seamus said turning to continue across the field.

"We also know that a rider in black is coming for her." Dan said.

Seamus stopped where he stood and turned back to the men. "Are you behind that?" He shouted pointing an arthritic accusatory finger at them.

"No sir," Lee said trying to calm the old man. "We were sent here by the Seelie Court to protect her from this figure."

"So what my little angel's been saying is true?" Seamus said his eyes growing misty.

"What has she been saying?" Dan asked.

"About fairies and pixies coming to tell her how special and important she is. At first I thought she was dreaming such fancies, but after the rider came that first night . . ."

"You've seen him?" Dan asked urgently stepping toward Seamus.

"Aye, five nights now he's come by our house. Each time we've had to stop little Kate from leaving the house. She says he sings to her." Seamus said. "My son and his wife Martha are sweet but they didn't see it for any harm. I'd known people taken by Jennie in the brooks of our glen when I was a lad, so I know the evil those devilish beasts can work."

"All we ask is that you let us meet her and see if she's the girl. If she is, we'll discuss our options then." Dan offered extending his hand to Seamus.

Seamus took it in his own and smiled. "I suppose it can't hurt for you to be lookin' at her."

Seamus led them around the wall through the field of wheat and came upon a small cottage with smoke lazily rising from the chimney. "This is the home of the McKendrick family. I've been here since me Molly passed, God rest her. My son, Canaan and his wife Martha built this house and have lived in it since they were wed. Little Kate is the first addition they've added to the family." Seamus said smiling at the pride he felt in his family.

He opened the small door to the cottage and stepped inside. "Where's the prettiest girl in the village?" He called.

"Right here," replied a small voice that Dan recognized.

A small red-headed girl leapt into Seamus' open arms and hugged her grandfather. Dan gasped as he saw the bright red hair on top of the child's head. Lee looked at the girl and then at his partner. Not a word escaped Dan's lips as he merely nodded his head in answer to Lee's unasked question. Kate caught sight of the men and the smile on her freckled face did not fade in the least, nor did she look at them with confusion. "Grandpa," she said. "They found me."

"Who did?" Seamus asked looking at Dan and Lee.

"These are the men the fairy said would protect me," Kate said leaving Seamus' embrace and walking out to them. She took each of them by the hand and escorted them inside. "Mom?"

"Yes dear," Martha called from the rear of the cottage at what Dan and Lee assumed was the kitchen as they heard the rattle of pans. "Can grandpa's friends stay for dinner?"

Martha came out of the back room wiping her hands on her apron. She stopped as soon as she saw Dan and Lee. Martha was a short woman with dark brown hair, her callused hands bespoke of someone familiar with manual labor. "And just who are you?" She asked examining the strangers in her home.

"I'm Lee Baum and this is my associate Dan Winston," Lee said bowing as Dan tipped his hat to the matron of the house.

"Well Mr. Baum, Mr. Winston, you're welcome to stay for supper if you like." Martha said walking back into the kitchen.

"Thank you," Lee called after her.

"So when do we leave?" Kate asked.

"Leave?" Seamus, Lee, and Dan all said in unison.

"Yes, Ms. Petal said you were going to take me away and protect me." Kate said looking puzzled at all the men. "Didn't anyone tell you?"

"No," Lee said looking at Dan who only shrugged.

"I don't fancy the idea of anyone taking you away from us deary," Seamus said gathering the little girl up in his arms.

"It's all right." The girl said stroking the old man's cheek. "They'll bring me back safe and sound. We've got to convince Daddy to let me go."

"That won't be an easy task girl, and you know it." Seamus said to his granddaughter.

"Ms. Petal has given me something to help convince him." The girl said winking at her grandfather.

"Okay," Seamus said releasing the girl from him. "Go play. Gents a word outside."

Dan and Lee left the small cottage, Seamus following on their heels. "Seamus, we had no idea we were supposed to take her somewhere. Our instructions were to find her and keep her safe." Dan said.

"I believe you," Seamus said. "Kate's been talking about this Ms. Petal for a few months now and Glorianna, whoever that is, but she trusts you fellows and seems to know about what's going on." Seamus looked at the men pleadingly. "If you know of a place that can keep her safe from that rider, then please take her. We'll convince my boy and his wife to let you take her. You best bring her back though."

"Seamus, if we take her. You have our solemn word that we will return her." Lee said placing a reassuring hand on the man's shoulder.

"Do you have someplace that you can keep her safe?" Seamus asked.

"We could protect her back in London," Dan said.

"That would take at least three days of driving non-stop. We would be hard-pressed to outpace any adversary we encountered." Lee said.

"Where's the nearest train depot?" Dan asked Lee.

"You can't be serious?" Lee replied.

"I am."

175

"Carlisle has one but do you really think that we can ride on the train." Lee said dumbfounded by the idea that Dan was putting forth.

"Those designs of yours, the ones that company bought for a new train," Dan started.

"They do run those on the tracks now but we have no way of knowing when we'd find one in Carlisle." Lee said. "Plus there is the matter of our gear and what would we do for transport once we returned to London."

"Rent out an old post car," Dan said. "There's enough room for the velociter and the Tin Man on them. We'll rent out the car nearest it so that we can be near our equipment should we need it."

"How far is Carlisle from here?" Lee asked Seamus.

"Several hours ride," Seamus answered.

"On horse?" Dan asked.

"Of course, I've never been in one of those new fangled three wheeled things." Seamus said.

"I can make it. I'll make all the arrangements and return as quickly as possible. Stay and have dinner with them. See if you can observe this black rider. The more details I have the better I can prepare." Lee said to Dan.

"Go on," Dan said. "I know how to do my job."

"I'll tell Martha one of our guests won't be staying for dinner." Seamus said going back into the cottage.

As the hours passed, Seamus told Dan tales of his family. Eventually, Kate's father Canaan came home from the fields. He was a lean man of hardened muscle from toiling in the fields most of his adult life. Seamus introduced him and Dan to one another. The men went into the house and were greeted by a table set for five. The table was covered with potatoes, peas, carrots, and pheasant. The chairs were hard wood and most likely made by either Seamus or Canaan. The family held hands as they said grace. "Wouldn't you like to remove your coat, Mr. Winston?" Martha asked.

"Thank you," Dan said removing his coat.

He saw Canaan look at his pistols and then meet Dan's eyes. "What line of work are you in?" Canaan asked.

"I'm an exterminator," Dan said evenly. "Or a bounty hunter, depends on who you ask."

"I'm asking you." Canaan said refusing to sit down.

"He takes care of the bad monsters. Don't you Mr. Winston?" Kate said smiling up at her father.

"That right?" Canaan asked.

"Yeah it is." Dan said sitting down.

The conversation faded as the plates were passed and filled with the food. Dan enjoyed the food, it had been a while since he had an authentic home cooked meal.

"Kate help your mother clear the table," Canaan said as he, Dan and Seamus sat around the table enjoying their full stomachs. "So why are you here?" Canaan asked Dan once Kate was out of the room.

"I'm here to protect her," he said. "Your father can fill you in on all the details."

Canaan gave an annoyed look at his father. "I'll tell you later son. Dan was sent to help with the rider."

"We don't need any help protecting our child," Canaan said as much to Dan as to Seamus.

"I don't think you know what you're dealing with," Seamus said. "You're a good father and you love Kate, no one would argue that but don't let your pride blind you to the real threat."

"Dad, I'll kindly thank you to stay out of this." Canaan warned.

"Will you at least let me stay so that I can see this rider for myself?" Dan asked.

"Sure you can stay and when you see we have everything in hand, you can leave." Canaan said.

"Agreed," Dan replied. "How long?"

"Another hour or so yet. That's when he normally rides past," Canaan replied.

"Good," Dan said producing a cigar from his shirt pocket. "Either of you care to join me?"

"I will," Seamus said standing from the table. Canaan merely shook his head.

Dan and Seamus sat on the small bench outside the front door enjoying the cigars. "Don't mind Canaan. He's a proud father and thinks he knows what's best for his little girl." Seamus said.

"Not the first time I've met someone like that," Dan said. "Happens more than you'd think in my line of work. They always think it's harmless until it harms them."

"Aye." Seamus agreed blowing the blue smoke of the cigar into the evening dusk. "Do you think your friend will be back in time?"

"I doubt it." Dan said. "He'll have everything ready by tomorrow though. Hopefully we'll be able to convince Canaan we know what we're doing."

"That may take some doing," Seamus said thoughtfully.

Dan considered this as he smoked his cigar.

The hour passed, Seamus and Dan sat on the bench waiting for the arrival of the rider in black. Canaan and Martha stepped outside and stood beside them as the time drew near. "He'll be heading from the woods soon," Seamus said.

"Then you'll see it's harmless, Mallory thinks it's just a ghost." Canaan said.

"Well Mallory also thought that white cow dung was a ghost, so I wouldn't trust his knowledge on the subject." Seamus said, causing Martha to cover her mouth to keep from laughing.

"Still, the rider hasn't bothered us and no one's been able to find hide nor hair of him in those woods," Canaan said.

"You'd be surprised how often I hear that and then I find a trail bright as all day," Dan said looking toward the woods.

A figure emerged from the forest at a fast pace. "Where's Kate?" Seamus asked concern obvious in his voice and posture. The oncoming figure frightened him.

"She's in her bed, door and window shut, with the shutters closed." Martha said.

The figure continued approaching. A rider in a flowing black cloak sitting a top of a black horse barreling across the wheat fields on a path that led right in front of the McKendrick's cottage. Dan looked to make sure that no one was in the path of the horse and saw a small figure in a white night shirt come around the side of the house. "Christ!" He exclaimed looking back at the cloaked menace.

"Kate!" Martha called drawing the attention of Canaan and Seamus to the little girl that had opened the window and made her way around the back of the cottage.

The rider leaned over to scoop up the girl and Kate opened her arms to be scooped up. Dan ran as fast as he could, having several dozen feet head start but lacking the large horse of his opponent. Seamus was sure Kate would be taken, but Dan scooped her up as the rider righted himself in his saddle and reared the horse up. Canaan and Martha were at Dan's side as he turned back to the rider. With a fluid motion, the rider drew a black bladed saber from under the cloak. Dan handed Kate to Martha. "Get inside, all of you." Dan ordered as he turned back to face the present danger.

Martha hurried off cradling her daughter in her arms. Canaan backed away from the rider, not looking away from the ominous figure. Seamus clapped a hand on his son's shoulder. "Get inside lad, this is a matter for him not us."

The rider sat still, the horse's breath steaming in the chill evening air. The cottage door closed and the figure looked to the closed door and then back to Dan. "Are you my challenge?" The rider asked, his voice seeming to come from all around Dan like the wind rather than a voice.

"I'm here to protect the child." Dan said reaching toward his pistols. "So you tell me am I a challenge?"

"No," came the omnipresent voice as the rider rushed toward Dan, saber bared for a decapitating strike.

Dan dropped to the ground, missing the blade and firing both pistols into the horse and rider. Rolling away from the stomping horse, Dan stood and took stock of the rider. Both rider and mount seemed to not notice the seven shots Dan had fired directly into them. The wind stirred Dan's hair. The top of his hat blew off of his head leaving the brim attached. "Not bad," Dan said.

The rider sat looking in Dan's direction. It bothered Dan that no eyes or face could be seen within the cloak. Taking careful aim, Dan sent a single shot into where the middle of the forehead should have been. The bullet did not pass through the cloak and no sound escaped indicating that it had struck anything. The rider sat unmoving as before. "Are you ready for the final blow?" The voice asked as the rider turned his horse toward Dan.

"Empty threats, come on!" He screamed challenging the rider.

The rider started towards him and Dan turned the side of the house, knocking over a loose bowl, the water inside the bowl flowed across the yard and the rider turned to ride around the small sliver of running water. Dan dove in front of the horse almost getting trampled but missing the killing blow the rider tried to strike. There was a door in the rear of the kitchen and Dan ran toward it. The door opened as he pressed against it. Dropping onto the floor, the saber rushed through the space that Dan had occupied the moment before, striking into the door frame. Martha screamed. Canaan and Seamus rushed in logs from the fireplace in their hands. Withdrawing the saber, the rider looked at the family standing before him and then turned his gaze on Dan. "Next time you will be removed," the voice said as the rider, sheathed his saber and rode off back toward the woods.

"You all right lad?" Seamus asked Dan.

"Yeah," Dan said pulling the remaining half of his hat off of his head. "My hat's not so lucky though."

Martha ran to Dan and hugged him. She kept repeating thank you to him. Canaan refused to meet his eyes. "You saved my girl," Canaan said extending his hand.

Dan took the offered hand. "Why was she out there?" Dan asked.

"She claims that she heard someone singing and she just had to go outside, couldn't stop herself," Martha said wiping the tears from her eyes.

"Sounds like some of them sirens from the water." Seamus said.

"Not like any siren I know of," Dan said. "They only draw male sailors and they don't offer to take them. It is some kind of glamour. Lee will be able to tell me more about it."

Dan was alert as he made his way back to the inn within the village walls. There were no surprises waiting for him. Although each shadow held threats. Never before had Dan come across a fey that did not react to being shot. Even if it wasn't the trick to killing them, bullets still hurt them. The rider had not moved. As Dan made sure that no other perils awaited him, he thought of his encounter with the cloaked rider. The sky overhead echoed, with thunder and lighting racing across the sky in the distance. Dan hoped Lee hurried back.

It was almost midnight when Lee returned. "Everything is tended to," he announced as he opened the door and saw Dan sitting on one of the beds. "How did it go?"

"Not like I expected." Dan said. "It almost got the girl. I shot it and it didn't even flinch. It was like nothing I've ever seen."

Lee sat his bag on the floor and removed a few of his books. "I need you to tell me everything that you can remember about the rider."

Dan told his tale of meeting Canaan and the entire meal and gave every detail he could remember from his encounter with the rider. "Nothing else?" Lee asked.

"That's it." Dan answered. "He sat there while I shot him clean through where his head should have been and didn't budge, then he came after me, destroyed my new hat by the way. Only time he did anything other than try to kill me was when he sidestepped some water I spilled."

"Running water?" Lee said.

"I guess, it was running across the yard."

"Perfect, I might just have our course of action then. Give me until tomorrow morning and I'll see what I can come up with." Lee said. "You should get some rest."

Dan rubbed his hand across his face. "I suppose. It was the weirdest thing I've ever seen. Seven shots right into it and the horse and nothing. Like I hadn't shot at all."

"Ironhill told you your normal approach wouldn't work," Lee reminded Dan.

"Indeed he did," Dan said laying down and pulling the covers up.

11   Dan and Lee woke to find the sky bright but the dark storm clouds remained in the distance approaching on a slow moving wind from the south. "Think it's another one of the sons of Donar?" Dan asked.

"Doubtful, they are very rare and I'm sure the dead ones are even more so." Lee replied still looking over his books. "Did you say that the girl remembers singing and she had to go outside? You're sure?"

"I didn't ask her myself, but the mother said that she had to go outside." Dan confirmed. "Why?"

"I want to talk to Kate about it." Lee said. "I've two possible culprits and the answer to that question will be the determining factor."

"Should we go now," Dan said, running his hands through his thick brown hair trying to tame it. "Wish I had a hat."

"Go see about one in the local shops, I've still got a few things to look after." Lee said turning back to his papers and books.

Dan returned and Lee was packing up everything. Sitting on Dan's head was another bowler hat. "Why don't you buy a proper hat?" Lee asked him.

"This is as proper as I need," Dan said smiling. "You ready to go now?"

"Yes, but first tell me did you see anything beyond the hands of the rider? Exposed I mean." Lee asked.

"As far as I know he was wearing gloves and I never saw anything else. Like I said he was pretty swallowed up by that cloak." Dan answered. "Why?"

"That is just curiosity on my part," Lee explained. "Let's take the velociter, I feel that we may need the speed to make our escape."

"Velociter or not, that horse is fast." Dan said remembering the speed the rider's horse had made across the wheat fields.

They stopped at the Horned Snake and looked in. Seamus was not inside. Dan and Lee continued on their way until they saw the McKendrick's cottage. Seamus was sitting on the bench, Kate playing near him. The old man's complexion was pale and his eyes had a haunted look to them.

Dan raised his hand and waved at the youngest and oldest members of the family. Kate waved back and smiled. Seamus sat on the bench and barely lifted his hand. "Mr. Baum, Mr. Winston," Kate said as they exited the velociter. "Thank you for saving me. Ms. Petal said that all was almost lost."

"Tell Ms. Petal I said she's welcome." Dan said.

"Kate," Lee started. "Why did you go outside last night?"

"I heard the song and I had to go. I didn't want to because I was told to stay in bed but I opened the window and climbed out."

"Thank you child," Lee said patting her fiery red mane of hair. "Would you go tell your mother that we would like to see her?"

"Yes sir, what about me dad?" Kate asked.

"Him to." Dan answered.

Kate ran into the house. "You've got to take her," Seamus said to them as soon as Kate closed the door behind her.

"Why the change of heart?" Dan asked.

"The display last night proved we aren't suited to handle this." Seamus said looking down. "Also the wailing woman of my family spoke to me last night."

"A banshee?" Lee asked astounded.

"Aye," Seamus said looking across the field. "I heard her crying last night and went about the field to find her. She was gorgeous. Told me I had made my fathers proud. Today's my last I'm afraid. It'll happen as I stand against the rider."

"Seamus," Dan started.

"None of that." He snapped. "I've lived me life as I saw fit and now I'm going to give that life to see that the next bunch of us to come along can grow old to."

"Seamus, you realize that standing against that rider isn't going to be necessary if we can get Kate away from here," Lee said.

"It'll be necessary. But you let me worry about that," Seamus said.

"You don't have to die, there's a chance you can live through this." Dan stated.

"Lads the banshee isn't meant as a warning, she's sent by my fathers to tell me I've lived a good life. I know proper folks see her as an omen but she's a comfort and a friend." Seamus explained.

"So you're just going to give up without a fight," Lee said.

"Haven't you been listening? Today may be the day but I've still got a spine about me. If I fall it'll be in front of the rider, and you lot had best be on your way." Seamus said, fire in his voice. "I'll not be dying for nothing."

"Have you told the others?" Dan asked motioning toward the cottage.

"Aye, they know." Seamus said. "Martha's having trouble with it but Canaan's a good son, he understands."

"I take it they still don't want us taking Kate," Lee said.

"They'll go along with it but don't expect them to be happy." Seamus warned.

Canaan came out of the cottage. "Lee Baum," Lee said introducing himself.

"Canaan McKendrick," Canaan said as they shook hands. "So you're the other one wants to take my Kate."

"That does seem to be the best course of action," Lee said never breaking eye contact.

"Are you sure you can protect her?" Canaan asked.

"Sir, the place we wish to take Kate is protected from all manner of supernatural threats." Lee assured Canaan.

"Is that what you'll be taking her in?" Canaan asked pointing at the velociter.

"Only for the first part," Lee said. "We'll be going to Carlisle to meet the new steam turbine train."

"And you can keep her safe until you reach London?" Canaan asked.

"We will keep her safe," Dan cofirmed.

"Once we are in London we can have the Royal Marines stationed outside of the building if it will make you feel better." Lee said giving his best smile to Canaan.

"Nothing makes me feel better about trusting my daughter to two strangers." Canaan said.

"Easy son, they aren't the ones trying to harm her." Seamus said placing a hand on his son's shoulder.

"I know dad," Canaan said.

"Go inside and explain it to your daughter, let her know no matter where she is we all love her very much." Seamus said.

Canaan left and went into the house. "Do you know what you're going to do, your guns seemed to not bother it." Seamus said.

"I'm not sure," Dan said looking at Lee.

"Yes sir, we have a plan." Lee said smiling to Seamus. "Dan a word."

Lee and Dan went back to the velociter. Opening the leather pack, Lee unfolded a map and a book on German folklore. "Here's what we face," Lee said pointing. "Is this it?"

Sitting on the page was a woodcutting of the black cloaked rider sitting upon his horse. "That's it." Dan confirmed.

"The Erlking," Lee said. "No one has actually seen within one's cloak and no one has ever defeated one."

"So what do we do?"

"The only way men have escaped them is to cross over running water no matter how small," Lee said. "That was what Ironhill meant about natural walls being stronger. The old Celtic belief was that evil could not pass through running water, it forms a wall against them."

"Lee," Dan said. "How does that help us?"

"Between here and Carlisle is a river, I think it's actually a tributary to irrigate crops but it will serve our purpose. We'll cross the bridge here," Lee said pointing at the map.

"Won't the Erlking or whatever it is, cross with us?"

"Not if we use some of your dynamite and destroy the bridge." Lee said matching the smile growing on Dan's face. "It's wood and shouldn't take more than two sticks to blow the other end of it and the Erlking will be effectively trapped on the shore."

"Just in case, how do we fight it?" Dan said. "The old man's right, my bullets didn't do anything."

"There are two prevalent theories, one that it's all just fairy glamour, but the hat you lost last night proved that it was real. The other is that there is not a being of flesh and blood, it is merely cloth. The entire being is nothing more than cloak, so I think that fire may be our best weapon against it."

"And how are we going to make fire?" Dan asked.

Dan put the small sack of belongings Martha had packed for the girl in the compartment next to his shotgun. The family was standing outside gathered around as the youngest member was getting ready to leave. Steadily darkening skies seemed to echo the faces of the family as tears were threatening to fall from each of their faces. Martha was the only one openly crying. Seamus was the last to hug the little girl. "Bye Grandpa," Kate said kissing the old man on the cheek.

"Goodbye my angel. Remember Grandpa loves you." Seamus said kissing the little girl's forehead. "You be a good girl."

"I will."

Dan helped the little girl up into the velociter and into the space between the seats where they had made her a temporary pad to sit on. The rider in black bolted from the forest headed in their direction. "Now's the time lads," Seamus said walking past the velociter something under his arm.

Dan couldn't make out the object because it was covered in cloth. "Lee, we need to go," Dan cautioned. "Is there a way to the main road through that field?" Dan said pointing to the fields behind their cottage.

Canaan thought for a minute. "Aye, cut through the field and stay to your left and it'll bring you back to the north edge of the village and the road."

Lee started off through the field as the rider closed the gap between himself and the McKendrick's cottage. Dan looked back and saw Seamus McKendrick throw the cloth to the ground. The Irishman held in his hand an old family sword.

Seamus heard the vehicle rattle as it made its way through the field searching for the main road. He also knew he would not survive this encounter but that by his sacrifice, Kate would be safe. It had been the deciding factor in his choice. The rider charged onward paying no heed to the old man standing in his path. Seamus stepped to the side and took a swing at the rider and the horse, every ounce of strength in his aged body went into the blow. The blade bit into flesh and the horse reared up, stopping its pursuit. Seamus pulled the sword from the horse and watched dumbfounded as the place his blade had cut sealed back together cleanly. Confused, Seamus looked at his blade and saw no blood upon it. The rider turned toward Seamus pulled the saber from under the cloak and swung at the old man.

Despite the ferocity of the blows Seamus was able to block them. The rider turned to head after the vehicle again. "No," Seamus shouted as he thrust the sword into the back of the rider.

The rider turned quickly, tearing the sword handle from Seamus' grip. The tip of the blade was protruding from the chest of the rider. He looked down at it and then reached up with a gloved hand and pulled the sword completely through his chest. Shock filled Seamus' eyes but not fear, he had known the outcome of his stand and he had gladly made it.

The horse reared again this time knocking Seamus to the ground. He rolled away from the horse. Ending on his back he looked up at the rider. The rider threw the McKendrick family sword down into Seamus pinning the old man to the ground. He gritted his teeth at the pain. The rider started to turn away. "Too late," Seamus said to him and then the old man joined his forefathers.

The rider regarded the old man and his statement and then set off at a dash riding past Canaan and Martha McKendrick as they rushed to Seamus' prone form.

Lee was driving the velociter along the path as Dan continued turning around looking for the Erlking. "We're still clear," Dan said as he glimpsed back again.

"There," Lee said pointing at the road ahead of them.

As the velociter's wheels purchased the packed dirt of the road, the Erlking shot into the field following them. "Here he comes," Dan announced.

Lee sped the vehicle to its maximum speed as several of the dials peaked into the red. The Erlking's mount continued on the path gaining ground. "It's not possible," Lee said in shocked amazement as the horse began drawing on them. The saber clashed off the rear of the velociter's carriage.

"I'll see what I can do," Dan said starting to open the door. "How far 'til the bridge?"

"A few minutes," Lee responded.

Dan opened the door and climbed out with the wind whipping around them, lightning flashing in the sky, and thunder rumbling about. Finding a handhold, Dan left the safety of the carriage and clung to the side of the compartment, closing the door behind him. It was a short distance to the flat section where the engine sat, but there was not much room for him to maneuver, especially with the steamer trunks in his way. Reaching into the small bag that Lee had stuffed near the boiler, Dan felt the familiar flint of the flare. "Here's hoping you're right about this," Dan said as he pulled the flare from the bag and was about to remove the flint top and strike it when something lashed out at him from the other side of the boiler.

It was the Erlking, he had seen Dan and not forgotten him from the night before. Instinctively, Dan fell back and pulled his Bowie knife from his boot. He blocked the few incoming strikes with the Bowie and held dearly to the flare with his other hand. The Erlking's horse was having trouble maintaining its pace with the velociter, allowing Dan some respite, but still the length of the Erlking's saber kept him in reach. Dan pulled the flint top from the flare and struck it. Light blazed from the magnesium struck tip. The Erlking was perfectly illuminated as he tried to keep stride with the velociter. With a well aimed throw Dan was able to get the flare inside the hood of the Erlking. As the bright red flame passed into the hood, Dan saw no head or any indication that there ever was anything other than a hood. The red light was burning up from within the body of the cloak. Fire began to spring up on the body of the Erlking.

"Bridge!" Lee called out the driver's side window.

Dan fumbled for the two sticks of dynamite as the flaming cloaked rider lost ground to the mechanized vehicle. Digging through his pockets for a match Dan lit the dynamite as the rear wheels touched the first ruts of the wooden structure. Dropping the two sticks off of the back of the velociter, Dan crouched down beside the boiler waiting for the explosion. The dynamite exploded blowing half of the bridge into splinters. What neither Dan nor Lee had accounted for was the fact that without the other end of the bridge, the portion they were on would not stay up. The intact portion of bridge's anchors broke and the remaining portion of bridge dipped into the murky waters of the river. The velociter fought for purchase and maintained its ground, slowly gaining an inch at a time.

The Erlking his robe fully engulfed with flames eating his horse stood still on the other side of the river where the bridge had once connected. Dan watched as the fires ate away at the hood. The Erlking turned toward the water. Standing as a motionless sentry, the rider stayed on the other side of the river. Dan breathed a sigh of relief as the fire consumed the cloak. The cloak collapsed in on itself, the horse being consumed as well. When it was done burning fabric lay on the bank of the river. It had taken only a few moments for the Erlking to die.

There was a splashing at the edge of the water where the bridge was dipping into it. A green hand was protruding from the water grasping the boards of the bridge and pulling up a hideous green skinned woman with green algae like hair. "Greenteeth," Dan called to warn Lee. "Get this thing moving."

"I'm trying," Lee responded, maintaining his calm demeanor.

The green woman was dragging herself across the bridge boards attempting to reach the velociter. Her green fingers reached up and pulled her closer towards the place where Dan was. One green fingered hand grasped the rear of the velociter. Once her face was above the rim of the floor, the teeth which gave her her name grinned at Dan as a smell of rotting fish wafted toward him. He lashed out with his foot, planting his boot squarely in the face. Jenny Greenteeth's head snapped back and came forward unhindered by the tread marks that marred her skin now. Rising forward reaching out a green skeletal hand toward Dan, Jenny's progress was stopped when Dan pulled both revolvers and fired several shots off into her face. The impact from the bullets pushed her from the velociter back onto the bridge. "Any time now," Dan said keeping his pistols aimed on the edge of the velociter in case she tried to rise up.

Lee ignored the gunshots and Dan's words while fiddling with the velociter controls trying to get the vehicle up off of the bridge and onto dry ground. After turning the stick and adjusting the controls the wheels finally got the traction they needed and shot forward off of the broken bridge and back onto the road.

Dan breathed a sigh of relief as he saw the green form of Jenny Greenteeth still lying on the bridge reaching out towards them. Lee continued on for several miles, putting distance between them and the bridge. The velociter stopped momentarily to allow Dan to get back inside it. "So what did I miss?" Dan asked.

"Kate wanted to go visit her friend on horseback, but her desire and memory of it quickly vanished, which I must admit seems promising." Lee said looking at Dan.

"Seems the enchanted cloak theory was right," he stated, answering Lee's unasked question. "Where's the Tin Man by the way?"

"I left him on the train car," Lee explained.

"The train's waiting for us?" Dan asked confusion on his face.

"No, when they found out who I was they decided to arrange for a private car that would be joined to the train once we arrive. The Tin Man is waiting within that car. Apparently having the designer of the train onboard is a great honor." Lee said shrugging his shoulders.

"Do you think we'll make it in time?" Dan asked as the first large fat drops of water fell from the sky and splattered on the windshield of the velociter.

"Even with the weather chasing us we should be in good shape to make the train," Lee confirmed as more drops fell from the sky while they sought to keep in front of the storm.

By the time they reached the train station the storm had completely overtaken them and rain was falling in massive quantities, turning the ground around them to mud and slowing the velociter as it made its way to the tracks. A large car stood near the end of the platform, one of the engineers watching for something. He waved when he saw the velociter and began guiding it toward a ramp which connected the train car to the depot landing. Lee was able to guide the velociter across the landing masterfully. It went across the ramp and parked near the Tin Man's trailer so it could easily be connected.

Kate looked at the men with wonder in her face. "I've never been on a train before," she stated to them.

"Don't worry," Dan said helping her out of the velociter. "There's nothing to it. You just sit down and let the world pass by around you."

The little girl smiled at them and then yawned, her eyes growing tired. "Where do we sleep?"

Dan looked at Lee, Lee pointed toward the door connecting them to the next car. Nodding Dan picked up Kate and carried her along with her belongings through the door into the rubber covered passageway to the next car which was their own private quarters. He found it was lavishly furnished. The trains that Dan had ridden in before were nice but he had never seen anything like this, normally it was just a small compartment that you had to share with someone else, or in some cases, four to a room and there were no sleeping quarters; you slept where you could. This was a far cry from those accommodations. There were beds in the room, three of them and they were separated from each other by wooden screens. A small serving table sat against the wall with decanters of different types of brandy. Sitting on top of the table was a small cutting tray with bread, cheese, and salami. Dan carried the drowsy child to one of the big soft beds and laid her in it. She smiled up at him as he tucked her into the thick down blankets. "Thank you Mr. Winston." She said letting another yawn escape.

"Call me Dan," he said to the child.

"Thank you, Dan" Kate responded closing her eyes and drifting to sleep.

Dan rustled her red hair. "No problem," he said heading back toward the chairs sitting near the serving table.

Lee came in carrying the shotgun and its pack, as well as his Winchester and his own leather pack of books. "She asleep?" He asked.

"Yeah," Dan said looking at the occupied bed. "Fell out as soon as she hit the sheets."

"She's been through a lot." Lee stated, setting down the items he was carrying.

"Did you hear any news while you were in Carlisle about Brogan or Falls?" Dan asked.

"Unfortunately, no I did not. I do imagine that Roger can tell us all about it once we reach London." Lee said as he gracefully stretched, it reminded Dan of a cat.

"Lee," Dan said, looking around the train and the speed with which the countryside was passing by. "I don't know how you come up with all these things, but keep it up."

Lee smiled at the compliment. "I fully intend to," he confirmed.

"Good." Dan said, cutting a piece off of the salami. "Where can I wash up?"

"Should be a place on the other side of the beds," Lee said.

Dan found the small porcelain basin with a tap that actually worked. He was impressed and splashed his face and neck with water. What he really wanted was a warm shower or bath, but he had gone longer with worse so this would do. Stepping out of the small closet with the basin, he picked a bed on the far side of the car, allowing Lee to have the bed beside Kate. The covers were as soft and comfortable as they looked and Dan, like Kate, was fast asleep beneath the down covers.

Once again Dan was in Ironhill's war room, sitting at a table across from the dwarf. "Well we got the girl," Dan said to the dwarf.

"Aye that you did." Ironhill agreed.

"How long do we have to keep her?"

"Until this is settled." Ironhill responded. "You killed the assassin but unfortunately the Unseelie is not going to give up that easily."

"Why didn't you tell us about Ms. Petal?" Dan asked.

Ironhill looked up at Dan, the shock of the statement showing clearly on the dwarf's face. "How do you know about her?"

"Kate told us about her. So you knew about her and where she was but felt the need to use Lee and myself and play games with us." Dan accused standing up from the small table.

"We needed you to take out the obstacles in your path, to help our cause." Ironhill explained.

"I don't care about the reasons. You lied to me, plain and simple. You sent me into danger and didn't even have the courtesy enough to tell us what we were walking into." Dan said pointing a finger at Ironhill. "You wanted them dealt with you should have told us. That is our job, dealing with fey and all the other monsters out there."

"I know but we can't interfere too much," Ironhill said.

"We've got the girl and we'll keep her alive for as long as we can, or until we find a way to stop this, at which point we'll be more than happy to clean up after you, yet again." Dan turned away from Ironhill. "Next time I see you, you got a knock coming your way."

Dan woke in the bed, the night still held sway outside. Looking at his pocket watch on the bed beside him, he saw that he had only been asleep for a few hours. He got out of the bed, knowing it was useless for him to try and go back to sleep. The plush leather armchair sitting near the writing desk was comfortable and Dan sank down into the leather and reflected on what he knew. His and Lee's capabilities to protect the girl were going to grow more limited as time went on and the Seelie Court would also be of no help, while trying to protect themselves.

Outside the countryside sped past as Dan sat trying to formulate a plan of attack. Normally Lee was the tactician and Dan was the fighter, but this situation called for a change. Dan was shook from his revelry as a metallic clank echoed in from the adjoining compartment between the train cars. Looking over his shoulder Dan could see Lee and Kate still asleep. Forgetting the noise, Dan went back to thinking. Then the noise came again. Dan got out of the chair to see what was causing the noise, his hand poised on the lever to open the door, when Kate stopped him.

"Don't," she said, sitting up in her bed. "Ms. Petal says she'll make you see what you want to see or what she wants you to see."

Kate closed her eyes and lay back down in the bed. Dan remembered the village they had seen, the one that had vanished. It had been a strange looking fairy that had caused it. Choosing caution over action, Dan woke Lee and told him what had happened. "Did you see what it was?" Lee asked tired.

"No," Dan said looking back to the door. "I just think it might be smart to take a look but if we get glamoured while we're out there Kate will be helpless."

Lee retrieved the Winchester from his bedside.

Nodding Dan retrieved one of his pistols and went back toward the door where the echo had come from. He turned the lever and opened the door, checking the compartment between cars. There was no sign of anything out of place then he heard a sound come from the car where the velociter and Tin Man were being stored. Dan closed the door behind him and proceeded to enter the other car of the train.

Lee waited by the foot of Kate's bed for Dan to return. The door opened and Dan stood in the doorway. "Couldn't find anything?" Dan said entering the room.

"Aren't you forgetting something?" Lee asked.

A puzzled look crossed Dan's face and then he turned around and closed the door. "Sorry about that," Dan apologized smiling at Lee.

The pistol bulged in Dan's front pocket as he made his way toward the chair he had been sitting in before hearing the noise. "Oh Dan," Lee said.

Dan turned toward Lee and a shocked look crossed his face as in one fluid motion Lee raised the Winchester and fired into Dan's chest. Holding a hand to the wound in his chest, Dan looked at Lee surprise evident on his face. "How?" He asked.

"I told you, you forgot something." Lee said watching as Dan's body started to shrink.

Falling behind the chair, the being that Lee shot stayed there making gurgling noises. Once the final noise had abated Lee crept closer to the chair. Leaning over the leather back he saw the dark fairy that had made them see a distressed village earlier in their journey. Her black wings were motionless and her eyes stared vacantly across the floor. The bullet's exit wound was clear between the two wings. Glistening silver blood seeped onto the carpet from the bullet's entrance. The door opened and Lee aimed at the center of the mass that stepped through. It was Dan holding his head and staggering in.

"Dan?" Lee asked, gently placing his hand on the trigger.

"What?" Dan responded, his voice carrying agitation with it.

"Didn't you forget something?" Lee asked once again to make sure that this was not another imposter.

"I'll close the damned door in a minute. If it's so all fire important do it yourself." Dan responded.

Lee lowered the rifle. "So what happened?"

"Got me when I went back there. Damn fairy glamour, it made me see someone digging through one of our trunks. I was ready to surprise them when something caught me from behind." Dan said still rubbing the back of his head, and then he saw the body lying on the floor. "That one?"

"Same as before, only she didn't have your winning personality or lovely manners." Lee said smiling.

"Good," Dan said. "Guess we should dispose of it."

"Indeed, off the back of the train?" Lee suggested.

Dan and Lee each hefted the fairy under an arm and carried her through the car where the velociter was stored. It was the final car in the train. Opening the rear door, they saw the darkness from the uninhabited wilderness through which their train was traveling. The two men let go of their grip and the fairy fell through the open door and onto the tracks below.

Kate was sitting up in bed as the men returned. "Ms. Petal said I could wake up now." Kate said. "I wanted to wake up when I heard Mr. Baum shoot but she told me not to."

"Well all the excitement's over so you can lie back down." Lee said smiling at the child. "Warm milk?"

"Yes please," Kate said. "Ms. Petal doesn't think that this is the last of the trouble. She told me earlier that the worst is yet to come."

12   The train pulled into London around noon the next day. Dan and Lee took care that Kate was between them the entire time they were exposed on the platform. They both breathed easier when she was sitting on her small pillow in between their seats. "Why didn't Roger meet us here?" Dan asked.

"Maybe he misunderstood the message," Lee said. "It was not necessarily the clearest message I've ever sent."

Driving the velociter with the Tin Man's trailer once more attached, Lee made his way through the crowds of people at the train station until he was back onto the streets of London. They were crowded by the normal throngs of vehicles and people. Kate took it all in, her mouth gaping in awe at the sights around her. It took longer than expected but Dan and Lee made it back to their flat without mishap. Parking the Tin Man's trailer inside of the shed and then the velociter under its shelter, Lee assisted Dan in carrying in their steamer trunks. They took Kate with them on their first trip.

Ms. Edwards' door opened as they were almost in front of her door. "Gentlemen," she said. "I did not expect you back so soon."

"We didn't expect to be back this soon," Lee explained.

"Mr. Roger is here for tea," she said looking at the men. "Does this have something to do with you?"

"Most likely," Lee said.

"Ms. Edwards would you mind getting some of that tea and any biscuits you might have for our newest friend Kate McKendrick?" Dan asked looking down at the child between him and Lee.

Ms. Edwards put her hands up to her face. "Well pardon me, young lady I did not see you. Would you like some tea?"

"Yes ma'am. Thank you very much." Kate said curtsying.

Ms. Edwards escorted the young lady into the tea room. Dan and Lee carried their things into their flat. Brackish Thumtum greeted them as they entered the flat. Of course not realizing who they were, he dashed at them with a large knife from the kitchen. "Hey!" Dan yelled.

The goblin stopped in his tracks and dropped the knife. "Sorry, I thought you break in. I no know it you." He said sheepishly.

"Brackish so glad to see you made it." Lee said walking past the goblin and entering his bedroom.

"Many nice tinkers here," Brackish said waving at the mechanical things in the room.

"Did you mess with any of them?" Dan asked looking Brackish over suspiciously.

"No, only look. No touch." Brackish said picking up the knife, blade first, and returning to the kitchen.

Dan set the steamer trunk that was across his shoulders in his room. Lee and Dan made one more trip to the velociter to gather the rest of their things. Roger appeared in the doorway as they passed. "A word," he said. His face told them the same thing that the tone of his voice did. He was aggravated at something they had done.

"One moment Rog," Dan said walking past him.

"Brackish," Lee said pushing the door closed behind him.

"Yes," Brackish said sticking his head from around the kitchen doorway.

"You're going to need to hide we have someone coming that will not be happy that you are here." Lee explained.

Brackish turned back into the kitchen. Dan went to grab the goblin and make him hide even if he had to put him in a box and sit on it. The kitchen was empty. Dan looked at Lee and shrugged his shoulders.

Nodding Lee went back to the door and went down the stairs. He returned with Roger. "So what's the problem?" Dan asked.

Roger's dark hair now had wisps of gray in it, no doubt due to his encounter with the wight. "The Queen has seen fit to keep up with your progress and has been providing us with your bounty count. Nice job with those orcs, I believe she said over one hundred. We will pay the bounties when you come in to collect them. The reason I am here is because of the information you gave to James Brogan."

"What's the Scot done now?" Dan asked putting a pot of coffee on to brew, while Lee prepared one for tea.

"He led a small army of hunters to that village and proceeded to try and exterminate the rest of them." Roger explained.

"I'm sorry, but why is that a problem?" Lee asked looking perplexed.

"Over half of them did not return. Brogan did of course. He's harder to kill than you two." Roger said. "The problem though is that now we have an unknown number of orcs roaming the English countryside, because instead of allowing Her Majesty's Marines to do their job, you sent off your bounty hunting brethren."

"Actually, we told Brogan about it after we sent the message to you. Not our fault those men went off seeking some easy money, and from what we saw, the orcs were in the countryside before Brogan went and pushed them out." Dan said.

He and Lee recounted their experience in Falls. Roger listened, his face expressionless. "Does her Majesty understand the severity of this orc problem?" He asked when they had finished.

"You would need to ask her," Lee said. "I imagine that someone has made her aware. Did she tell you why we went where we went?"

"No," Roger said looking at his feet. "Only that you had been sent by order of the crown and that your bounties would be relayed to me with no proof of demise."

"Then we can't tell you anything more." Lee said. "You understand."

"I do," Roger said. "But why send that little girl to me?"

"We expected that she had information you could use, plus she's very special." Dan said.

"I imagine so, since you wanted her here with Ms. Edwards." Roger said.

"I beg your pardon," Lee said looking at Dan. "She's here?"

"Yes," Roger replied looking confused at the two men. "She relayed your message and then said that you wished her to stay with Ms. Edwards until you returned."

"Did we?" Dan said as the corner of his mouth twisted up into a knowing smile.

"From my understanding, Ms. Edwards filed papers to become the girl's legal guardian the day after she arrived here." Roger informed them, still confused.

"Apart from Brogan did you have anything else that you wanted to share with us?" Lee asked.

"The last of the sisters has been seen," Roger said.

"Meg," Lee said looking out the window.

"From my understanding you shot her into a burning house. The accounts I've heard from Brogan and the others is that the house you described was the one that had been blown completely apart. She's obviously much more powerful now." Roger said.

"You know how their power works don't you?" Lee asked.

Roger shook his head. "It's simple." Dan said. "In most families if a witch is born they have a small amount of power, nothing much. In the case of the Cairn sisters all three were born with more power than most. That power is connected to them by blood. When one of them dies the power goes into the remaining ones. With Meg being the last left she has the collective power of all three of them."

"Yes it makes her a great deal more deadly than most of the witches in this country." Lee said.

"Great and as I recall her sister was trouble with less power." Roger said.

"Indeed she was," Dan said remembering the battle.

"We will deal with her when we must." Lee added. "What we need to know is if there has been any strange activity nearby?"

"A few things have crossed my desk. Giant wolfs in the city, rat-kings in the sewers, and a few other things that some of the more superstitious are calling bad omens." Roger looked at the men as their faces grew dark with worry. "What is it?"

"We don't know Roger. That is the truth of the matter." Lee said.

"If I were you, I'd inform the queen that we've returned and would love an audience with her." Dan stated.

Roger stood and went to the door. He turned back to the men. "I'll see what I can arrange," he said as he left the flat and walked into the London streets.

"Okay Brackish," Dan called.

The goblin appeared once more from the kitchen and walked over to the men. "You draw tinkers?" He asked Lee.

"Indeed," Lee said looking at Dan. "Did you do anything with them?"

"No, only look. They look fun," the goblin said with a mischievous smile.

"They are and they ain't for you." Dan said.

"I know, never hurt look." Brackish said.

"Gentlemen," Ms. Edwards said, opening the door and entering with Kate and Elizabeth following behind. Her next sentence froze in her throat as she saw Brackish.

Both the goblin and the woman let out a small shriek. Dan leaped forward to catch the swooning Ms. Edwards while Brackish ran away into Lee's room. Elizabeth and Kate giggled as little girls are want to do when adults find themselves in situations children are unfazed by. "Hello Elizabeth." Lee said.

She curtsied. "Good afternoon Mr. Baum and to you as well Mr. Winston."

"Indeed," Dan said carrying Ms. Edwards to the nearest sofa and sitting her against the arm of it. "So we wanted you to wait with Ms. Edwards?"

"I am sorry for the deception sir, but I have a feeling that you may need my special talents at other times." Elizabeth explained. "Where would you like for Kate to be staying? Ms. Edwards does not feel that she has room in her quarters for two young girls."

"She'll stay here." Lee said. "In the event that you should sense anything sinister approaching, Ms. Edwards and you should come here immediately. It will be the safest place in the building if something attacks."

"I haven't seen anything of that nature," Elizabeth replied. "But if I do I will be sure to come here with all haste."

"Where shall I sleep sir?" Kate asked.

Elizabeth put her arm around Kate's shoulder, both girls smiled at each other. "My room's less filled with mechanical get ups." Dan said.

"True, that might be the best option." Lee agreed.

"If you'll stay here with Ms. Edwards for a few moments, I'll go clean up and make it fit for a lady." Dan said excusing himself to his room.

"Is the little beasty always here?" Kate asked Lee.

"He's a new addition to the household, just like Elizabeth. No permanent decision has been made about his lodgings." Lee explained looking at the closed bedroom door where Brackish had fled.

"Ms. Petal won't like this at all," Kate said.

"Unfortunately Ms. Petal is not the chief voice of authority here," Lee stated. "So she will have to deal with our decisions."

Dan came back into the room carrying a box full of things. "I think it's ready for you," he said.

Kate walked toward the room that Dan had cleaned quickly. "Thank you." She replied sheepishly as she disappeared into the room.

"I miss something?" Dan akesd looking at everyone.

Before anyone could answer Ms. Edwards moaned. Lee sat beside her patting her hand and speaking soothingly to her. "Tea," Dan said pointing towards the kettle.

Elizabeth went to it and found a cup on the counter. She poured the hot tea into the cup and brought it to Lee. The old land lady opened her eyes. "My goodness what happened?" She asked looking from Lee to Dan.

"You had a bit of a fright, but here have some of this." Lee said handing her the cup of tea.

She took a tentative sip of it. "How embarrassing," she said. "What frightened me?"

Dan and Lee exchanged glances. "Go ahead, she might as well know." Dan said. "Didn't you get our letter about someone coming to help out?"

"Indeed I did, but the young lad has yet to arrive." Ms. Edwards said; a bit of her normal cheer returning.

"Brackish," Lee called standing outside of his bedroom's closed door. "Please come out."

The door opened and something was walking across the floor. Ms. Edwards' view of it was blocked by the other sofa. "Did he arrive with you?" She asked Dan.

"Not exactly," Dan said as Brackish cleared the sofa.

Ms. Edwards gasped. "Now Ms. Edwards. This little guy is going to be helpful. Aren't you?" Dan said.

"Yes, I help anyway I can." Brackish said. "We clan."

"We'll explain that later," Lee said to Ms. Edwards. "However for the time being know that he is not one of the monsters we hunt. He has sworn an oath to us and will not harm anyone unless they try to harm him or one of us first."

Brackish nodded his head vigorously then he smiled at the woman. She looked away as the lips drew back revealing black gums and sharp teeth. "Like this," Dan said demonstrating a smile while keeping his lips together.

It took a moment but Brackish was able to get his lips down and cover his teeth. Ms. Edwards looked at Brackish and knew there was no point in trying to argue with Lee and Dan. "Very well," she said extending her hand. "I am Ms. Edwards very pleased to meet you."

Ms. Edwards flinched as the goblin grasped her hand the best he could with his smaller cold hands. "Brackish Thumtum," the goblin said. "Nice meet you."

"If I need any assistance, I shall contact you." She said placing the saucer and cup of tea on the table and standing. "Come along Elizabeth."

Elizabeth walked behind her and winked at Brackish as she left the room and went back to her quarters with Ms. Edwards.

"I scare her." Brackish said, his shoulders sagging.

"Give her time, Brackish." Lee said placing a hand on the small shoulder. "Once she sees that you aren't evil she'll be okay with you."

"Yeah," Dan said. "About that, are we really sure we can trust him?"

"We clan, I protect clan." Brackish said thumping his small fist on his chest.

"We did form a clan with him," Lee said, reminding Dan.

"All right, put 'er there." Dan said shaking hands with Brackish. "I don't know how things are done in your world but here a handshake is an unbreakable bond. Understood?"

"Yes. Clan bond." Brackish said solemnly.

"So why didn't you introduce yourself to Ms. Edwards?" Dan raised an eyebrow at Brackish.

"She would scream and beat at me with cleaning stick," Brackish explained.

"We'll have to work on that, but for now we need to determine our next course of action." Lee suggested

"All right," Dan said taking the kettle of coffee and pouring a cup of it. Dan opened the cool box and reached in for a piece of ham and stopped. "Did you drink my beer?"

Brackish looked around for cover. "I thirsty." He explained. "Nothing else to drink."

"Water," Dan said pointing to the tap in the kitchen.

"Blech," the goblin said sticking out his tongue. "Elixir better."

"Dan," Lee said stepping into the argument. "We'll get you more beer. Brackish if you do as you're told we will also provide you with some beer."

The goblin danced and clapped at the announcement. Dan sat down with the salted piece of ham and tore into it. "Fine, so what do we do next?"

"First things first, we should inspect our gear. Then depending on how long it takes for the Queen to respond to our request perhaps it's time to work on some upgrades to our current inventory." Lee said smiling.

"What've you been up to?" Dan asked returning the smile.

"I know that reloading your shotgun can be time consuming so I was wondering how would you feel about an eight round magazine that you could replace?" Lee asked.

"Replace, how?"

"Much like Colonel Colt's designs suggest, you would carry the magazine which would fasten into place and when it was empty you would drop it out for a fully loaded one that you could carry. Of course you would need to reload the spent magazines once you ran through all of the full ones." Lee said. "I know you have more shots now but if I can get you six to seven of the eight round replaceable magazines you'll be able to keep up a steadier rate of fire than if you have to reload the entire tube after finishing the magazine."

"Okay, I'm on board." Dan agreed. "What are we going to do about Kate?"

"She will be fine." Lee said. "Apparently Ms. Petal is going to object to Brackish's presence here and I informed her that Ms. Petal is not in charge."

"Oh well, she'll come out eventually." Dan added as he stood and retrieved the shotgun and his pistols from their place by the door.

After inspecting their weaponry, and cleaning what needed to be cleaned, Lee set to work modifying the shotgun. His first step was to remove the current extended magazine from the body of the weapon and then add new gripping hooks on the barrel and the stock that would lock one of the new magazines in place and also allow it to be ejected when needed. Then he would work on putting a small lever in the stock to allow the hooks to release the magazine. Lee spent the most time designing the trigger attachment. With the design he was using the magazine could not be released while the trigger was being depressed. It would also render the trigger immobile until a new magazine was in place and the lever was released.

Brackish watched from one of the tables in Lee's workshop. The small goblin had seen black powder clan tinkerers build different tinkers from pieces but he had never seen anything as well executed as what Lee was doing. Watching for hours, the goblin drifted to sleep while Lee toiled long into the night on his new modification. Brackish rolled off the table and awoke when he hit the floor. Laboring without noticing the goblin's fall, Lee was still at his table working on the shotgun. This time watching from the floor Brackish saw the progress that Lee had made. The gripping hooks were in place and the trigger mechanism was taken apart but the lever attachment had been completed. All Lee had to do was reassemble the remainder of the trigger. "Curses!" Lee exclaimed looking up from the table.

He went to a table against the wall and began sorting through springs of all sorts and sizes. After several moments of searching, he rose and removed the goggles that he had been wearing. "That's all for now." He said to Brackish.

"Why? Tinker done?" Brackish asked.

"Not quite, I don't have the right size spring that I need." Lee pointed to a chair across the table from him.

Brackish climbed up and stood in the chair. Lee then explained all the modifications that he had made and explained that without the spring the magazine release lever would not function properly. "I'll see if I can't procure one today." Lee said as he left the workroom.

The sun was shining outside. Dan and Kate sat at the table and were eating a breakfast of eggs and bacon. "Bangers in the kitchen," Dan said seeing them.

Lee walked into the kitchen and saw the pan with the bangers browned within it. He turned on the burner to allow the sausages to warm up. After he was content that they were warm he turned off the burner and sat them in two separate plates. Scooping eggs into the plate, he took a piece of bread and walked to the table, handing Brackish the other plate of bangers. Brackish looked at it strangely. "Get some eggs,"

Lee explained pointing to the small mound of eggs he'd left for the goblin.

Brackish did as he was told and sat at the table with the three humans. Watching as they ate, Brackish mimicked them. He found that the eggs were not bad but the bangers as they had called them were delicious. His stomach was filled to bursting and the others humans finished their food before any of them spoke. "I really must apologize for my behavior," Kate said. "It was rude."

"It's quite all right," Lee said patting her hand. "Did you inform Ms. Petal of Brackish's presence?"

"She was aware of it," Kate responded. "She told me that if you trusted him and felt he was safe then she would trust your judgment."

"Glad to hear," Dan said finishing the last of his coffee. "Went to market this morning for some milk and juice, of course the breakfast we just ate, and I got a few more bottles of beer. Not for you," Dan added as Brackish's face lit up with excitement.

"Of course," Brackish said, looking down.

"I might be able to be convinced to share though," Dan said taking his plate into the kitchen. "How'd everybody else like breakfast?"

"It was delicious," Kate said. "Thank you very much."

"Human food tasty. Liked bangers," Brackish said looking at Lee. Lee nodded as Brackish said the word properly.

"Boy, you like that stuff, when all this blows over I'll make you some of my famous flapjacks, you'll never taste anything better." Dan said whistling. "How goes the work on Betsy?"

"I don't understand why you seek to name weaponry," Lee said. "Sometime, today preferably, I will need to purchase a spring to complete it."

"What if something happens and I need it sooner?" Dan asked.

"You still have the pump don't you?"

"Yeah I've got it, but I gotta tell you I prefer the one you fixed up," Dan stated.

"It's not permanent, but for the time being it will have to do until I have the spring I need."

"All right," Dan conceded walking toward one of the closets off of the main room.

He retrieved the shotgun from the closet and opened the hard case that it had been stored in. Sitting down in front of the coffee table, he began to disassemble the shotgun and clean it. Lee began to drift asleep sitting at the table. "I believe I will go to bed," he said excusing himself from the table.

"Our ride will be here at one," Dan called.

"What ride?"

"Roger got in touch with Victoria. She's sending a carriage for us." Dan explained.

"Wake me at noon," Lee called.

"Brackish," Dan said getting the goblin's attention. "Make sure he's up at noon."

Brackish nodded as he ate the remainder of Kate's bacon. The little girl just watched him curiously. "He's not going to try and hurt me is he?" Kate asked Dan.

"You clan, I no hurt clan." Brackish said drawing back at the accusation.

"I don't think he'll bother you. Seems we're his adopted clan, in goblin terms we're family." Dan explained, giving Kate a reassuring smile.

"Nice to meet you, I'm Kate." She said grabbing Brackish's hand and shaking it.

"Brackish Thumtum." He said practicing his smile without showing his teeth.

"Would you like to play?" Kate asked.

"What play?" Brackish asked.

"Oh lord," Dan said. "Little lesson for the two of you: goblins are not used to playing and playing does not involve black powder, bullets, danger, or anything sharp. Understood?"

Both Brackish and Kate nodded their understanding. "We could play a game," Kate suggested.

Brackish's face still held the confusion it did when she suggested they play. "You can play hide and seek or jacks, other than that all we've got around here is cards. You cannot leave the flat, cross the threshold on that door and you'll be at the mercy of anything that's after you. Brackish will make sure you don't do that, right?" Dan said as Brackish looked at the door and nodded solemnly. "Whatever you decide to play, you'll have to explain the rules to our newest friend."

"I will sir," Kate said. "Come on Brackish we'll play in the room."

Kate grabbed Brackish by the hand and almost dragged him into the bedroom she had commandeered from Dan. Chuckling to himself, Dan thought of the exposure to humanity Brackish was about to receive.

13   The motorized carriage carried them to the palace as it had before. This time Roger was not with them and one of the Queen's guards met them at the side door to the palace. The red coated guard led them to the same room they had met the queen in previously. "Please sit gentlemen, her Majesty will be with you momentarily." The guard said as he made a crisp turn about face and left the room.

It was Prince Albert that next entered the room. His face had aged more since they last saw him. Lee suspected it was also a result of the wight's touch as was Roger's graying hair. Both Dan and Lee started to rise but Albert stopped them with a wave of his hand. "Victoria is quite busy but we have made time to meet with you. Our first point of business is the condition of the girl?"

"Kate McKendrick," Dan clarified.

"She is doing well sir, currently being protected at our home." Lee said.

"Excellent, excellent," Albert said clapping his hands. "One moment and I will see where we stand with Victoria."

Albert excused himself from the room and left. It was only a few minutes and Queen Victoria came into the room, escorted by Albert. "Gentlemen, so good to see that your task was not as time consuming as we feared it might be," she said as the two men stood and bowed before her. "Please be seated."

Sitting back down, Dan decided to speak first. "Seems that Ironhill knew where she was the whole time but they wanted Lee and me to take care of some darker problems before we got to her."

"Yes. He told me you were quite upset with the ruse." Queen Victoria said. "I was not made aware of the deception until you had already departed on your journey. You do have my apologies for my involvement in the deception."

"Not necessary ma'am." Dan replied.

"Beg your pardon majesty, but Roger told us of some strange events going on within the city itself." Lee said. "Has the Seelie Court been in contact with you to gain their perspective on these phenomena?"

"As of yet we have not spoken with them for going on a week." She said, worry creasing her brow. "I fear the siege of their strongholds has been increased and we may have to deal with the coming maelstrom on our own."

"Have any precautions been taken?" Lee asked.

"As of this morning all military units are on high alert. We have the mobile artillery being dispersed to join units we believe will be in the locations most likely to see heavy combat. Apart from that my advisors have no other advice to provide me." Victoria sat with her hands sitting in her lap, the weight of the country on her shoulders.

"We did hear that these German creatures were coming here through the stone circle," Dan offered.

"What is the stone circle?" Albert asked from his position behind Victoria.

"We don't know that, but it's all we've got." Dan said.

"We'll have some of our people look into it." Albert said.

"Now where is the child?" Victoria asked.

"He just asked us the same thing?" Dan said pointing to Albert.

"I most certainly did not," Albert said standing up even straighter.

"When you came in while the queen was busy." Lee said.

"Albert has been by my side all morning." The queen said.

Dan and Lee bolted out the door to get back to the carriage. As they burst out the side of the palace, the carriage was gone. Its driver lay dead on the cobblestones, his neck cleanly snapped.

"I say what is this about?" Albert asked breathing heavy as he caught up to the two men.

"You should stay with the queen," Dan said.

"It seems that a shape shifter entered the palace grounds, took your place to find out the location of the girl and then stole the carriage." Lee explained as he and Dan looked around for transportation.

Two guards were strolling around the perimeter on horseback. Dan and Lee ran toward the men. "We need your mounts," Lee said.

The guards reached for their rifles, mounted into carriers attached to the front of the saddle. Dan grabbed the guard nearest him and pulled the man off the horse. "Ain't got time for this," he grumbled climbing into the saddle and turning the horse towards the gates.

The other soldier pulled his rifle out and aimed at Dan's back. "Stop this instant." Albert commanded. "Give this gentleman your mount."

The soldier quickly dismounted and handed the reins to Lee, who promptly quickened after his partner.

Dan raced through the streets of London, on horseback, trying to catch up to the motorized carriage that was working its way through the streets of the city. He raced along the cobblestones, the horse's shoes sparking off of the stones. People darted to get out of his path while he tried to remain vigilant of velociters and other transports that were larger than the horse. Even with the traffic the carriage was nowhere to be seen in the street ahead of him. Searching around the crowded alleys and streets he saw no further way to proceed without taking the horse onto the sidewalk with the pedestrians. *So be it*, he thought as he pulled the reins leading the horse onto the sidewalk. He pulled the rifle from the front of the saddle and fired a shot into the air. All of the commotion and noise on the street instantly faded as the shot echoed off of the buildings. "Move or get rode down!" Dan shouted as he started the horse at a trot onto the sidewalk.

The mass of people parted and Dan was able to excel past the trot until he came to the next cross street. Since it had fewer markets and businesses on it, there was less traffic. This caused him to take the horse back to the street and push the animal into a full gallop. Unbeknownst to Dan, Lee was close behind. Adrenaline pulsed through Dan's body as he neared the flat.

Kate and Brackish sat on the floor playing jacks as something hit the door. Both of them jumped. Kate opened the door to a slim crack and looked out. She pulled the door open and saw Dan standing in front of the door looking over his shoulder. He was breathing heavy. "Kate," he said taking deeper breaths. "We've got to go."

"Okay, let me get my stuff." She said as Brackish stood beside the sofa his hand resting near the bottom of the cushion.

"No time, something's coming. We have to go now." Dan demanded.

"Where's Mr. Baum?" Kate asked noticing that Lee was absent.

"I lost him," Dan said still looking over his shoulder. "Now come on."

Dan held his hand out toward the child. She hesitated and then started to take it. Before she could Brackish leapt over her, in his hand was the dagger Lee kept under the sofa cushion. The small goblin caught Dan by the ear and stabbed the dagger into Dan's shoulder near the throat. Brackish held on tightly as Dan fell back against the wall and then onto his back where he slid down the stairs. The dagger made a wet sucking sound as it was pulled from the body. Adjusting his grip, Brackish plunged the point where the heart should have been. Ms. Edwards opened the door and screamed at seeing Dan dead on the floor not more than ten feet from her door. Kate also screamed and shut the door. The body Brackish was standing on started to change and shift into pale translucent skin, shrinking in size until a featureless, genderless, corpse was lying on the floor.

The front door to the building opened and Dan stepped in with the rifle in hand. Brackish pulled the dagger from the body and stood in a warrior's stance. Sniffing the air, he lowered the dagger and came up to Dan. Ms. Edwards took her eyes off the body and in seeing the latest arrival to her door, she ran to Dan and hugged his neck. Her petticoat knocked Brackish into the wall. "Somebody want to tell me what's going on?" Dan asked, shocked at the reception he had found waiting for him.

"I would like to know that as well," Lee stated entering the door, a matching rifle in his hand.

"Lord Almighty, I thought that beast had killed you." Ms. Edwards said. She turned and pointed to the white body in the hallway. "I don't know how but it looked just like you sir, right down to your clothes."

Dan looked at the body and then to Brackish. Brackish did not meet Dan's eyes but looked at the floor embarrassed by the attention. "Good job," Dan said.

"No smell right, not like you. Tried get Kate," Brackish explained. "I scare her."

"Don't worry about that, we will explain it to her." Lee said. "Is that my dagger?"

Brackish handed the dagger to Lee handle first and smiled at the man. "Sorry," Brackish said.

"Ms. Edwards sorry to bother you, but there may be other attempts to abduct Kate therefore in the event that Elizabeth or either of us request your presence in our flat, please make all haste in joining us. Your well being may depend on it." Lee said. "Again I am truly sorry that we have brought such distress into your home."

"I appreciate your consideration," Ms. Edwards said taking Lee's hand in her own and patting the top of it. "Given that I know nothing of these things I'll honor your request."

"Thank you," Lee said.

"Sorry to interrupt," Dan said dragging the dead fey down the hall. "But I'm going to need some help getting it in the carriage."

Lee excused himself and helped Dan carry the corpse back into the street. Their horses were both tied to the rear of the motorized carriage. After unceremoniously throwing the body into the passenger compartment they went back inside. They both cautiously approached the door. "Kate," Dan called.

"Kate," Lee said a little louder.

"Who is it?" She said.

"It's the lodgers of this fine place." Dan said. "Open up and take a look at us."

"No, the goblin killed you." She said her voice cracking as she fought back tears.

"The goblin actually killed a shape shifter that was trying to get to you." Lee said. "Just like the one that came onto the train."

She opened the door a crack. "Where's Brackish?"

The goblin peered around the legs of Lee and Dan. "Sorry scare you." He apologized.

She ignored the apology. "And you're not dead?" She said looking at Dan.

He raised his hand. "Promise."

She opened the door all the way. "If you're who you claim you are then try and cross the door," she challenged.

Dan, Lee and then Brackish all three stepped into the doorway. Kate threw herself into the legs of the men and squeezed them tightly crying freely. "I thought you were dead!" She exclaimed.

"We know, Ms. Edwards got a similar fright," Dan said. "But I'm not."

"Brackish knew that it was not really Dan so he did what we had told him to do and kept you in here and protected you." Lee said kneeling in front of the child. "We have to go back to the palace now but stay in here, Brackish will protect you."

The child looked cautiously at the goblin. "You clan, I keep safe." He said trying to once again explain his actions.

"I understand but it still scared me." She said.

Brackish nodded as the little girl walked into her temporary room, the jacks half played on the floor. Lee walked back to the sofa cushion and placed the dagger under it. He winked at Brackish. Brackish winked back. Dan fastened his gunbelt across his hips. "You know they won't let you in with that," Lee said.

"They can try and stop me. Given the circumstances I think old Victoria just might understand." Dan said.

"Very well," Lee replied as he set about securing the pistol in his shoulder holster.

Dan and Lee drove the motorized carriage, with the horses keeping step while tied to the rear of the vehicle, back to the palace to try once again to meet with the queen. The guards that met them at the door did not look pleased when they handed over rifles taken from their fellow soldiers. "Sir," one of the guards said, a lieutenant judging by the rank insignia on his shoulder. "No weapons allowed within the palace."

"Too bad, the queen's going to have to allow an exception this time." Dan responded.

Lee stood quietly and watched as the Private in front of him turned his rifle on Dan. The lieutenant reached over to retrieve Dan's pistols. "I would not do that," Lee warned.

"Frankly, your opinion is of no consequence to me. I have my orders." The lieutenant replied.

"He's warning you because he knows soon as you lay a finger on my irons I'm going to break your jaw." Dan explained smiling at the guards.

Prince Albert opened the side door to the palace. "Let these men pass." He ordered.

Both guards stood at attention. "Sir, these men are armed." The lieutenant explained.

"I don't care. These men are trustworthy and here at the invitation of the Queen herself." Albert replied. "Do I need to explain further?"

"No sir," Both guards said in unison and stepped to the side allowing Dan and Lee entrance into the palace.

As the men walked down the hall back towards their meeting room, Albert spoke "I trust you were successful in dispatching the spy?"

"We'll answer once we are with the Queen and can make sure you are in fact Prince Albert." Lee said.

"Of course, good thinking." Albert said.

As they opened the door an older gentleman in a suit stood and bowed to the queen. He passed the men without making eye contact. "Gentlemen welcome back." Victoria said. "I trust that you were successful."

Dan looked around and made sure no one else was in the room. "Yes ma'am. The little girl is still safe. Unfortunately the changeling that was sent after her was killed."

"Oh," she said. "I have tried to contact the Seelie Court itself but have had little success. I fear that we may have greater problems than we had initially anticipated."

Dan and Lee both raised an inquisitive eyebrow to the queen. "Do you feel we should tell them?" Albert asked, further raising questions in Dan and Lee.

"They may be at the center of this storm," she responded to her husband. "So far our information is not confirmed but it seems reliable at this point. Mobilization has begun. Creatures have been spotted throughout the countryside; they seem to be converging on London. We are not sure of their intentions but we have begun moving soldiers into positions to intercept them. All regent wardens are contacting their charges. All bounty hunters are being called up to assist in defending the city. All save you gentlemen."

"With all due respect, we can be a massive help out there." Dan said.

"I agree you can be, however I feel the greater importance is to keep the child you are currently guarding alive, do you disagree?" Victoria asked.

"No ma'am," Dan said. "I've just never been one to sit out of a fight."

"We are not asking you to do so now," Victoria explained. "We are requesting that you stay with the girl and if the fight comes to you that you do as you have always done in the past."

"It would be an honor," Lee said giving a slight nod of his head toward the monarch.

"We'll do as we're asked." Dan said. "When does your group suspect this thing will start?"

"Best estimations," Albert started. "Are that we can expect the first waves of attack to meet our defensive positions tomorrow afternoon."

"Here?" Dan asked incredulously.

"No, we have set defensive interception positions related to the sighting of gathering forces. Several have been placed at different location around London but most of our forces are being arranged to meet the enemy in open ground where superior firepower will account for more." Albert said stiffening with pride at what had been his plan.

Lee sat back considering the options. Dan waited to see if he would be able to think of a better way. Finally Lee sat forward. "What would happen if these defenses were overrun?" Lee asked.

"That is why we have different regiments stationed about London," Albert responded. "Given the nature of our enemy we don't expect more than one or two of the defensive posts will be overtaken."

"But if they do we are going to be scarcely outnumbered," Lee said.

"Yes, but we don't anticipate this occurring." Albert repeated.

"Right then," Lee said standing. "We have several defensive articles that we need to prepare just in case we need be called into the fray."

Dan stood and placed his bowler hat a top his head. "Hopefully, everything will be fine and we won't have to come back until this entire situation is over."

"That is our hope Mr. Winston," Victoria said as the men left the room.

Lee stopped at a clockwork shop on their way back to the flat. After he returned to the carriage, Dan started the conversation. "What are you thinking?" He asked Lee. "You backed down too easily with Albert."

"Simply put, it seems that it might be a ploy to lure forces outside the city," Lee stated. "Drawing attention to the tactical short sightedness of Albert would do nothing but build enmity with the monarchy. I would like to avoid that at all costs."

"So what do you expect to happen?" Dan asked looking at the sky where it was gray and overcast, in part from the vapors and fumes the new technology emitted.

"One of two things: a small force will enter London undetected and seek to take Kate from us or the small rabble that has been sighted will actually bypass the defensive positions and show up to wreak havoc in London almost completely unopposed." Lee stated not liking his own feelings regarding the coming attack. "Either way I feel we will have to be on complete guard and prepared for the drop of the hammer, as it were, at any moment."

Lee retrieved the spring from the bag and examined the ends of the coil. "Is that the piece you need?" Dan asked.

"Yes, it won't take me long once we arrive to complete the modifications." Placing the spring back in his pocket Lee looked out at the city. "I feel our poor corner of the city may look like a war zone before this is through."

"Well let's at least make sure we're secure before it happens," Dan said staring out at the brick fronts of the buildings as they passed by.

Once they arrived back at the flat they did not find the house in the same state of excitement as it had been previously. Kate and Brackish were contentedly sitting playing a game of jacks, the goblin wearing a curious look as he watched Kate's hands deftly retrieve the jacks. Elizabeth was being taught how to properly prepare afternoon tea by Ms. Edwards. After minimum greetings, Lee went to his workshop to complete the modification to Dan's shotgun. Dan rummaged through different shelves and gathered different supplies from all over the flat, after he was content that he had all the necessary supplies, he made his way about the house.

The minced garlic herbs that he had gathered were mixed with olive oil and the mixture spread across the outside vents to prevent any type of vampire from invading the property. Next he fastened hawthorns and wolfs bane across all the locks on the windows and above the door frames. "What are you doing?" Ms. Edwards protested.

"Taking precautions to keep you ladies safe," Dan responded as he continued about his task.

He spread small amounts of salt and brick dust under the windows and across the threshold at the front door. The lack of knowledge they had regarding the German creatures was the greater threat. Between the two of them, they could handle any British or American beast but this was an entirely different situation. It set both Dan and Lee on edge but they prepared as best they could. Using silver shavings, Dan laid them about outside hoping that in the event any werewolves were about they would touch the shavings and announce themselves.

Without knocking, Dan entered Lee's workshop as he was bent over working on installing the spring into the shotgun. "Yes?" Lee said annoyed at the interruption.

"What about giants and other things that can just bust in the room or don't adhere to traditional wares?" Dan asked.

"I don't think they will be sending giants and if they do, then we do not need to worry." Lee said.

"Why not?"

"The giants make very good targets for the military so I assume they'll take them down first," Lee stated. "If not then I wouldn't be too concerned, we'll have to use the Tin Man to take care of the problem."

"Best we got?" Dan asked hoping for something else.

"I've got something that might work in the event it comes to that. I don't think it will though." Lee said turning back to his work.

Dan understood the message and left Lee alone to finish his modifications.

While Kate took a bath and prepared for bed, Dan and Lee explained the situation to Brackish. "We're counting on you to be our last line. If something happens to us, you protect them." Dan explained.

"Brackish keep clan safe or die," the small goblin swore, making a small crossing motion over his heart. "Gun?"

"Not yet," Lee said. "If you need one and something happens to us, you'll know where to get one."

Brackish nodded and looked at his feet. "No trust me?"

"We don't know how good of a shot you are or whether or not you can handle one of our pistols and we don't have time to find out." Dan explained. "You've proved yourself so we trust you."

The goblin smiled at them. Dan and Lee both fought against the urge to react to the goose bumps that the smile raised. "We need you on alert, if you hear anything that you suspect may be something trying to get in, get one of us immediately."

"Yes," Brackish said. "Il wake you and we fight."

"Something like that," Dan said patting Brackish on the head.

During the night as Kate slept in Dan's bed, Dan slept in the armchair, Lee finished working on the modifications and then slept in his bed, and Brackish the goblin stayed alert through the night sitting by the fireplace occasionally throwing new logs onto the fire to keep it lit and warm. His main focus was the winds blowing outside the window. They told him that something was moving near them but the winds swept in from the North and the East and it carried many strange and worrisome noises with it. Although throughout the evening Brackish stalked the hallways making sure that nothing had entered the house through the wards that had been laid by Dan and Lee. Nothing attempted to breach the defenses and to the best of Brackish's awareness nothing had tried to. During the night further removed from London, otherworldly forces had moved closer to the borders of the city.

During his sleep, Dan's dreams transported him once more to the war room of Ironhill. The dwarf seemed older, his armor was now bloodied and tarnished, his axe seemed dull. "What's the good word?" Dan asked evenly, his anger at the dwarf still not settled.

"Very few good words are to be had these days," Ironhill said. "All of us are besieged save one or two hidden enclaves. We've had limited contact with any others these few days. The child's guide Petal is busy with fighting and I imagine she'll be unable to talk with the child for the coming days until this comes to a head. Needless to say I've been unable to find the information you need on the stone circle or the necromancer."

Ironhill removed his helmet; a great bandage took up a large portion of the right side of his head. "Can you hold out?"

"Aye," Ironhill said. "No one has ever forced a dwarf from his home and I'll not be the first."

"Are you aware that a force is mobilizing to march on London?"

"Aye, I am." Ironhill said. "Don't trust the soldiers to deal with this problem."

"We don't," Dan said. "We also don't think that this is the real fight, just something to draw attention away from the city itself. The real fight is going to come to our doorstep."

A cry arose from nearby. "I can stay no longer. May your fight go better than that of my brothers," Ironhill said as he picked up his axe and walked toward the door.

The sun woke Dan as it shined in through the curtain less window. He woke up and rubbed the sleep from his eyes. Brackish still sat upright on the couch cushion where he had been when Dan had finally drifted off to sleep. The goblin's spine stiffened as he turned and looked at Dan. "Anything?" Dan asked stifling a yawn.

"No," Brackish said looking back out the window. "Strange noise on the wind, no more."

"Okay, so you up for some breakfast?"

Brackish licked his lips. "Sausage?"

"Yes, I think we still have some. I'll see what I can cook up. Go wake Lee."

Brackish made his way noisily through the flat and knocked on Lee's door. Lee opened the door in his house jacket and slacks. "Breakfast," Brackish said cheerily.

"Very well," Lee said as he left the room and walked into the small dining area.

Dan was rumbling around through the cupboards and cabinets, metal clanging on metal and occasionally the sizzle of butter or grease in a pan. "Go wake Kate, it won't be but a few minutes," Dan said.

Lee told Brackish to stay at the table and went to wake the girl. A brisk knock on the door, went unanswered. "Kate," Lee tentatively called. "Kate!" He said more forcefully when she didn't respond.

With a light push, Lee opened the door and stepped in. Kate was sleeping peacefully in the bed. Gently, Lee shook her shoulder. The girl's eyes flew open and she sat bolt upright in bed. "Where's Ms. Petal?" The girl asked tears filling her eyes.

"What?" Lee asked puzzled.

"She told me she would visit me every night but last night she didn't." Kate explained to the puzzled adult.

"I'm sure it's fine," Lee said placing a comforting hand on Kate's back.

The child wrapped her arms around Lee's waist and shuddered. "Come now, Mr. Winston is making us breakfast again." Lee offered.

He had to lead Kate from the bedroom to the table. "What's wrong with her?" Dan asked.

Brackish looked at Kate sensing that something was wrong from the change of disposition. "Ms. Petal," Lee said.

"I wouldn't worry," Dan said. "It was told to me on good authority that Ms. Petal is out there keeping the bad monsters away and she'll be back to talk to you real soon."

Kate's face lit up like the morning sun. "Really," she said.

"Really," Dan confirmed. "Breakfast?"

Bringing in pans with meat, potatoes and eggs, Dan set the food out for everyone as they began eating their breakfasts. Once the food was finished and the plates had been cleared from the table, Dan informed Lee of his latest conference with Ironhill. "So what happens if they fall?" Lee asked.

"I assume that Kate becomes less important to them as a target," Dan said. "And also we're going to be up to our ears in dark fey and all other manner of monsters."

"Any advice from them?" Lee asked hopefully.

"None. We're basically on our own." Dan said.

"Well since things may get worse before they get better let me introduce you to the latest adaptations to your shotgun," Lee said escorting Dan to his workshop.

Dan spent the next few hours practicing with the weapon so that he could eject and replace the spent magazine easily. After he was able to perform the task blindfolded he placed the shotgun back on the workbench. "How about spare magazines?" Dan asked.

Lee held up a strange fabric that looked like it had long pockets in it. Looking at Dan's confused glance Lee chuckled to himself. Holding up one of the spare magazines Lee dropped it into one of the pocket openings. It fit perfectly. "It fits on around your leg and will hold eight, five on your thigh and three across your shin." Lee explained.

"I like it." Dan said admiring the weapon.

14   Private Louis Smithson stood at his post behind the hastily dug entrenchment. The purpose for the entrenchment was to allow the two mobile artillery units to have a clear line of fire over the infantry men. The private was wondering what sort of blunder had led to them being stationed in the middle of nowhere. They sat miles away from the nearest village and yet they had been positioned facing toward one of the forests a few hundred paces away. "Sir," Louis said to Corporal Brigham who was over his squad.

"Yes Smithson," Brigham replied never taking his face from the telescope he had to his eye.

"Why are we stationed here, sir?"

"Because we were told to be here," Brigham said. "It is our duty as the Queen's soldiers to obey our orders regardless of reason."

"Yes sir," Louis said knowing that the corporal did not know any better than they did.

Louis wondered if it was the Prussian forces. They had taken the Germanic military in less than a year, a feat no one would have believed until it was done. There were rumors that they had converted some of their flying balloons into carriers that could drop entire battalions on the battlefield. It was nervous to think of such things but perhaps that is why they were there. The Prussians had set troops down nearby and they were approaching through the trees. Louis stopped himself, his foolish daydreams were just that: dreams. Deep down, he knew that there were no Prussian troops. In all reality he assumed they had been called out on another readiness drill. The sun beat down and then arced above their heads and as Dan inspected his modified shotgun, the first rumblings of an approaching force came to Louis' platoon.

The loose dirt on their dugout trenches shook and then grew more furious in their movement. Sergeants relayed orders that were then echoed by squad leaders and corporals. All the soldiers placed their Colt B-3 rifles onto the top of the entrenchment. The Colt B-3 was a lever action rifle specifically designed for the British army. It had a larger caliber bullet than the comparable Winchester and also a larger magazine to allow for more ammunition. This was effectively their first live combat testing. Trees in the forest started shaking. Louis swallowed as a giant shape rose up from the trees and stood several feet above them. Louis' realized it was a giant, just like the one in his favorite story with the beanstalk. "Corporal?" Louis called.

"Hold fire!" Brigham ordered.

The mobile artillery opened fire and began pelting the nearby trees with explosive shells. Finally a combination of shells hit the giant directly in the head and shoulders causing the behemoth to tumble to the ground where a large scattering of birds took flight as the forest and nearby earth trembled with the impact. Black shapes skirted the edges of the woods, Louis thought that the enemy may have been sizing up the resistance in their path. "Sir," Louis started. "Why are we fighting bogles? Don't the bounty hunters do that?"

Brigham slapped Louis across the face, bringing the panicked private to his senses. "They are where they are and doing what they can. We are here and we will hold this line. Clear?"

"Yes sir." Louis replied turning back to his rifle.

A few rounds of the artillery were lobbed into the edges of the forest causing explosions of dirt and trees.

After the deafening roar of the artillery, the silence that grew on the field had an eerie quality. Only the most experienced of the soldiers were breathing normally. Most of the inexperienced men in the trenches were holding their breath waiting. Shadows began to slink from the forest, gradually taking shape as they neared the edge of the canopy. The smaller trolls that were not allergic to sunlight and orcs on their warg mounts edged onto the field. As a clear line of enemies became apparent Louis suddenly felt very scared. His platoon had to be outnumbered at least ten to one. Swallowing back his fear, he sighted down the barrel of the rifle and waited for the order. The mobile artillery began firing rounds into the line and shifting to hit other portions of the enemy as the small army of monsters charged from the woods and ran across the field. A small rock mound had been made to indicate at which time the artillery would have to stop firing and the infantry would have to take up the fight. The front line of the rushing army was almost to that marker.

Louis' squad was in the front trench. "Fix bayonets," Brigham ordered.

The soldiers retrieved the sharp blades from their scabbards and placed the bayonet in its position and then prepared to fire into the oncoming horde. Once the first line crossed over the marker, Brigham gave the order to open fire. The artillery continued firing into the bulk of the oncoming enemies hurling their broken bodies into the air. The steam driven Gatling gun that was set up in the trench down from Louis' squad began firing sweeping across the entire field of vision of the operator. The Gatling gun looked strange sat on top of the large oak barrel that contained the machine workings that allowed for the rapid rate of fire.

The oncoming force was met by a hail of bullets from the infantrymen and the front lines collapsed as those behind them pushed over the dead bodies and continued forward. Louis' rifle clicked empty.

237

With the dexterity that he had shown during training, Louis reloaded the rifle from the bandolier of cartridges hanging across his shoulders and waist. All the soldiers had them, but Louis seemed to have the easiest time reloading. Corporal Brigham was screaming as he attempted to fire his empty rifle into the oncoming rush. Then the rear group of orcs let loose a barrage of arrows. The barb tipped darts fell around the trenches, in some cases hitting soldiers causing only minor injuries that did not require the soldier to retire from the field. In most cases it appeared they were not aimed and fell harmlessly into the ground. Corporal Brigham was not as fortunate. The arrow that found him caught him right in the top of his head and dropped through the cloth of his cap and killed him instantly. The soldier fell limply to the floor of the trench. The rest of Louis' squad started to flee the trench. "We don't have time for that," Louis shouted over the gunfire as he continued firing into the ever encroaching horde.

The other soldiers turned and continued on at their post. The Gatling gun continued firing as arrows fell from the sky. Soldiers screamed and blood was spilled but the soldiers stayed at their post. The platoon's commanding officer ordered the young man who had been assigned as their runner to take his mount and ride until he could ride no further. He gave the young man a sealed letter. The runner saluted and ran for his horse. The galloping of his horse was drowned out by the din of the battle as the man rode from the fray to carry his message to company headquarters.

Louis remained firmly entrenched until the orcs were riding almost right on top of them. "Fall back," he called as they scrambled from the trench and retreated back the ten paces to the next trench.

Louis' squad turned and fired into the oncoming mounts, riders were thrown from their positions. The Gatling gun was firing wildly, its operator having been killed when the orcs hit the trench. One of the orcs looking to cease the gun cracked the barrel with his cleaver and damaged the interior workings causing them to build pressure with no release. It effectively turned the Gatling gun into a bomb that quickly detonated throwing shrapnel and fire into the oncoming horde. The artillery stood silent and prepared to retreat their vehicles from the front to a reserve position to provide covering fire. Seeing the explosion and realizing that the front trench was empty of British military personnel, the two operators opened fire in unison pounding into the confused orcs and trolls turning the open field into a sea of viscera. There were two clearly marked forces after the artillery expended their ammunition. Those that had been behind the explosive barrage and retreated into the relative safety of the woods and those that had been in front of the barrage and had no choice but to press forward. Some of them made it to the second trench. They fought like demons and were better accommodated to the close quarters combat than the British troops.

A troll was beating one of the officers against the trench wall until a few of the men brought it down with close concentrated fire into its exposed back. The orcs were different, the mounts were useless in the enclosed space, one well-placed shot and the beast was nothing more than a blockade. Some of the orcs that had already lost their mounts leaped into the trench swinging at anything occasionally striking an already dead soldier but not caring and turning to go after the next. It was one of these blood drunk orcs that made its way to Louis. He stood as the rest of his squad dealt with an orc on the other side of their location. The orc let out a screech and rushed at Louis, blood coating the outer layer of the beast's armor. Louis prepared himself and slipped the bayonet off of the rifle. The orc came in and swung his cleaver at Louis. Using the barrel of his rifle to block the blow, Louis was shocked to see that the cleaver had cut through the wood of the rifle and stopped only after biting into the metal barrel. Kicking out, Louis sent the orc back into the trench wall. Grabbing the orc's hand that held the cleaver, Louis leaped on top of the orc stabbing repeatedly into the orc's exposed side. He had been hearing a fierce scream as he stabbed. When he was sure the orc was dead, he realized it was his own scream.

Looking around, he saw the rest of his squad staring at him fear in their eyes at the ferocity he had shown. One of the three men was pressing his shirt against his side where blood was seeping through his fingertips. The British defenses held despite losses that exceeded their expectations. The sun set on gore drenched battlefields across the lands surrounding London. It had been a gambit on the dark fey's part. The stone circle opened and deposited more of the deadly forces to protect the portal in the English countryside. More of the English fey of the Unseelie Court were going to join them in order to insure that the plan did not fail.

As British commanders were receiving the word that their forces had defeated the enemy advancements and forced a retreat, a small contingent of fey both foreign and domestic with a few monsters not fully affiliated with either the Unseelie Court or the Council of the Black Forest made their way into London. The main thoroughfares into the great city were guarded, but this infiltration force did not enter into their consideration. It was anticipated that a large force would enter from the roads; this force did the opposite and used the waterways and sewers to make their way unnoticed within the city. Large beings of animated stone left long scrape marks in their path, the fey represented were imp, troll, red cap, and one of the enchanted amalgamated beings bred in the dark forests of Germany, they were rarely seen by man at all. One lone human figure followed at the end of this parade of monstrous intent. They knew where they were to go. The changeling that had been silenced had told them the location of the child. Placing a hand against the stone the German fey assured the others that no mortals were on the street above them. In anticipation of a coming attack, Queen Victoria had issued a curfew. This effort to limit loss of life assisted the fey. The golems with their large stone bodies stood and pushed back the cobblestones that formed the street. Many of the local residents heard the noise but did not go to their windows to look, fearing that while looking out something would see them and drag them into a situation they dearly sought to avoid.

Brackish leapt up from his place on the sofa and ran into the kitchen when he returned he had a cleaver and one of the larger butcher knives clutched in his hands. "Something coming." He stated looking at the windows.

Someone ran up the stairs and began to beat upon the door. Lee came from his bedroom, while Dan crossed to the door from his arm chair looking over his shoulder at the goblin. Holding one of his pistols in one hand, Dan opened the door. Elizabeth leaped into the room out of breath. "What's the matter child?" Lee asked still looking around confused.

"I saw it." She said. "A small group are nearby they were sent to take Kate. I couldn't wake Ms. Edwards. Mr. Winston, I don't know what exactly will happen but it is not going to go well."

Lee walked to his room and retrieved the Winchester and the newly modified shotgun and pneumatic power pack. He started to hand them to Dan but the American waved them away picking up the older pump action shotgun that he had previously retrieved from the closet. "When I get back with Ms. Edwards I'll strap in." Dan left the flat as Lee told Elizabeth to join Kate in Dan's room.

The small force of evil stalked through the streets all of them attempting to move stealthily, except the golems whose stone bodies made it impossible and the redcap whose iron shoes sparked and clanged off of the cobblestones. As they approached their destination the Germanic creature shrouded in its cloak ordered the golems to the end of the street to prevent anyone from coming to the aid of the humans in the building. The imps grew more excited as the task at hand approached. The red cap flexed his eagle taloned claws and removed one of its iron spears. The troll moved along not reacting at all. Uncomfortable movements made the man following the parade grimace. "Shed your fool's cowl," the German ordered, a voice as harsh as winter winds sweeping through the Alps.

The man stopped and lowered to the ground. His body began to shiver and within a few seconds the bipedal werewolf stood in the viscera that he shed when the change overtook him. Flexing newly muscled limbs and jaws that had reshaped themselves and grown stronger, the werewolf stood and stretched in the night letting out a short howl.

Dan stopped at the door to Ms. Edwards' room when he heard the howl in the night. "Not far," he said to himself as he pushed open the door. "Ms. Edwards!"

The older woman sat up pulling the covers tight about her. "Mr. Winston, what is the meaning of this?" She demanded.

"Something bad is about to happen," he said. "You need to get to our flat now."

Ms. Edwards started to retrieve her house coat not comfortable in just her nightgown. Dan took her by the arm and half pulled her from the room into the hallway. "Mr. Winston," she protested.

"We don't have time," he answered.

Lee stood in the doorway to their flat looking down into the hallway as Dan and the clearly disheveled Ms. Edwards exited their landlady's personal quarters. Something scratched at the front door of the building. "Hurry," Dan ordered pushing the woman towards the stairs as he stood there, shotgun trained on the door.

The door burst in and a werewolf sat hunched at the doorstep. A small bald headed old man stood behind him just barely visible over the beast in the doorway. Dan saw the iron shaft in his hand and the odd looking red tint to his head. "Red cap," he called as the diminutive figure hurled the iron spear at Dan.

Turning, Dan was barely missed by the deadly projectile. Dan fired once with the shotgun taking part of the werewolf's shoulder and the red cap's face with the blast. "Werewolf! I don't have any silver." Dan called.

"Leave it to me," Lee responded, as he used the lever action of the Winchester to unload all the standard shells and then reload with two silver bullets at the front of the load and then the remainder with standard cartridges.

Ms. Edwards refused to look back as she climbed the stairs, Lee trying to see around the woman. Once she was safely in the room he directed her towards Kate and Elizabeth. None of the forces entered the building. The barriers that Dan and Lee had set up appeared to work. Dan swore under his breath as the German creature took a tentative step over the line. Lee dropped to the floor to see the creature. He saw a long slender hand like a woman's extending beyond the sleeves of the cloak; they were as white as porcelain, her fingertips appeared to be covered in ice.

"She's the most dangerous," Lee called down to Dan. "She's not normal, she's a mixed breed."

The being shot small bursts of lightning towards the door. Lee rolled clear of the blasts. Once the bursts had passed Brackish ran to the door to see the creature. "Abomination," he called pointing at the cloaked figure that stood in the hallway.

Dan fired into the figure at point blank range throwing her through the sheet rock of the hall and leaving a hole in it. Turning back he saw that she had broken the line of salt and brick dust, the fey moved in, their werewolf bounding at him first. He turned to run.

"Down," Lee ordered.

Dan dropped as two shots were fired and something thudded to the floor behind him. Taking the stairs quickly as he could something grabbed his hand and spun him around. It was a troll. Trying to maneuver the shotgun to fire at his attacker, he found that the stairwell leading up to the flat was not wide enough for such an action. The imps tangled around his shoes, their miniscule bodies working to trip him up.

Letting go of the shotgun he grabbed his pistols and prepared to fire into the troll. Realizing what Dan was attempting the troll took his wooden club and bashed Dan on the head. "Take him," the German creature said from the hallway behind the confusion.

Dan fell at the troll's feet, unconscious. Lee raised the Winchester to fire at the troll when another small bolt of lightning flew near him driving him to the ground. Brackish undeterred by the display of power, leaped onto the chest of the troll and buried the butcher knife to the hilt. With the cleaver, he began to cut into the beast's face. Brackish leapt free as the troll tumbled backwards. The cleaver embedded in its skull. The three imps looked at Brackish and rushed toward him. He swatted one into the wall where it fell, then picked up the other one and using his knife like teeth bit off its head. The last imp fled down the stairs screaming.

A small bolt of lightning struck Brackish in the chest and launched him into the flat. The redcap that Dan had shot and another fellow redcap entered the house, the wounded redcap shuffling along obviously in pain. "Take him," the cloaked German said pointing.

Lee leapt into the door frame rifle ready and saw one of the redcaps ready to throw his deadly spear. Before Lee could fire, the spear flew from the wielder's hand and struck Lee clear in the chest driving him back to the floor. The cloaked beast took the tip of her finger and began to write on the wall, scorch marks following after her finger. Stepping back to admire the note, the figure turned toward the waiting redcaps as they stood holding the prone figure of Dan Winston.

The motorized carriage driver knew that curfew was in effect but he had received a message from Glorianna's Prison that he was to go pick up Dan Winston and Lee Baum from their home. Zipping through the streets at a speed that was normally impossible with the London crowds, the driver made the approach to make the final turn to his destination. The gaslights lining the sidewalks were lit and revealed just how empty the streets truly were. As he took the final turn, the driver did not realize how final it would be. A stone statue loomed up before him and to the driver's horror the statue moved and struck the carriage. It stopped dead in its tracks and the driver flew over as the rear of the vehicle lifted from the ground at the sudden stop. He saw the stone giant begin to tear into the body of the carriage and then the cobblestones raced up to greet him and he laid on the cobblestones, his body broken in more places than he could count. Mercifully the impact had rendered him unconscious and he could not feel the pain.

The golem continued ripping apart the metal frame as its twin stood watch at the other end of the street. Finally reaching the metallic sputtering pieces under the driver's seat, the golem squeezed the components into an indescribable clump. Unknowingly the combustible fuel was further compressed, and coming into contact with the other heated pieces of the motor caused an explosion which destroyed the golem's arm. Since the hulking monstrosity was made of stone, it did not feel the loss and remained at its post.

The cloaked figure exited the building followed by the redcaps as the motorized carriage's engine exploded. Under the cloak, the figure scowled at the sound. Despite the sounds they had made on their way to the building they were now leaving, the explosion was more than most people would tolerate. Calling to the golems in the native German tongue they responded to, she stood in the midst of the street and waited.

Once they reached the designated spot, she ordered them to open a hole in the street to the tunnel system that they had used to enter the city. The redcaps wanted to split open Dan and use his blood to replenish the coloring on their bald heads. Their leader forbid it and silenced the grumbling of the redcaps with a clear display of her power by having the two armed golem crush their red stained heads. The newly one-armed golem was ordered to stay and prevent anyone from following them through the tunnels. The cloaked figure led the two armed golem through the tunnel with Dan resting in its arms.

Once all the commotion outside quieted and they were sure no other monsters were in the house, Kate, Elizabeth, and Ms. Edwards exited the room. They found Brackish with Lee's head in his lap, a large metal spear sticking from his chest. All three of the females let out a cry and ran to the downed man, Ms. Edwards looked into the hall and closed the door. She had visibly paled at what she saw. Brackish's shirt had been singed and beneath the singed hole his flesh was a darker color than his arms and face. "Are you okay?" Elizabeth asked the goblin.

"No, I fail clan," he said stroking Lee's hair.

"I meant your chest?" Elizabeth said pity for the small creature.

"It will heal," he said never looking up from Lee's face.

Lee opened his eyes and tried to sit up but couldn't because of the three people and one goblin crowding around him. Brackish leaped to his feet, letting Lee's head drop to the floor. "Not dead!" He exclaimed.

"Of course not," Lee said. "Why would you think . . . oh I see." He said taking note of the spear standing up from his chest.

Wrapping his hands around the iron shaft he tried but could not remove the spear. "Excuse me ladies," he said as he unbuttoned and removed his shirt revealing the brass vests that he had made for Dan and himself.

The iron tip of the spear had penetrated the vest but only enough to get itself stuck and cause a small scratch on Lee. Unbuckling the harness and sliding out of the damaged vest, he went to his room and returned when he had put on a new shirt. "Where's Dan?" Lee asked looking around, rubbing the back of his head where a knot was beginning to rise.

When no one answered, Lee made his way to the door and opened it. He saw the dead troll with their kitchen cutlery still protruding from its body and the body of what must have been the werewolf before Lee had put two silver rounds into its head. A small headless body oozed a black ichor on the stair and another tried to stand and continued to fail in its attempts. "Brackish," Lee called.

When the goblin arrived, Lee pointed to the remaining imp. Brackish disappeared within the flat and returned not two seconds later, this time brandishing a fork. Preparing to spear the imp, Brackish snarled at the diminutive figure. "Not yet," Lee said looking at the imp. "He has some questions to answer first. Take him inside and put him in a bottle."

Brackish grabbed the imp by the foot and carried it at arm's length into the flat. "Make sure the top is secured before you leave him," Lee cautioned.

Looking at the burned marks on the wall, Lee realized that they were letters. His mind still not focusing due to the knock on his head he had taken when the red cap spear had knocked him to the floor, he forced himself to calm down and see the words as they were written. His mood was not helped by the message that met him.

If you wish to retrieve your friend, bring the fire headed child to the stone circle by midnight tomorrow.

The message stopped but it was clear that they thought a trade would be accepted. It was obvious that the fey over estimated humanity's capabilities for compassion but they were right about one thing, Lee would be coming for Dan, but first he had to find out where the stone circle was located. As he made his way to enter the flat, a rumbling erupted from outside.

Carefully coming to the bottom of the stairs, he looked out the shattered remnants of the front door and saw the large one armed golem standing in the middle of the street throwing large handfuls of cobblestones at people who had wondered from their homes. The cobblestones forced the people to retreat. Lee Baum, who had always been a temperate man, not prone to anger or aggressive displays, was overcome with outrage at what he was witnessing. Given the attempts that had been made on his life and now the abducting of his best friend and partner, he could stand no more. He walked to the rear exit of the flat and down the stairs into the garden. He threw open the doors to the shed where the Tin Man stood on his trailer, waiting until Lee charged the dynamo and brought him back to life. A devilish smile crept across Lee's face. It was a look that had never been on his face before, it felt alien but at the same time appropriate. If the forces of evil sought to invade his home he would meet them head on and send them back to their master's damnable thrones in pieces.

The Tin Man tore through the fence that separated the front yard from the rear yard. Unmoved by the newcomer the golem turned and hurled a handful of the cobblestones at the approaching automaton. Lee heard the sounds as the rocks struck and in some cases dented the Tin Man. Looking through the periscope Lee came within ranged and lowered the three barrel cannon and opened fire. He expended every shell he had loaded and when he finished the golem had been reduced to rubble and a fine gray powder. Lee then proceeded to return the Tin Man to the shed and went back around to the front to inspect the gaping hole that the golem had guarded. Looking down into the darkness, Lee saw no sign of the forces carrying his friend. He noticed the crumpled body of a man, going to the form lying in the road, Lee could see a clearly marked envelope in the man's coat pocket. It was marked for Dan and Lee. The man moaned. "Stay still, help is on the way." Lee said as he read the news from Roger that Queen Victoria had one more mission that might end the current ordeal they were so engulfed in.

15   The driver had been carried off by the hospital carriage. Lee sat staring at his maps and charts trying to determine what course of action to take. A small group of soldiers had already descended into the sewers, the message lay on Lee's desk unopened. Elizabeth stood looking at Lee. The man noticed the child and gave a weak smile. "You should open it," she said indicating the message. "It might give you the answers you need."

Lee opened the summons from Roger. It was a request for Lee to come to the palace to consult on a piece of intelligence that had been gathered recently. Lee set out for the palace in the velociter immediately. Ms. Edwards was staying with Kate and Elizabeth. Brackish had set up guard at the door of the flat, both of Dan's dropped pistols in his hands and the imp was currently sitting in the cold storage in the kitchen. When Lee returned the imp would be willing to cooperate with the information he requested. The palace was completely lit and there were guards well outside the gates waving their arms to slow him down. Several sets of guards sat behind quickly erected barricades, rifles trained on the velociter. *We weren't the only ones to be visited,* Lee thought as he opened the window.

"No admittance until further ordered sir," the Major said.

Lee held out the paper summoning him to the palace. "My orders should be sufficient." Lee said.

The Major took the paper and then walked over to one of the small lamps near the guard stations. All the riflemen in the area did not lower their rifles or flinch at the weight of the weapons they were aiming at Lee. The Major picked up a small round device and spoke into it. Lee could not make out much in the dim light but he saw what appeared to be a cord attached to the back of the device. After he had finished speaking, the Major placed the device up to his ear. A few nods of his head and the Major spoke back into it, sat it down and made his way back to Lee. He handed the paper back to Lee. "Go directly to the gate. They will give you further instruction there." The major instructed.

Lee drove the rest of the way to the gate where he saw a heavier armed group of soldiers with several of the automatic Gatling gun barrels in place. Stretched in front of the palace were barricades with soldiers and the mobile artillery units spread across the grounds, most likely forming a perimeter around the palace. Lieutenant Colonel Cole, a man easily recognized to anyone familiar with the London newspapers, was standing waiting for him. Lee looked at the officer unimpressed.

"You are expected sir," Cole said. "If you will please pass through the break in the barricades there and place your vehicle near the main entrance to the palace. The Queen's Guard will be out momentarily to escort you. Any deviation from that course will result in her Majesty's Forces considering you a hostile force and opening fire upon you."

Lee did not flinch at the comment but merely turned away from Cole and headed toward the place he had been directed. Once the velociter was parked and Lee was out of it, four of the queen's guards trotted down the steps and stood still. "Sir," the front guard said with a half bow. "Please follow us."

The guard turned and led Lee with the other three guards bringing up the rear. Turning to face Lee, the front guard stopped his procession. "Before we continue, we will need to inspect you for weapons." The guard explained.

Lee dropped his jacket and allowed the soldiers to procure his pistol and search his pockets and shoes. Satisfied that the revolver was the only weapon he had on his person, they continued onward this time to a different room located deep in the center of the palace. The guard opened the door and announced Lee then stepped out allowing Lee to enter. The room was void of any windows and had four suits of armor arrayed around it, each directly across from a different doorway leading into the room. Prince Albert and Queen Victoria sat on large stiff backed chairs, both of them appeared to have aged just within the short time that Dan and Lee had last seen them. "Your Majesty," Lee said bowing to the monarch. "How can I be of assistance?"

"Our reports indicate that there was some disturbance at your home," Albert said.

"Yes, it seems a small force infiltrated the city and set about to kidnap or destroy young Kate McKendrick." Lee explained. "What they succeeded in accomplishing was the abduction of Dan Winston as a hostage hoping we would exchange Kate for him."

"I am sorry to hear that," Albert said shaking his head. "Of course you know we cannot give them the girl. Our defensive forces were met with combat tonight but were able to route the enemy, given the current situation it seems that it was an elaborate ruse to allow this force you spoke of to enter into our streets unnoticed."

"So it would seem, sir." Lee agreed. "According to the message, I was asked here to assist with some recent intelligence?"

"Quite right," Albert said. "We believe we have located the stone circle the troll referenced." Albert produced a leather file from beside his chair and handed it to Lee. "Please sit and look through this."

Lee saw the empty chair not too far across from them and sat down in it. He opened the file and removed the photographs within along with the hand written notes. The notes detailed times and corresponding events. The photographs showed those events in blacks and whites. At first the photographs were of what appeared to be a growing light source and then shadows were being disgorged as the photographer was forced to move further back. The final photograph showed the hilltop where the light source had grown to fill the encircling structure. The silhouetted shapes left no doubt as to the location of the phenomena. "Stonehenge," Lee said looking up. "What are these figures representing?"

"Each time the light source grew it would drop a contingent of unwanted creatures onto the hilltop. As you can see the photographer and his military escort were forced to withdraw. That last photograph was taken this afternoon shortly before sunset. Information coming in would indicate that enemy forces are still being dropped and pushing out, creating a formidable force that we will have to roust once our forces are in position." Albert said. "We also believe that Mr. Winston is being taken here to take back to the other side of that . . . portal, I believe one of our advisors called it."

"It would seem to explain the message I received." Lee said.

"A small contingent of troops was sent into the sewers after word of your troubles arrived. They followed the pipes until they came to an exit where it appeared something had been anchored," Albert looked to Victoria before he continued. "Unfortunately, I have to inform you that Mr. Winston may not survive this. We have a plan to close the gateway and then move in to destroy the invading forces."

The photographs and papers fell to the floor. Lee stood up shocked at what he was hearing. "What bloody plan do you have?" He demanded, a very dangerous thing for a man like him to do towards the monarch but he was overcome with the indignant manner they were willing to throw away Dan's life.

Albert stood. "Calm yourself. You are a guest here." Albert was silenced by the cold metallic hand of Victoria that grasped his forearm.

"Tell him Albert, we've asked so much of both he and Mr. Winston. He has the right to know." It was the first time Victoria had spoken and the broken edge to her voice told Lee that she had not reached her decision lightly.

Albert took his seat and motioned toward Lee's overturned chair. Lee righted it and sat down, preferring to be standing and moving to burn off some of the anger that boiled inside of him. "I am sure you are familiar with the flying ships the Prussians used against the Germans. Also how they used airborne explosives to render greater damage. We are in the process with fitting an airship with such capabilities. At sunset tomorrow we suspect that it will be prepared and by the time Big Ben chimes seven the bombs will be used to destroy the gateway on what we hope will be both sides and hopefully take out a great deal of the enemy forces."

"Where is the airship taking off from?" Lee asked.

"It should be docking several miles outside of London at the armory depot station." Albert said raising a suspicious eyebrow. "Why do you ask?"

"Put me on the ship. I'll prepare the Tin Man and we'll go through the portal on the drop at seven. All I ask is that you give me an hour. After that, drop the bombs and hopefully the portal will close, I can attempt to shut down the portal from the other side while locating Dan." Lee said. "You have got to give him a chance. He deserves that."

"I see no reason to postpone the . . ."

"Albert, he will have his hour." Victoria stated firmly quieting her husband. "I cannot give you more time than that. Do you know of the armory depot Albert spoke of?"

"Yes your Majesty," Lee replied.

"Then Godspeed." The queen said.

"Thank you," Lee said bowing and leaving the room through the door he had entered.

The guards returned his pistol at the front entrance and watched as he drove back using the same route he had previously taken. This time Lieutenant Colonel Cole let him pass without stopping as did the major that initially greeted him.

Lee returned to the flat to find Brackish still standing on the top step brandishing a pistol in his hands and the other one tucked into a belt he had cinched extremely tight to keep his pants from falling. It would have been a comical sight except for the seriousness of the situation. Outside a small group of soldiers had set up around the crater in the street. Rumor was a similar crater was found several streets over. Brackish lowered the pistol at the sight of Lee. "Nothing happen," he informed Lee.

"Good," Lee said opening the door and stepping past him. "Come on in, I don't think they'll try anything else tonight."

The goblin gave another look to the hallway and then stepped over the threshold and closed the door, setting the pistol on the table. Sitting near the table was the newly modified shotgun with its pack. Lee headed toward his workshop. "Brackish, I need some assistance."

Running, the goblin hurried to assist Lee. Confusion crossed Brackish's face as he saw Lee with large cloth materials spread out on his worktable. Motioning to the stool across the table, Lee spread out more tools and a quick plan he had whipped up in a few seconds. It was not as detailed as his other designs but with the lack of mechanical parts, it did not need to be. "What tinker we make?"

"We're going to take the Tin Man into the sky and float him down again." Lee said.

Brackish's face told of his hesitancy that he felt toward the possibilities of dropping out of the sky in the large metal creation. "I wouldn't do this normally you understand, but it's the only hope we have of rescuing Dan. It's for the clan." At that all hesitancy left the goblin's face and his hunched back straightened.

"What I need do?" The goblin asked his face completely serious.

"Here's the design, I need you to get the scissors and start cutting to these measurements. Can you do that?" Lee asked.

Brackish held up a finger and ran out of the room. When he returned he had a pair of scissors and Elizabeth by the hand. "Mr. Brackish says you needed my help measuring?" The freshly awakened girl stated.

Lee smiled at the goblin's ability to find a way to help. He handed the papers to Elizabeth. "Measure this out and then show him where to cut," Lee instructed.

Elizabeth looked at all the different materials gathered on the table. "Which one?" She asked.

"All of them," Lee answered turning to one of his tables filled with wires.

Dan opened his eyes. His head was hurting him and there was very little light wherever he was. The sound of water lapping on the side of a boat came from all around him. Something large was passing in the water near him. He moved his head so he could see and that made his head swim even more. He lay back down for a moment and took it slowly. His eyes gradually adjusted to the darkness and he saw the darker shape standing out in the front of the boat and a much larger and ominous shape in the rear, most likely the oar man.

"Do not struggle," a female voice said from the front, it was the shape. Lithe movements were barely noticeable under the cloak she wore. Before he could fully follow her she was lying across him. "If you struggle, we will be forced to end your life now. We would not want that."

"You aren't from around these parts," Dan said noticing the hint of an accent on the voice.

"Neither are you," she said rising off of him. "Englishmen do not fight as you fight. It seems we are both strangers in a strange land, no?"

"No, I'm pretty well acquainted with the land." He said trying once more to sit up.

A large weight pressed on his chest keeping him on the floor. The breath squeezed out of him and he expected the sound of his breaking ribs to pulse from him. With a single word from his female companion the weight disappeared. "My friend does not like you to move. I suggest you do not attempt that again. Golems can be so unpredictable."

Dan coughed as he tried to force the air back into his lungs. "So I've heard. German?"

"Of course, you are fortunate." She said again.

"I shot you," Dan said ignoring her last statement.

"I must admit that it stung a little but I am unlike any fey in this land you abide in." She stated standing up in the bow of the boat and dropping the cloak from around her. "My blood is not pure and full of inbreeding as these races here. My mother was a Sylph, my father a human magically bonded to a Jotun hierarch as a tribute from his village. He learned to tame the storm through this bond, only the storm was my mother. He fled with her as I grew within her. A child of three races, I am of the chosen warrior of the master." The woman turned and looked at Dan, he saw her clearly for the first time. Her face was frighteningly beautiful but her skin had the look of pristine snow with eyes the color of storm clouds. "You are going to meet the master. He has requested you until they arrive with the child." Dan laughed at the woman who turned a fierce gaze upon him and sent a small shock of lighting into his foot. His leg went numb and he jerked at the spasming muscles. "I do not enjoy mocking."

"Lady, I ain't mocking you. Your master is wrong. They'll never trade that girl for me." Dan said. "You guys clearly overestimate my value."

The woman came close enough that their noses were almost touching, Dan could feel the cold emitting from her face. "If they do not, then the master will kill you. I may beg to use you for my own enjoyment first." The woman gave Dan a wicked wink and returned to the bow of the boat.

Elizabeth had measured the strips to the plans that Lee had drawn. Brackish cut perfectly along the indicated lines. Lee stood instructing them on how to lay out the cloth. Once they had the cloth in the correct arrangement Lee set about inserting small rings through which the string would be run. "Please run the two lengths of string through as the diagram shows," Lee said heading out to the Tin Man.

Stepping up into the body of his creation he began using the torch to open up the top of the Tin Man's head. Once he had succeeded he began to attach small bolts to the underside of the head directly onto the body of the Tin Man itself. He had wished that he would be able to field test the device but given the shortness of time he had no choice but to proceed and trust that he had done the math correctly. Brackish came into the trailer and stood watching as Lee was pulling himself off of the floor while holding onto the newly attached bolts. The goblin sat staring at him until Lee turned around. "Elizabeth say we finished like plan shows," Brackish said explaining his presence.

"Very well, let's go gather it up shall we?" Lee said putting down the torch and removing his goggles before heading into the house.

The boat rocked up onto the shore line and Dan was picked up and placed across the stone shoulder of the golem. "Where are you taking me?" He demanded.

"Quiet or I will freeze the breath in your lungs," his captor said in a whisper.

The golem followed the cloaked woman for several hundred feet and then stopped under a large oak tree. With a hushed word from the woman, the golem stood completely straight putting a hand on Dan's back. Something shuffled in the nearby darkness. Dan strained his eyes but could not make it out. The smell that assailed his nose, was one he was familiar with; it was the same scent that he had caught a whiff of while in Falls. Something growled from nearby and the woman gave another hushed command and Dan was laid across the back of something breathing and covered in fur. Calloused greasy hands took chains and bound him across the rear of the warg. "Let me go," he said and the golem squeezed across him tightly until he began to lose consciousness from lack of air. The woman gave an order and the golem turned and marched back toward the city.

Dan began to take deep breaths as the woman gave a click of her heels into the flanks of the warg and the beast lunged into the dark with its great strides. The chains that held Dan in place were tight and uncomfortable but they did prevent him from falling off or bouncing around on the back of the beast. He could see the hood fall back from the woman's face as she rode the large wolfen beast across the darkened countryside.

The golem climbed the hill making his way toward the old stone bridge to enter London, as he had been instructed to do. As the lights from the bridge cast shadows across the stone body marching toward the city of London, the soldiers on the bridge became alerted to the coming threat. Orders were given to stop and identify itself, but since the orders were not in the language the golem had been built to understand it gave no heed to the orders. Soldiers put their rifles to their shoulders and gave one final warning to stop or be fired upon. The golem continued on, unheeding of the warning.

Shots rang out as the soldiers fired into the stone frame chipping away pieces. The soldiers were shocked when their bullets had no effect on the creature approaching them. Reloading their weapons they continued to fire upon the walking statue with no effect. "Artillery," the commanding officer called as the stone giant continued marching toward the blockade across the bridge. The mobile artillery unit drove forward, blocking the path of the golem. The golem continued on showing no change of pace or direction. "Fire!" The commanding officer ordered.

With a deafening roar the artillery launched the shell at the stone figure. The shell struck the golem in the dead center of its chest, exploding and sending small pebble sized pieces of the stone raining down. An unforeseen effect of the artillery's shot was that the explosion had also weakened the bridge. The soldiers carefully traversed the damaged bridge on foot and set up barricades on the other side. They then made their way back across the bridge to take up their old positions. Damaging the bridge was the last part of the infiltration forces mission, with the nearest bridge destroyed all forces leaving London would have to be rerouted and sent several hours out of their way. Once the explosion had echoed into the night, both Dan and his captor had heard it, and the woman with her white face gave a harsh laugh into the night.

Lee had left the flat in the velociter, pulling the Tin Man with it. Brackish was sitting in the passenger seat that was normally occupied by Dan. Both the man and the goblin heard the explosion coming from the outskirts of the city. Lee felt compelled to see what new evil was occurring but could not force himself to turn from the path he was on. Dan needed his assistance if he was going to have any hope of surviving and returning to London. Brackish opened the window and leaned out sniffing the air. Closing the window the goblin fell back into the passenger seat. "Other rock man," Brackish said. "Boom!"

Lee was glad that the other golem had been destroyed, they were known to cause all manner of chaos and destruction even when not being controlled by those with malevolent intentions. Turning his attention back to the course of action before him, he headed out to the east of the grand city towards the depot where he would board the airship with the blessing of the crown. The sun was still several hours from cresting above the horizon and Lee hurried because he knew at just over twelve hours he would be involved in the biggest battle of his life.

"Lady, you got a name?" Dan asked as he lay bouncing along the back half of the warg.

The smell had become easier to deal with the longer he was around it. What he could not get over was the beauty of the woman that had captured him.

"My father called me Freyja." She said. "The master has given me a new name, he has deemed me Valkyrie."

"So you choose those that die in battle?" Dan asked.

"You know more than I would have believed."

"Every fighter knows about Valhalla," Dan stated. "Aren't you supposed to be a lover of heroes?"

"You see yourself as a hero?" Valkyrie asked looking over her shoulder at him.

"I don't see myself as a villain," Dan said. "I get the feeling you don't see me as a villain either."

"Enough of this pointless chatter," she said turning back to the road ahead of them.

Dan smiled. He always knew how to rile up a lady, especially when telling the truth. The warg's pace, as incredible as it seemed, quickened making the ride more uncomfortable for Dan. Tirelessly, the warg ran through the dark never stumbling or stopping, never altering its pace. Hours passed as Dan sat resting, as soon as his body became used to the rhythmic gallop of the beast. Before long he was snoring, much to the chagrin of Valkyrie. She preferred him sleeping as opposed to talking, for his speech had caused her to anger at his assumptions.

As the night crept on and the warg raced to its destination, they passed several groups of soldiers on the road marching to the stone circle on the hill. The warg was able to outpace the march of the soldiers and continued on without incident. The warg finally began to slow its descent and Dan woke as the rhythm of his sleep was disrupted. He then smelled a stench as strong as that in Falls if not stronger.

The sounds of clanking metal and snorts and grunts told him he was among hostile forces that he had met before. Valkyrie spoke to them in the same language she had used to address the golem and the forces around her seemed to calm themselves. Dan raised up his head to take a look around then lowered his head again. It seemed that the stone circle was now being guarded by a force of several hundred orcs, judging by the torches and sounds Dan heard. His odds of escape seemed to be deteriorating. Valkyrie slid off of the warg and called to something nearby. Dan's was removed from the warg and a pole was slid down his back underneath his bound hands and feet. With a grunt something lifted the pole pulling Dan free of the warg, his shoulders burned as his arms shifted and his entire upper body was suspended by his wrists. He did not grunt or make a sound. Instead he looked and saw several larger beasts carrying the pole between them. They were headed near what Dan assumed was the stone circle and a swirl of white and blue lights. Valkyrie entered into the swirling lights and vanished. The lead creature entered with the front end of the pole and the march continued until they were almost upon the portal and then Dan was carried into it.

16   Lee pulled the velociter to the gates of the depot. Several heavily armed soldiers were positioned behind large barricades and suspiciously looked at the velociter and the trailer it carried. Opening the window, Lee called to the soldiers. "I have clearance from the queen herself."

One of the soldiers came forward while his fellow sentries maintained their aim on Lee. Holding out the paper, Lee looked about as the soldier examined the orders. It was clear that there was a large airship on the grounds of the depot. The large hydrogen filled balloon was visible from several miles away. It was clearly on the ground, but impossible to hide without deflating it. "I'll have to show these to the commanding officer," the soldier said turning away from Lee.

Lee waited as the soldier disappeared inside the fence and was lost amidst the buildings. Brackish sat on the floor out of sight of the soldiers, he and Lee were anxious with good reason, trying to sneak Brackish onboard would get them both shot. After several minutes had passed the soldier returned, the orders still firmly in his hand. "Sir," the soldier handed the orders back. "Once you enter the base please keep to the left and proceed to lot F-12."

Lee nodded as the other sentries lowered their rifles while the soldier who had carried off his orders opened the gate for him to pass. "Well we are in," Lee said. "Still please do not cause any trouble and keep quiet until we are in the air."

"I know, I know," Brackish said.

"Good. These men will not hesitate to shoot either you or me." Lee warned. "They do not know about you and neither does the queen. I'll make the introductions once this ordeal has passed us by."

Lee took the route he was given and drove to the far end of the depot near the edge of the base's property. He drove ever closer to the looming airship. He saw lot F-12 painted on a white sign beside a large warehouse facility that was set further away from the other buildings. A sign reading explosives told him all he needed to know about the reason that F-12 was sequestered at the rear of the depot. Parking the velociter, Lee exited telling Brackish to stay put where he was. He made his way to a ramp in the rear of the airship that was lowered where military personnel were using small steam driven motors to push large pallets into the rear of the ship. A man in a crisp uniform consisting of a navy blue blazer, white slacks and a navy blue captain's hat stood with a clipboard inspecting the oncoming pallets.

"Are you Lee Baum?" The man asked as he noticed Lee approaching.

"I am, are you the captain of this fine vessel?" Lee asked.

"No," the man said. "I'm first mate Jonas Hanson. The captain is currently onboard plotting our course. Once these men finish loading their gear we'll be able to load on your equipment." Jonas looked over at the velociter and the trailer. "We will not be able to accommodate freight of that size."

"That is merely my means of transportation. I assure you my equipment will take up no more room than one of these explosive devices." Lee said smiling.

"Who said anything about explosives?" Jonas asked studying Lee.

"Do not take me for a fool. I can recognize black powder and what I assume is a phosphorous ignition device that upon impact will trigger and cause an explosive reaction." Lee said. "If you do not need anything else, notify me when it is time for me to board the ship."

Lee walked away, shock still clear on Jonas' face. He knew that they were transporting explosives but he did not know nearly the detail that Lee had just demonstrated with a cursory glance.

Brackish stayed in his place in the floor as Lee came over and opened the door and started reaching around his diminutive companion. He tossed a canvas bag onto the floor. "Climb in," Lee said.

Brackish slid the bag over himself and waited as he was lifted from the seat and carried somewhere else. Lee was careful not to be rough with Brackish, carefully sitting the goblin on the floor of the Tin Man's compartment. Lee looked around to make sure that no one was watching. "Stay hidden until I give you the all clear." He ordered.

Brackish stayed in the bag as Lee loaded Dan's upgraded shotgun along with all of the spare magazines for it, several boxes of ammunition for Lee's own Winchester, several bundles of dynamite, and before he closed the compartment, he loaded the Tin Man's cannons to capacity. "You can come out but keep your head down," Lee said as he shut the compartment.

Dan opened his eyes and found himself in the middle of a dense forest where trees different from those of the English forests grew. This forest was old and the tree roots scoured the ground. Looking around he saw that several stones were arranged to form a circle with a smaller blue and white light swirl on this side of it. The creatures carrying the pole set it down on a nearby stone slab and disappeared into the darkness of the forest about them. "You do not seem to be the one we were looking for," said a withered old voice from beside Dan.

"Yeah, I get that a lot." Dan said. "Any way I can get out of this truss?"

There was movement from nearby and his bonds were loosened. Valkyrie stepped away taking his bonds with her. Dan sat up rubbing his wrists where they had chafed. He saw the being that had spoken to him. A cloaked figure sat in a throne formed from the contours of one of the large trees. "So whose party am I at?" Dan asked.

The creature leaned forward, removing his hood. Underneath was a wizened face with a thick beard and one of his eyes was clearly missing. The scars on his face spoke of great battles fought, but the place with the missing eye was not scarred by battle. A crow called from one of the roots near the man. "Odin," Dan said marveling at the realization.

"Ha," the man laughed. "Once I was known by that name. Now I am known as Wotan. The faith of others has diminished and thus my realm has grown smaller, but I see I am still remembered by some."

"Why?" Dan asked. "Why go through all this trouble to try and kill a child?"

"Kill a child?" Wotan asked giving a confused look at Valkyrie. "I do not seek innocent blood. It is true I sought the child to bring here and open up the talks with the ruling court of your land once again, but killing the child had never been broached by us in council."

"You've spoken with them before," Dan said, something was not sitting right with him but he didn't think he was getting that feeling from Wotan.

"One of their representatives met with my council to discuss the transfer of my people from this war torn land to your land." Wotan explained. "We were refused and forced to side with those that we had long since stood against."

"Was that also when you threw your lot in with the Unseelie Court," Dan accused.

"Who are you speaking of?" Wotan asked. "The only members of your races that we have met with was the one that came representing Glorianna."

Wotan nodded his head about him and Dan saw the gathered orcs, bugaboos, and trolls. "Why did the force that captured me travel in the company of the Unseelie Court? Why are you invading our land?"

"The werewolf was one of ours. The small men with the spears came to us as allies several weeks ago; they have been attempting to get Glorianna to reconsider. As for invading," Wotan said laughing. "We've merely sent warriors to protect the portal, nothing else. Unless you speak of the Erlking but you destroyed him. What blood must run through your veins!"

"Wotan, I must ask this. Who was sent to talk to you about coming to England?" Dan asked.

"It was a little man, they called him Ironhill." Wotan said.

"Did you send the orcs to conquer and slaughter the small village of Falls?" Dan asked, pieces were starting to fall into place for him but he had to bide his time when fewer of the dark beasts of this land were present.

"You continue to speak to me in riddles and besmirch the name of great Wotan. I have wrought war and destroyed men in times past but it was always for their indiscretion. The men of England have done nothing to me, and because of that I have seen no reason to wage war upon them." Wotan said standing up.

The old man towered over Dan. "Take it easy," Dan said. "I meant no harm, was just asking questions about some of the stuff I've seen. You know anything about necromancers?"

"Those that tamper with the dead are of the lowest filth," Wotan replied.

"Glad to see we agree on that," Dan stated.

Lee stood beside the Tin Man as the airship left its mooring in the depot and began to rise into the sky. Brackish was moving about within the Tin Man, Lee could hear the occasional footstep. There were two soldiers standing guard at the hatch to the explosives. They had been placed to insure that Lee did not tamper with the pallets and cause a catastrophic event aboard the ship. His attention was focused wholly on the ship and workings of the large rotor engines with their turbines and propellers and the occasional notches he saw in the railing along the walkway that wound its way around the windows of the airship. Given the method he intended to use to get the Tin Man onto the ground, if it proved successful it would be easy to form a pack for a soldier to wear that would allow them to assault from the air. Looking at the pallets of black powder, Lee came to realization that these were not the same as the bombs the Prussian's had used.

These bombs did not have the metal casings that made the Prussian bombs so deadly. "Excuse me," Lee said to the nearest guard. "I need to speak with the first mate."

The guard spoke into a round instrument attached to a brass tube. It was not long before Jonas appeared from the storage facility. "Can I help you?" He asked.

"No," Lee said. "I can help you. I realize what you are trying to do with these bombs but they are going to be less effective than their Prussian counterpart."

Jonas looked over his shoulder at the pallets. "I beg your pardon?"

"Prussian bombs have the hard casing that turns into shrapnel upon detonation. All those bombs are going to accomplish is an explosion and some fire afterwards." Lee explained. "Anything that could be wrapped around them would be advantageous."

"I will pass your recommendation onto the captain," Jonas said making a crisp turn on his heels and exiting back through the door.

Shortly after his exit Lee heard Jonas giving orders to a group of soldiers to begin wrapping metal wiring around the bombs. It would not be as effective as the Prussian bombs but it would make the danger these bombs posed to enemy forces that much greater. The city of London was sprawled ahead of the airship and it was a breathtaking sight for Lee. Here the city could be seen without the haze that hung in the air from the fumes the vehicles and factories put off. It was still a lovely city but at times while one walked through her streets it was difficult to see it.

Lee opened the rear compartment and saw Brackish trying to hide. "It's all right," Lee whispered. "You have to see this."

Lee used the periscope controls and turned the Tin Man's head until the view was outside at the sights that he was seeing. With a wink to Brackish, he closed the compartment. Listening, Lee heard the goblin stand on top of something and then a hushed sound came from within.

The guards did not take any notice of it. Taking notice of how far the ground was below them, Lee swallowed back the fear that started to well up within him. His latest addition to the Tin Man was principally sound but Lee was less concerned with theory and more concerned with reality. If it worked then all would be well. If not then Dan's only attempt at rescue would end before it began. Lee pushed these thoughts from his mind. Lee continued running over the plan he had devised and making sure that it was covered. He intentionally did this to make sure that he did not drift onto the results if the new addition failed.

Dan was fed food he did not recognize but he was assured that it was not poisoned and would do him no harm. Some of it tasted fine and was not too different from foods he had in England. They brought him something made from cooked cabbage and he ate it but had to hide his grimace as it went down. Wotan had left him in the care of Valkyrie as he held council with the rulers of the Council of the Black Forest. From what Dan had pieced together, Wotan and the others that were the equivalence of the Seelie Court had made peace with the darker forces of Germany in order to find a place for all their people.

Given the things that Dan had seen and witnessed while trying to find Kate McKendrick, he knew that forces had been on English soil and destroyed, at least, an entire village. Something was wrong and Dan smelled treachery.

"Your thoughts betray you," Valkyrie said from beside him.

"My thoughts aren't the ones I'm worried about betraying." Dan responded looking at the orc guards in the hall.

"Wotan is wise above all, surely you know of how he lost his eye." Valkyrie said.

"Yeah I've heard the stories, but in my experiences even wise men make bad decisions when they do them for the right reasons."

"Wotan would not do something as such for he is more than a man."

"I suppose so," Dan said, waiting for Valkyrie to respond.

When she failed to Dan looked at her and saw that what he had said caused her to stop and think. Now when she looked at the orcs guarding the forest there was a shimmer of distrust in her eyes that had not been there before.

The sun was sinking low on the horizon while storm clouds were beginning to form in the channel. Lee stood watching all of this realizing that they would soon be in place and that he would have to test his latest improvements to the Tin Man. "Sir," the guards behind him said, snapping to attention.

Lee turned and saw a man with a white beard standing in the doorway. His uniform was almost identical to the first mate except the chest held many more medals and the shoulders revealed a higher rank. "Captain," Lee said to the man as he strode past the Tin Man and shook Lee's hand.

"Glad to have you aboard." The captain said. "We will be ready for you to drop in half an hour. You'll need to position your contraption at the end of the ramp. Once it lowers and it's safe to remove, you'll be given an all clear. I have to return to the helm now but Godspeed to you."

"Thank you sir," Lee said.

Once the captain had left Lee cranked the dynamo to create the power needed to operate the Tin Man. He connected the controller and before he wrapped himself in the cord he snapped one of his brass chest plates on. Lee had made some slight modifications to both his and Dan's. Now there was a small brass piece that rose up and offered protection to their throat and mouth. Pulling the straps tight, Lee began to wrap the control cord around him. Opening the compartment he stepped over the shotgun's pack and stood in the small space closing the compartment behind him. Brackish stared at him. "Remember the plan?" Lee asked.

"Yes," Brackish said.

In the goblin's hand was one of Dan's pistols. The other one was in a belt that Lee had initially carried. The loops around the belt contained bullets. Because the belt was too big for the small goblin it was strung across his shoulders where Dan's other pistol sat in its holster hanging at Brackish's thigh. "Silver in the holster?" Lee asked.

"Yes," Brackish said. "Only I need it, use normals keep reloading."

Lee nodded his head as he used the periscope to guide him to the ramp as he had been instructed. "Soon we'll find out if this will work," Lee said giving a smile full of confidence.

Brackish returned the smile while both of them felt somewhat anxious about their proposed plan of attack. The time sped past until there was a knock on the back of the compartment, Lee opened it. Jonas stood outside the compartment, a serious look on his face. "Three minutes," he shouted over the sound of the wind rushing past and the airships engines.

The ramp was opened and Lee nodded his head. "What's the signal?" Lee asked.

Jonas held up a flare. "When you see the green smoke that's the all clear," Jonas explained.

Lee nodded his understanding and closed the compartment back up. Pressing his eyes up to the periscope to make sure he could see the smoke, he attached his brass chest plate to one of the new metal loops he had installed. "Strap in," Lee told Brackish.

The goblin secured the shotgun and its pack and then tied himself to the wall with leather cord. Green smoke trailed behind as the flare was thrown across the Tin Man. Lee worked the controls and led the Tin Man to the edge of the ramp and then the large metallic construct was free falling through the air. The large treads on the bottom making sure that it did not fall end over end. Brackish screamed as they plummeted to the ground.

Dan was sitting on the stone slab that he had originally been placed on. Valkyrie stood off to the side of the slab looking around, completely aware of her surroundings. She carried herself in a way that let the other races know that she was formidable. Dan's glances at the strange beauty with him began to last longer. Wotan entered the hollow within the woods and took his place on the tree throne. Entering behind him was the largest orc that Dan had seen yet, the bones that were being worn as decoration most likely indicated that this was a very important chief. Dan paid little attention to the bones other than a cursory inspection but noticed the long barb pointed spear the orc carried. The orc took up a position on Wotan's left side and a cloaked figure that remained completely hidden within the shadows of the forest sat on his right.

"I hear you have some interesting things to tell us," Wotan said.

"I do." Dan agreed. "First of all I think you've been done dirty. I think that your friends here have been playing for the Unseelie Court the whole time, and I think they intend to destroy your people."

"Proof?" Wotan asked his face a mask of grave seriousness.

"I saw a village destroyed by orcs and those big dogs. All but one person had been slaughtered." Dan said remembering the terrors he had seen in Falls. "Also I know that forces of both German fey and Unseelie Court have been attacking the members of the Seelie Court. Finally, when your rider failed to secure the girl, a mean spirited water spirit with the habit of drowning children tried to snare her. If you aren't working with the Unseelie Court then why is it that I keep finding traces of them in your dealings?"

The sky above rumbled. "You dare challenge me!" Wotan shouted. "I am the wisest of my people, you are but a speck of dust before me."

"I forgot the best part. A dead son of Donar was controlled by a necromancer and attempted to destroy me and my friend."

"A son of Donar?" Wotan asked, his face growing haggard.

"Yeah," Dan said. "So tell me where would a necromancer get access to a recently deceased one?"

"My grandchildren," Wotan said, ignoring Dan.

His massive hand wrapped around the throat of the cloaked figure at his side. The hood fell away revealing an unassuming looking woman. "What do you know of this Trude?" Wotan demanded shaking the woman.

"He speaks with a beguiled tongue. None have ever dared command the dead of the Wotan's seed." She said, begging.

Wotan released her from his grasp and turned back toward Dan. "Do you speak true to me?"

"It's the only thing I've been doing since I got here." Dan said. "Look a terrible storm started in on us, I challenged him to a fight, then he came down and begged me to free him. I did."

Wotan grabbed Trude by the hair and threw her onto the stone slab at Dan's feet. "She knows of the necromancer, don't you Trude? Of course you look over all the practitioners of your foul art here."

Trude, the Queen of the German witches, rose and her features remained the same but took on a harsher aspect. "You are a fool Wotan, desperation has made you blind. I desecrated your kin's corpse and will do the same to you," Trude said pointing a crooked finger at Wotan.

"What treachery do you speak?" Wotan demanded.

The orc chieftain remained in his place beside Wotan, bored with the scene playing before him. "You ask of treachery. Treachery abounds before you Wotan, and you will die." Trude announced.

"Valkyrie . . ." Wotan began.

"Now!" Trude cried cutting short Wotan's words.

From his position beside Wotan the orc chieftain leaped into the air and buried the barbed tip of his spear deep into Wotan's chest, pinning him to the tree. Valkyrie let out a strangled cry. Blood spreading across his robe and frothing from his mouth, Wotan reached for his great spear. While Trude stood before Dan cackling at the sight of the dying being. Spear in hand, Wotan gave a great heave and hurtled the weapon of steel and wood. It hit the witch center of her chest and threw her body back. Dan dropped to the floor as her body sailed over him landing just in front of the portal. Trude wrapped her hand around the shaft of the spear and then her body went limp and she remained where she lay. Dan looked up and saw the old Viking god's vacant eyes and knew that he had died. The orc chieftain started giving orders to the dark creatures surrounding them. Dan hurried to Valkyrie who stood staring at Wotan's body, tears glistening in her eyes.

"Mourn later, you start now and we'll be joining him sooner than I'd like," Dan said as the creatures began making their way toward Valkyrie and Dan.

They stood back to back as the evil forces approached them. Valkyrie called out to the trees and there was a great rumbling from within the earth. Several large figures appeared, rising from the ground around the trees. The monsters stopped their advance giving out surprised shouts as they turned and saw the new foes. Golems began making their way through the crowds, swinging their giant stone arms sending orcs and trolls flying through the air. Dark shadows raced toward them, moving with a purpose and liquid quality that ordinary shadows did not possess. It was the bugaboos. Creatures notorious for lurking in closets and under beds where darkness reigned supreme, they came from these places at night to frighten people feeding off the fear.

They proved to be a hazard for the golem as well, despite the lack of fears that the stone men possessed. Their shadow forms solidifying into beings that were able to land blows on the golems. Like all creatures of the otherworld they were stronger than was naturally possible and their mighty blows cracked and damaged the golems. This distraction allowed the orcs and trolls to get away from the golems and continue their approach toward Dan and Valkyrie. "Stay at my back," Dan said. "No matter what happens, stay at my back."

The creatures continued approaching, gaining speed as they came until they began leaping into combat with Dan and Valkyrie. She was able to put several down with the lighting charges she was casting. Dan had to rely on his fists until one of them dropped the cleaver it had been wielding and then Dan commenced hacking at the crowd of attackers. Both he and Valkyrie were cut and bleeding from dozens of small wounds, surrounded by their vicious adversaries, when something unexpected happened.

17   Lee and Brackish had been falling for three seconds, which seemed like an eternity to them, when Lee pulled the pin that released the circular cloth pieces out of the top. "Cross your fingers," Lee said to Brackish.

Brackish did not get the point of crossing his fingers, but did it just in case the tinker required it to work.

The different colored sections of cloth began to blossom out of the top and, as the wind caught underneath them it pulled the cloth completely free of the Tin Man and slowed their descent. "It worked!" Lee screamed triumphantly, excitement filling his words.

Brackish began to breathe again and then realized he had not been breathing since Lee had been given the signal to exit the ship.

Jonas watched from the ramp to make sure that everything went as planned. He was confused when he saw the first patches of cloth coming out of the top of the Tin Man but then the wind pulled them completely out and slowed their descent. "Bloody brilliant," the first mate mumbled to himself.

The orcs on the ground were pointing at the giant metal man descending from the sky. Curious about the large circular cloth patterns they saw emerge. As the Tin Man got closer they became more frantic, finally they fired arrows that bounced off of the metal undercarriage. Primitive fear driving them they abandoned their posts to clear a space for the floating device.

The Tin Man settled onto the ground with little impact. Lee cut the straps to the cloth and the wind took them across the hill and away from Stonehenge. "Ready?" Lee asked unhooking himself.

Brackish let loose a war cry and untied the leather strap binding him to the side.

"Very well then," Lee replied.

Unwrapping the cord from his body, Lee began to steer toward the glowing lights. There was no doubt that these were the same lights that had discharged the orcs, which stood at defensive positions around the hill. Closing his eyes against the brightness, Lee steered the Tin Man through it. There was a slight rattling sound and the ground beneath them became uneven. Lee opened his eyes and looked out. He was not within the stone monoliths of Stonehenge anymore, but wherever he was he recognized the orcs and trolls about him and in the middle of them was Dan standing back to back with some woman.

Lee opened the compartment and leaped out, Winchester in one hand, Dan's shotgun in the other. If they had not been surrounded by weapon wielding monsters, Dan's befuddled look would have been amusing. Giving a great underhanded heave, Lee tossed the shotgun with its pack to Dan.

Brackish leaped from the back of the Tin Man and saw the orcs and trolls standing bewildered around the metal device. He started firing into the nearest orcs and trolls, killing them. Once the orcs and trolls recognized the threat, they turned their attentions to the newcomers. Lee began firing into the beasts as they turned to attack. "We need to thin them out," Lee said stepping into the Tin Man and readying the cannons.

Dan knelt down and shrugged the pack onto his back. Valkyrie continued fighting as the orcs and trolls began to take the fight to Lee and Brackish. Smiling, Dan saw the three barrels drop from the Tin Man's chest. Grabbing Valkyrie by the arm, Dan pulled her to the ground and covered her with his body. Valkyrie was trying to push him off of her to return to the fight. "Hold on," Dan said into her ear.

Then the sound of the cannons firing started to echo among the trees, and the explosions turned the orcs and trolls into wet pieces of meat and bone. Dan had never heard the Tin Man's cannons fired so continuously. Once the cannons stopped, Dan was not sure if he was deaf or the cannons had stopped. Then he heard the familiar voice. "Dan!"

Jumping to his feet, Dan almost dragged Valkyrie trying to get to Lee. Lee was standing in a small crater not far from the Tin Man waving. Raising his rifle, Lee fired just off of Dan's shoulder and something yelped and then came the sound of armor falling to the ground. Jumping into the crater, Dan laid his back against the earthen wall. "I'm really going to need more than eight shots." Dan said.

"Here," Brackish said with the magazine holder that Lee had shown Dan.

A wicked smile crossed Dan's lips as he fastened it onto his leg. A brass chest plate landed at his feet. Dan raised a questioning eyebrow to Lee. "No arguments. If you'd had it earlier you probably would not have so many lacerations." Lee said, firing a few more rounds and then reloading the rifle.

Dan shrugged off the shotgun's pack and strapped the chest plate into place. With some assistance from Brackish he was able to get the pack back on.

Grunts and clanging armor were coming from all around them. "What happened to your rock friends?" Dan asked.

"They have all been incapacitated by the bugaboos." Valkyrie said, then with a warrior's cry she hurled lightning about her and left four charred smoking orc corpses.

Lee raised an eyebrow at Dan. "Is she the one that came to . . .?"

"Yeah, yeah I'll tell you all about it later." Dan said cutting Lee off.

Valkyrie continued striking out with lighting but the blasts were losing their intensity. She sat down breathing heavy. Lee continued firing off shots toward their flank. "Dan, we're going to need your new toy front and center," Lee said looking over his shoulder.

Dan raised his head just above the nearest root and saw the small contingent of approaching orcs; they were hidden behind trolls that were carrying shields of tree bark. This force was not his main concern when he saw several of the liquid shadows approaching their position. "Bugaboos incoming!" Dan announced.

"Here," Lee said tossing several of the magnesium flares to Dan.

Striking them Dan laid them around their protective crater and then concentrated his attention on the approaching force. "Ain't even fair," he said pulling the switch and listening to the familiar sound of the piston starting its action.

Standing up from the crater, Dan smiled at the oncoming force as he squeezed the trigger. One strafe with the shotgun and the bark shields were shredded as were those that had carried them. One more strafe took out half of the orcs and then the shotgun was empty. Dan left off the trigger and then turned to look at the new mechanism. Upon seeing it, his memory of how to operate it returned and he ejected the spent magazine, retrieved another magazine from his thigh and pushed it into place. He did this as the pack continued its rhythmic chant of the piston.

The orcs that were now running toward him were cut down before they were close enough to spit on him. Taking his trigger off the shotgun, Dan switched out the magazine just to have a fully loaded one ready.

"I got to tell you, I love this." Dan said patting the shotgun.

Brackish was shooting at random approaching villains, not caring if they were troll or orc. One of the liquid shadows rose in front of him taking on its form of nightmare proportions. It snatched up the goblin from the ground and opened its gaping maw of a mouth revealing several rows of sharp teeth. Brackish laughed at the sight, showing no fear. The bugaboo dropped Brackish at his laugh and its form began to waiver. Knife in hand Brackish leapt, cutting at the bugaboo. When he was finished the frail thing on the ground bleeding black ichor would not have frightened the frailest of children. "That reminds me," Lee said looking at Brackish.

Brackish pulled Dan's bowie knife out from under his vest and tossed it to his friend. Dan quickly put it inside his boot and returned to watching the forces that were trying to assail their position. "I never did ask, what's the plan?" Dan inquired.

"Destroy path, go home." Brackish said firing off another shot before he opened the cylinder and started ejecting spent casings.

"Concise but appropriate," Lee said as he continued shooting at targets outside the range of Dan's shotgun or Brackish's pistol. "We need to destroy the stone circle here in order to close off the portal. If we do not her Majesty is going to bomb the portal on our side and hope to close one side or the other. I would much prefer it if we were not here when that happens."

"What'd you have in mind?" Dan asked. "You fired off all the cannon rounds."

"I brought your little helpers," Lee said.

Dan looked at Brackish. Brackish looked back and frowned at him and pointed towards the Tin Man. Dan made sure there were no imminent attacks and ran to the Tin Man where he saw several bundles of dynamite. He laughed as he carried them back to the crater. "I can lay them but we'll need to be ready to go before I light them up."

A howl erupted from the trees. "Do you have any silver?" Dan asked.

"Yes," Brackish said as he retrieved the pistol still in its holster.

"Are those my pistols?" Dan asked actually taking the time to look at the guns.

"Not now," Lee said. "Brackish."

The snarling werewolf bounded into the clearing, running on all fours, it made great strides to reach the crater. Brackish took careful aim using one of the roots to balance the barrel of the pistol. A squeeze of the trigger and the werewolf fell crumpling against the roots, a revealing hole in his head. "Two others," Lee warned.

Dan looked and saw them come in from opposite directions. Brackish was able to get the shot off at the one nearest Lee, landing a killing blow on it. The one coming in from Brackish's flank was upon him before he could fire. Dan rolled and pulled out the other revolver and fired the four loaded chambers into the belly of the beast. It staggered back, but did not fall. The distraction gave Brackish enough time to fire two shots into the creature's thick muscular chest and kill it with a bullet through the heart. Placing the revolver with silver bullets in the holster, Brackish took the empty revolver from Dan's hand and started reloading it. Brackish gave Dan a thumb's up and Dan couldn't help but chuckle. Valkyrie looked at the men confused as she tried to hit the forces gathered within the trees. Her power was waning and her bursts were growing less effective. "Might as well rest," Dan said. "Conserve your strength."

"What do you know?" Valkyrie asked, appalled that Dan had seen fit to give her advice.

"I know you ain't hitting squat at the moment." He gave her a wink. "Did you bring me any fuses?"

Lee looked at the pouches along his belt and retrieved several long loops of fuse and tossed them towards Dan. "Wonderful," Dan stated examining the different lengths. "I can give us two minutes at most."

"It will have to do," Lee said.

Dan took another look around and saw several of the trolls making their way forward. "I can light and run, dropping as close to the stones as I can get. I don't think they'll get all of the bundles," Dan looked at the trolls as they tried to stealthily make their way to the crater. "Trolls, ten, all the way to one."

Lee took aim and started firing. Brackish started firing at them as well. He was hitting them but not making the accurate kill shots that Lee was. While the men were distracted the orc chieftain made his way around their flank. He was determined to bury his spear in the man they had brought to them, the one that had wrought havoc on his minions in the village of Falls. Rising up quickly, the chieftain caught Brackish's arm in his mouth and crunched down tasting blood and feeling the crunch of the bone. A wail escaped Brackish's mouth and the others in the crater turned to see the orc chieftain rise up with Brackish suspended by the arm from the foul creature's mouth.

The spearhead still dripping with Wotan's blood was poised to be hurled at Dan. At seeing the struggling goblin, Dan let loose a cry and ran at the orc. Knocking the spearhead clear with his shotgun, Dan reached down and came up with his knife, burying the blade of the Bowie deep into the center of the chieftain's skull. Brackish fell to the ground as the chieftain's mouth dangled open. Then the rest of his body went limp and slid off of Dan's knife. Wiping it off on the chieftain's coarse hair, Dan replaced the knife and hefted the spear. The orcs had stopped their approach and stared at their fallen chieftain. Raising the shotgun in one hand and the spear in the other, Dan let out a horrifying cry that caused the orcs to flee back to the trees. Throwing the spear into the dead chieftain's body, Dan knelt and picked up Brackish. The goblin looked at him, his arm mangled beyond repair and hanging on by a few shreds of tendon. Lee was beside Dan, removing the gunbelt. "Brackish, we can't save the arm," Lee informed him. "If we remove it now and cauterize it you won't bleed to death."

Brackish nodded his understanding. "Get me a flare and your knife," Lee said to Dan.

Handing first his knife, then one of the lit flares to Lee, Dan watched as Lee used the flare to warm the blade of the knife and sterilize it. Dan put a bullet in Brackish's mouth. "Bite down," Dan said.

Brackish closed his eye and bit down on the bullet. Lee used the razor edge of Dan's knife to make a clean cut of the damaged tissue and then held the flare to the amputated arm and cauterized it to prevent further blood loss. Brackish's eyes opened wide as the flame touched flesh and then they closed as the pain sent him into the waiting arms of unconsciousness. "I hate to disturb you but they seem to have retreated for the moment," Valkyrie announced from behind them.

"Now or never," Dan said as Lee wrapped a bandage around Brackish's shoulder.

"Agreed," Lee said carrying Brackish into the Tin Man.

"I'm going out on foot, take her." Dan said.

"I will not leave until every one of those dogs is dead," Valkyrie stated.

"I was afraid of that," Dan said, landing a punch clearly on her chin, knocking her out.

He caught her before she fell. Carrying her over his shoulder he sat her in the compartment. Lee used some strings to tie her against the wall with new bolts in place. Dan raised an eyebrow. "I'll tell you later," Lee said. "Go lay the charges. Once we exit we'll be surrounded by orcs."

Dan smiled and patted the shotgun. "I'll be ready."

Picking up the discarded gunbelt and wrapping it across his hips, he also picked up the pistol that Brackish had been using when he was attacked and placed it inside the gunbelt. Next he picked up the bundles of dynamite and started placing fuses in them. Flare in one hand, dynamite in the other, Dan began to jog around the perimeter of the stone circle, placing fuse to flare as he passed one of the stones and dropping the lit bundle as he went. The orcs were making sounds from the woods but there were none in sight. Just as well, he didn't have any free hands to shoot with. One of the bugaboos materialized almost directly in front of Dan.

It reached out with ghoulishly long fingers toward him but Dan was able to discourage it by jabbing the flare at its face. The form shrunk away from him staying on his periphery, waiting until the flare ran out. Dan continued until he was out of dynamite. Lee had already positioned the Tin Man to head out, and with one of his hands free Dan held onto one of the revolvers. The bugaboo appeared nearby, Dan tossed the flare at it striking the shadowy creature. The thing shirked and shrank and Dan fired the remaining cartridges from the pistol into the bugaboo. The figure danced with the impacts and fell away dead. "Go Lee," Dan called as he ran toward the Tin Man and the portal, by his guess they had less than a half a minute before the dynamite blew.

Lee began guiding the Tin Man back to the portal aware that he was heading directly into another fight, only this time he would have to stay within the Tin Man and he was out of cannon shells. Dan ran along hopping onto the small space at the rear of the Tin Man just above the treads. He felt the same strange sensation and then he was aware of a change in climate and sound. Opening his eyes, he saw the familiar monoliths of Stonehenge and heard the sounds of the orcs, it sounded as if they were already engaged in some form of combat.

From the other side of the portal there was a large explosion and it created a temporary vacuum almost pulling Dan free of the Tin Man then when he looked back the portal was gone. Stepping off of the Tin Man, Dan saw the orcs fighting amongst themselves but they seemed to realize that they were not alone anymore. One of the orcs leaped onto the front of the Tin Man and the others crowded around. It tried to climb up the side of the device. Lee turned on the piston arms as Dan cranked his shotgun pack. The piston rammed straight through the chest of the climbing orc and pounded the orcs standing in front of it. If it did not kill them then it effectively took them out of the fight.

A loud roar came from the other side of the orcs and those at the rear turned to face a new foe. Dan could not see what was drawing their attention as he opened fire with the shotgun killing orcs. Given their crowded conditions he was able to sometimes hit three with one shot. He kept replacing magazines until he was out of ammunition and by that time the orcs had been so devastated by Dan and Lee in the center and the attacking force of British soldiers and bounty hunters that the surviving members of the invasion were retreating in every direction. The soldiers were giving chase and shooting after their foes.

Dan stood amidst a pile of bodies almost up to his chest when he saw a familiar figure. James Brogan sat astride one of the wargs, his sword covered in foul smelling blood in one hand, a smoking pistol in the other. "Hello boyos," he said dismounting. "Good days work aye?"

"How did you get to ride that thing?" Dan asked as the docile warg came up and sniffed at his hand.

Lee opened the compartment of the Tin Man. "Unbind me," Valkyrie demanded.

"Better do as she says," Dan said.

Lee untied her and she stepped out of the compartment followed by Lee. "Medic!" Lee called.

A soldier with a doctor's bag and a white cross on the breast of his field coat came running towards Lee. Lee took him to Brackish and explained the situation. Turning away from the Tin Man, Lee stood mystified by the warg. "How did you do that?" Lee asked astounded.

"I was just wondering the same thing," Dan stated.

"You struck me," Valkyrie accused, causing Dan to look back at the woman.

"Don't believe I've had the pleasure," James said, giving a roguish smile to Valkyrie.

She held up her finger and a small burst of lighting sparked from it. "I am speaking to this one," she said.

"Sorry, about that." Dan said. "I wasn't leaving you to die. You're too pretty for that."

Valkyrie stood shocked into silence, her glare at Dan softened. "I am sorry, but . . ."

"It's okay," Dan said smiling at her. She returned his smile tentatively.

Valkyrie watched as several soldiers came towards her, their weapons raised. She tensed. "All right, you boys stop it right there," Dan ordered. "So help me God if you don't I'll see to it every one of you suffers."

Lee, Dan, and Brogan stepped in front of the woman. The soldiers hesitated. "You know we are here by Royal Order straight from Queen Victoria herself," Lee said. "I assure you shooting her envoy will not please her."

The soldiers looked at each other. "He's right." Lieutenant Colonel Cole said from the rear of the group. "I suggest you lower your weapons."

The soldiers did as their commander ordered. Cole turned and walked away surveying the battlefield around him. "Terribly sorry sir," one of the soldiers said to Dan.

"I know heat of the moment," Dan said giving the soldier a dismissive wave. Tossing an arm across Valkyrie's shoulders, he turned back to Brogan. "Now Brogan about this beast?"

"That is a story," Brogan said. "We made camp outside of Falls waiting on sunrise and this beast comes wondering near our fire from the woods. It had been shot by some fool."

"That would most likely be me," Lee said.

"So I tossed him some scraps of meat and he kept hanging around. By the morning we were proper mates." Brogan laughed heartily. "You should have seen the look on those beasts' faces when I rode through the village slaughtering them, riding on one of their own. The saddle the orcs used wasn't too difficult to get used to."

"If I hadn't seen it I would've never believed it." Dan said shaking his head. "How are we getting home?"

Lee looked at the Tin Man seeing the dents and dings it had taken during the onslaught. Brackish was resting on the floor of the compartment as an army medic attended to his arm. "We have arrangements." Lee said looking up.

Dan followed his gaze and saw the massive airship as it came into view above them. Slowly several large baskets were lowered down. Valkyrie looked puzzled at the baskets as did Dan. The army medic stood up. "I can't do much for him but I've given him something for the pain. I'd get him to a doctor of his own kind." The medic walked away, a look of disgust at having to treat Brackish.

Lee ignored the man and took the controls for the Tin Man in hand and guided the metal giant into the basket. Looking at Dan and Valkyrie, he nodded toward the empty basket. They stepped in the empty basket, Lee followed behind. "Brogan, a pleasure," Lee said nodding toward the Scotsman.

Brogan saluted with his sword. "Aye it has been." He said.

Lee removed a large oversized pistol from the interior of the basket and aimed it into the sky away from the airship. Squeezing the trigger, he sent a red flare arcing through the sky. The baskets began to climb. Dan and Valkyrie held onto the sides of the basket, Brogan stood watching as they lifted into the sky.

It took several long minutes for the baskets to reach the airship. When they were locked into place Dan saw the large spool of cable that had been wound up to retrieve the baskets. Lee gave a cursory greeting to Jonas and went to the Tin Man where he carefully lifted Brackish off of the floor's compartment. "I need your medical facility," Lee said.

Jonas stood staring at the goblin. "Now!" Dan said shaking Jonas into action.

"Of course, right this way." Jonas said leading them all to the medical room.

18   Several weeks passed and as the siege against the Seelie Court races died out, as supply lines for the German fey were severed, things began settling back to normal. Kate McKendrick was escorted back to her home with a squad of Royal Marines. Before she left she had told them that Ms. Petal wanted to thank them. Her final comment to them had been: "I'm going to start training for my role on the court." Dan and Lee had understood the comment, while the others around the child wore confused looks.

Dan and Lee collected the largest fey related bounties to date, in part to the orcs they'd defeated at Falls. It was not long after receiving it that they had been called to meet once again with Queen Victoria. As on their first meeting, Roger escorted them to the side entrance of the palace. They were shown into the meeting room with the lovely windows and view of the garden.

Dan, Lee and Brackish sat on the small sofa waiting on the queen to arrive. Ever since taking Brackish onto the airship it had become well known that he was their latest partner, having taken up residence in their flat. Brackish had lost his arm but Lee had seen that only as a new challenge and set about fashioning one that would connect to the nerve endings and feed off of bioelectric energy as Queen Victoria's did. The prototype he had come up with was not a perfect remedy but it would do until Lee could perfect it. His prosthetic arm was larger and longer than his natural one and it only had two fingers and a thumb as opposed to his other hand which was almost human except for the black nails and greenish hue. Still this was Brackish's first time within the palace and he was taking it all in. Eating biscuits from the tray in front of him, he examined everything that was in the room.

Queen Victoria and Prince Albert entered from their usual door. Lee and Dan stood up. Brackish looked confused but slid off of the sofa to stand beside them. After Victoria sat down, they also sat down. "Well gentlemen," she started and then looked at Brackish. "I don't believe I've had the pleasure."

"Pardon us," Lee said. "This your Majesty is Brackish Thumtum, our newest partner."

Brackish slid off the couch and held out his prosthetic hand for her to shake. She placed her brass hand in his. "A kindred spirit I see," she said winking at the goblin. Brackish smiled, not showing his teeth as Dan and Lee had taught him, and retook his place on the couch. "We also have another guest."

Albert opened the door and Ironhill stepped into the room, wearing the suit he had worn on their first meeting. All three of the bounty hunters stood up ready to attack the dwarf. "Gentlemen!" Victoria cautioned. "He is a guest within these walls and you will show him the proper respect."

"Fellas," Ironhill said climbing onto the sofa beside Victoria. "Sorry about everything that happened but you saved the girl and the day. The court owes you a great deal."

"About that," Lee said. "It has come to our attention that your German counterparts met with the Seelie Court and were told in no uncertain terms that they were not welcome in the British Isles."

"Nonsense," Ironhill scoffed. "We would never turn our back on a possible ally."

"Of course not," Dan said. "Unless you were the one calling the shots."

"I don't know what you're accusing me of," Ironhill started.

"I'm accusing you of selling us out," Dan announced standing up once more. "Sorry ma'am." He said as he got control of his anger and sat back down.

"That's just ridiculous." Ironhill said. "Who's told you boys such lies?"

"Wotan," Dan said.

"It seems that he was unaware of his compatriots' alliance with the Unseelie Court and was merely attempting to kidnap Kate McKendrick in order to reopen negotiations with the Seelie Court." Lee explained. "It was because of this that they killed him when the opportunity arose."

"Sorry to disappoint but I never met any Wotan or anyone else from that side of the world, other than the ones we slew when they tried to kill me as well." Ironhill said.

The door opened and Valkyrie stepped in with the most beautiful woman that any of them had ever seen. Her skin was like porcelain with hair that looked like spun gold, she seemed to glow. A tear escaped from Brackish's eye. "Glorianna," Ironhill said breathless.

"Yes Ironhill," she said her voice as soothing as the ocean when it laps against the shore. "Is that him my dear?"

Valkyrie nodded. "He came and spoke on behalf of your court, and denied us refuge." She said never taking her eyes off of Ironhill.

"No!" Ironhill exclaimed. "She is lying."

"No," Glorianna calmly replied. "There is no deception in her words, but your words bear the bitter taste of dishonesty. Why Ironhill? Why would you betray us so?"

Victoria stood and moved away from the dwarf, fearing he may lash out. "Why?" Ironhill said spitting the word at her. "Remember the

Limestone Massacre? Whose kin were senselessly slaughtered like pigs? Mine. Rather than pay an eye for an eye what did you do but make peace with them. I was there, buried in the limestone. When dark fell I dug my way out and escaped if not they would've butchered me as well."

"You brought this upon the world when you revealed our existence." Ironhill continued. "So when I was contacted by the Germans I told them they were denied admittance by you yourself, forcing Wotan to join forces with the Black Forest Council. I dropped word to the Unseelie Court of what was transpiring and then you sent me to meet with that mortal wench," Ironhill pointed at Victoria.

"Then why did you have us clean up the German invaders?" Dan asked.

"So I did, I thought I was sending you fools to your doom. Yes, Wotan only wanted to hold the girl until we agreed but the Unseelie and the Black Forest wanted the same thing, to destroy the humans on this island and to rule it. They wanted something that I wanted. To purge the humans from this land so that we can continue to live undisturbed."

"Enough," Dan said rising from the sofa and punching the diminutive figure. Ironhill's head slammed into the wooden top of the sofa and he bounced forward onto the floor where he remained unconscious. "I told you I'd thump you next time I saw you." Dan said pointing at Ironhill.

"Word has been sent, Ironhill is no longer leader of the dwarf guilds, a new leader is being chosen. We will take him now," Glorianna announced.

Two small dwarves appeared behind her, they entered stepping around, not speaking to anyone in the room and bound Ironhill's hands and feet in thick set chains. Then, as if nothing out of the ordinary was happening, they carried him away. Queen Victoria curtsied. "Thank you so much for your help in this matter."

"It was my pleasure. I am only sorry it had to occur." Glorianna said returning the curtsy.

Glorianna turned and began to leave the room. Valkyrie turned to follow her. "Wait," Dan said reaching out toward Valkyrie. "You could stay."

Valkyrie smiled. "I am staying." She said.

"Where?" Dan asked.

"She is going to assist her brethren in relocating to our shores," Glorianna answered. "Queen Victoria has been most gracious to allow them travel to our lands, provided the Black Forest Council stay firmly on their own soil."

Glorianna turned and walked away, the glow in the room fading as she went. "I'll be by once everything is settled, but it will take a while." Valkyrie said. She gave Dan a gentle kiss on the lips.

She left the room and Dan turned around, his composure intact but his posture gave away his sadness. He sat down on the sofa where he had been. Brackish patted him on the arm.

Dan was in a melancholic mood on the ride back. Roger still unaware of just how far reaching their assignment had been, was prying for information while trying to appear as if he wasn't. Brackish merely listened and occasionally would respond with something that made no sense to Roger. Lee had to hide his smile as the motorized coach made its way through the bustling streets. Dan's mood did not improve as they arrived at their flat. Elizabeth and Ms. Edwards greeted them as they came into the building and started up the stairs.

Nodding and putting on a halfhearted smile, Dan continued on. Lee and Brackish followed him. As they entered Dan was in the kitchen rummaging around. Brackish went in and came out with a bottle of beer. The goblin was smacking his lips as he went back to the sofa. "I'll have one of those to," Dan said reaching into the fridge and bringing out another bottle.

"Do you want to talk about it?" Lee asked.

Dan gave him a warning look. Lee held up his hands and went into his workroom. Brackish sat on the couch happily drinking his beer. "Here's to the woman we want that never want us," Dan said holding out his bottle.

Brackish clinked his bottle against Dan's and they both took a large swig from the bottle. "I better than cow squeezings," Brackish said.

"I've told you that's milk. It's good for you." Dan stated taking another drink. "Although I've got to agree I like this stuff better myself."

"If you're going to get drunk with Brackish, please go ahead and take your boots off. Last week you nearly broke the sofa when you were dancing on it." Lee called from the workshop.

"Yes mother," Dan called falling back onto the sofa and pulling his boots off.

Lee came out of the workroom with a map of England on a piece of cork. Several different colored pushpins had been placed in the map. "What's that?" Brackish said.

"Hopefully our next job," Lee said.

Brackish put the stopper back in the beer bottle and leaned forward to look at the map. "Dan?" Lee asked.

"What?" Dan asked looking annoyed.

"What challenge do you feel like tackling?"

"Sobriety," Dan responded.

"This is no time to drown your sorrows. I'm sorry about Valkyrie or Freyja or whatever she wishes to go by, but her decision has been made. Since when did the great Dan Winston, slayer of monsters and righter of wrongs, ever mind the loss of a woman?" Lee asked. "You are obviously going soft."

"You know better than that," Dan said taking another drink.

"Perhaps we should change the name to Brackish and Baum, what do you think?" Lee asked Brackish. "He's obviously not going to be much help."

Brackish considered the offer for a moment then shook his head. "Something else," he said.

Dan made a disgusted noise and went to his bedroom.

"What choice we have?" Brackish asked looking at the map.

"There have been several roaming bands of orcs in different parts of the country, they seem to be left over from the invasion and are just trying to survive. They are what the green pins indicate." Lee said pointing to the five green pins.

"Which one pay most?" Brackish asked.

"These two are the largest groups of orcs," Lee said pointing to the corresponding pins.

"Well than that settles it," Dan said emerging from his room wearing his standard bounty hunting clothes. "We'll hit those orcs first."

Dan had his pistols strapped across his hips. The shotgun and its pack strapped across his back. "We should wait until daylight," Lee said.

"Why?" Dan asked.

"That's when the velociter will arrive from its location at the depot." Lee reminded him.

Brackish laughed. Dan cringed but since Brackish had removed himself from the goblin community his laugh had gradually become less malignant.

In the morning, once the velociter was returned, the three of them packed for the trip. Dan dressed as he had been last night upon emerging from his room. Lee in his long travelling coat, pistol in his shoulder holster, Winchester in hand, and leather bag filled with books for research. Brackish brought up the rear with the new belt that Dan and Lee had commissioned for him. It still had a holster for the new revolver in it and all the standards where he could carry ammunition but it also had a small sheath along the side that Brackish kept a knife in. The two men had come to learn that Brackish was good with a gun but he was better with a knife.

Lee looked at the Tin Man's shed. "How long?" Dan asked.

"It'll take me several days of hard work to complete the modifications." Lee said.

"I don't think we'll need it, we'll just make sure not to get trapped in any villages with them." Dan said. "Besides we've got competition to catch them. Brogan will be after them and that warg will give him an unfair advantage to track them."

"Daylight burning," Brackish said.

Dan and Lee both gave the goblin an incredulous look. They could not believe what he had just said to them. "You heard him," Lee said.

Dan laughed as they pulled away from the flat looking for the next bounty.

THE END

Winston, Baum, & Brackish
will be back in
The Seven Mummies of Sekhmet
coming soon!

Winston & Baum can be found on Facebook at
www.facebook.com/WinstonandBaum1

Other works by Seth Tucker

Friedkin's Curse: A Werewolf Tale of Terror

Four friends, Jack; Emera; Ameth; and Owen, go to the Friedkin School for Girls. It's supposed to be simple, go pick up Emera and Ameth's sister Ruby, but the students have been seeing something in the woods; something monstrous; something not human.

That first night, Jack is able to hold it at bay. Now the army has arrived, but protecting the people at the school does not seem to be their top priority. Jack will have to rise to the task as the soldiers seem to be unable to stop the werewolf. His only hope of understanding the werewolf's origins and motives rests in the two old journals belonging to the house's former owners. Soldiers and civilians alike are dying. The werewolf seems unstoppable driven by an unholy desire. Jack and the survivors will have to last the night and destroy the werewolf or die trying.

Now what started as an overnight trip has turned into a fight for survival. The werewolf in the woods wants something that only it knows. In the dark of the night, evil walks the halls.

Available exclusively on Amazon.com for the Kindle!

Acknowledgement

This book would not have been nearly as good as it is without the discerning eyes of my alpha readers: Chris & Caralyn. I owe you a great deal of thanks for helping this book reach its potential.

Author's Note

Thanks for reading the first Winston & Baum adventure. I hope you enjoyed reading it as much as I enjoyed writing it. Winston & Baum was one of those ideas that came from a deep seated need to write something fun. After finishing Friedkin's Curse, I sat down and wrote an epic story. It was a draining experience and currently sits on a shelf in the back of my closet. How long will it remain there? I don't know, I'm not ready to go back and begin wrestling with it again. So after the ordeal I had gone through with the epic piece, I decided that I wanted to write something fun, action-packed, steam punk, and something incorporating my personal favorites, mythological creatures and monsters. It was from this need for "fun" that Dan Winston came sauntering into my mind. He is by far the most enjoyable character I've ever written (Lee coming in a close second). In the process of writing this book, the idea entered my mind for the second one (due out summer of 2013). Since then, I have been fortunate enough to craft five stories for these characters so far, dealing with different parts of the world and the mythology associated with those regions. So once again thanks for reading, I hope you enjoyed it. If you did please tell your friends about Winston & Baum.

About the Author

Seth Tucker was raised in a small village in the forest. At the age of three, he wrestled and killed a 30-ft anaconda and to this day wears the skull as an athletic supporter. At the age of fifteen, he began traveling America with a small performing troupe that catered strictly to Russian mimes. Entertaining mimes does not pay much and he eventually made the transition to a career in writing. He now spends most of his time writing novels that he is sure mimes enjoy, but are not strictly written for them. His turn-ons include peanut butter and bacon, but never at the same time (unless of course it's called for). You can follow his adventures at lagomorphflix.wordpress.com.